I0739070

BESSIE

The Monster in Lake Erie

By: Deborah Tadema

BESSIE

The Monster in Lake Erie

Published by Isabella Media Inc 270 Bellevue Ave #1002,
Newport RI 02840
www.IsabellaMedia.com

© 2018 Isabella Media Inc
All rights reserved. No portion of this book may be reproduced in any form without permission from the publisher, except as permitted by U.S. copyright law.
ISBN-10: 0-9994459-5-2
ISBN-13: 978-0-9994459-5-2

For permissions contact: requests@isabellamedia.com

CONTENTS

CHAPTER ONE

From beneath the waves, Bessie watched the man struggle, his face contorted in pain as he bounced off the hard clay rocks. Water splashed over him, pulling him under. Arms and legs flailed madly about. He coughed and braced for another wall of ice-cold water that came straight at him. Fingertips scratched at the packed gravel on the cliff wall. The lake took him under again. When he surfaced, he choked, spit out mouthfuls of water, waited for the next assault.

The man managed to pull himself along the side of the cliff to the outer edge of the outcrop. From there, the lake opened up before him, the beach too far away. There was no fear in his eyes, just raw determination.

Bessie crawled along the bottom to get a closer look. She had watched humans drown before. They were weak and tended to give up too soon. Not this man. He took several deep breaths, swam out past the clay rocks and rode the large swells. The man didn't get far when he stopped for a rest, and shivered. She saw his breath in the wind. He hugged his side and winced at the hazy sun then tried again. She followed.

Humans had poor eyesight. Bessie had been able to get right up next to them before they saw her. Shock and fear would appear on their faces. They'd panic. Some died.

A huge wave grabbed the man and pulled him back out. She had lost him. Bessie skirted across the lake bottom in search for him. Waves thundered overhead. She found him again as he bobbed on the surface, eyes closed, head on his chest. He barely moved, barely breathed. She stopped and watched him, and waited to see how long he would hang on.

A wave crashed down in front of him, splashing his face, and jerked him awake. His eyes, the color of a cloudy sky, squinted down at her. She thought he had given up by this time, he looked tired. Or maybe he knew she was there because he moved closer; near her head and gawked at her with wide eyes.

She did not breathe; did not flick her long tail. Nor did she blow bubbles. Could he see her this far under water, through the muck that the lake had stirred up? Did her big bulk cast a shadow that shimmered as she moved? Bessie closed her eyes and waited, listening to the roar of the waves overhead. After several seconds, she opened them and watched him fight on. This time he seemed panicked, as if suddenly, he wanted to live. There was fear in his eyes now. He got caught in an undertow and was dragged down only to surface far out in the lake. He gasped for air and looked back at the shore. Did she read defeat in his eyes?

His arms and legs didn't have enough strength to keep him up anymore. Too exhausted to lift his head, he sank and was pulled out further. He had stopped his courageous fight. Bessie moved in close enough, so he could see her. His eyes were closed, his arms floating above his head as he drifted. She nudged him with her snout. There was no response. She pushed him toward the shore and lifted him up with her nose and rolled him onto the sand.

****

Port Stanley was at the mouth of Kettle Creek, nestled in between two large hills. It was an era of big flowered dresses, high boots and the miniskirt. Men wore single-breasted suits with collarless jackets, hats were becoming scarce. Bell bottoms had arrived, and someone had invented polyester. The Beverly Hillbillies played on television, along with Star Trek and the Twilight Zone. Color was new on the TV screen. Antennas stretched high into the sky like sentinels from every rooftop which replaced the set of rabbit ears that sat on top of the TV in the fifties.

Rock and roll was all the rage with the young crowd. Shangri-Las, Doors, Byrds and the Bee Gees were just a few of the bands whose songs blared from transistor radios and jukeboxes. Teenage boys banged on guitars and drums in garages and basements. Little girls played with Barbie dolls. Nobody wore seatbelts in the chrome laden cars. They didn't think twice about drinking from the garden hose or sharing a bottle of Coke. If you got into trouble at school, the punishment was twice as bad when you got home. And a loaf of bread was twenty-five cents.

Kettle Creek sliced the town in half where two fourteen-year-old boys sat on the edge of the dock swinging their legs. School had just gotten out for the summer. "You think it's still too cold?" Troy Jackson asked his friend. They had worn their bathing trunks under their pants today, just in case.

"Yeah, I do." Jason Webster answered as he looked longingly at the murky water below. "I really wish I could be practicing my diving. Remember last year, when I did a somersault?"

Troy laughed. "Yeah and all I could do was a belly flop."

"I bet I still can."

"Now?"

"Why not? It's been hot out for two whole weeks. I want to cool off."

"You just said it was still too cold," Troy reminded him. "Besides, I heard there's a sea monster in there."

"Do you believe in monsters? Are you still a baby?"

Troy watched a log float down the creek. "No, I just heard. That's all."

"I'll bet you a milkshake I can do it."

"You're on."

Jason stood, pulled down his pants and lifted his shirt off, dropped them on the dock to reveal his new red bathing trunks. "Count down," he said, as he flexed his arms and legs, showing off his scrawny body.

Troy backed out-of-the-way, counted down from five. Jason took off at zero and flew past him, landing in the creek with a big splash.

Troy ran to the end of the dock. A few seconds later his friend came up and spit water out of his mouth. "You did it, Jason," Troy said, excitedly. "Now you can get a blue ribbon at school if you can do it in the pool."

"Come on in. It's not that bad." Jason clenched his teeth.

Troy noticed they chattered and placed his hands on his hips. "Why are your lips turning blue?"

"It's not that bad down here, once you get used to it."

"You're nuts."

Jason ducked under and swam around, spurted water out of his mouth when he surfaced. "Come on, I'll give you the milkshake back."

"I don't even have the money to buy a milkshake," Troy told him. "Okay. I'm going to cannonball, so watch out." He threw off his clothes, determined not to show his friend his fear that the rumors might be true. He let out a loud "Geronimo!" And hit the water with a huge splash, surfaced and spewed water up at Jason.

"You're right." He realized Jason was gone. "Jason, where did you go?"

"Up here." Jason walked to the end of the dock pulling his T-shirt over his head. "I'm freezing."

Troy swam round to prove to himself that he was just as brave as Jason. A few yards out, he turned and smiled up at his friend.

"That's enough, Troy. You're going to get pneumonia or something. Come on out."

"I'm coming." He swam out further instead.

Jason suddenly started to yell. "Get out! Troy, get out now!"

"Why, it's not suppertime yet? The water's not that bad."

"Troy! Get out!" Jason's frantic voice finally sunk in.

"What's wrong?" Troy headed toward the ladder.

Jason pulled Troy up by the shoulders. "Hurry, Troy, get out of there."

"Man, you're scaring me, Jason. Don't do that."

"Look." Jason pointed to the center of the creek where Troy was only minutes before.

A huge shadow moved slowly under the water.

     Bessie — The Monster in Lake Erie by Deborah Tadema

Troy gulped. "What is it?"

"Maybe it's that sea monster of yours." Jason's voice crackled.

"I thought you didn't believe in sea monsters." Troy tried to hide the panic in his own voice.

Jason shivered. "Well, I didn't."

****

Bessie felt a pulse through her like never before. The blood stone the man on the beach wore called her, disrupting her thoughts. She had to get away to clear the ringing in her head.

She swam up the creek where the boats slept. She went back out into the lake, hid under the water and watched her man. His chest rose and fell ever so slightly so she knew he was still alive. The blood stone was their connection. A ring with a red stone embedded in it. Bessie sensed he was vital to her very existence. She could not kill this man if he had it. Bessie knew what had triggered the instinct to save him from drowning.

From further down the sand, she sensed something else. Another pull, from a different source. This confused her. Tom, her keeper, had walked up to her man on the sand. She stood guard. He had a ring with a stone the color of the sky and the water. It also called to her, in an unusual way. This stone, Bessie knew, made her lightheaded. It made her feel as if she could lift her flippers and soar into the clouds.

The two stones had come together. This Bessie sensed was important. Something was going to happen. She needed to keep these men safe, as long as they wore the rings.

****

Chilly water surrounded the man when he became aware of the scratchy sand underneath him. His legs raised and lowered with each swell of the waves that rushed to shore. Seagulls squawked overhead in the gray sky. A hazy sun filtered through the clouds. Unconsciousness threatened to overtake him again. Every inch of his body cried out in agony. The last thing he remembered was that his sailboat blew up. After that; everything was a blur.

A dark shadow crossed his face. Big hard hands grabbed his shoulders, dragged him on top of a dune, dropped him without ceremony. A grunt escaped the man's lips. The stranger paid no attention to him. Instead, he stood and glanced out at the lake.

In the faded light of late afternoon, the stranger he would come to know as Black Tom posed an eerie figure. A tall, ridiculously thin man, who wore all black, from his long coat to his big boots that he planted only inches from the man's head.

Tom scratched the stubble on his chin and sneered at him with stained teeth. "Looks like you'll live after all, eh?" When he bent down, alcohol and body odor emanated from him, made the man turn his head away. "For now."

Tom's deep voice sent ice picks down the man's back, which made him want to bury himself under the sand. All he could do was lie there, helpless and in excruciating pain. He moaned in agony.

Tom spat on the ground beside him. "You upset her, didn't ya?"

"I don't know what you mean," the man said through clenched teeth.

"I said you made Bessie mad."

"I was just sailing my boat, minding my own . . ."

"How did mind'in your own business sink your boat?"

"It exploded. I didn't . . ."

Tom's deadly look made him stop. After a few seconds, Tom turned his attention to the lake again.

Curiosity got the better of him; the man asked who Bessie was.

"Bessie, I told you," He spat again. "Yep, you made her mad, you know. You of all people can't afford to upset her. That's the last thing a keeper needs to do."

"What the hell are you talking about?" The man sucked in his breath as pain shot up his side. Through clenched teeth, he said, "What a lunatic."

Tom heard him. The pupils in his eyes grew as big as quarters. He flexed his fingers and his nostrils flared. He let out a deep laugh that

Bessie — The Monster in Lake Erie by Deborah Tadema

penetrated the man's nerves. He got no answer. Instead, Tom bent down and riffled through his pockets.

"Hey! What are you doing? Get your filthy hands off me, you bastard."

Tom grinned at him and stuffed his wallet, a set of keys and change into his coat pocket. The man tried to twist away, the pain held him back. He wanted to kick Tom when he was being robbed of his watch and a priceless ring. Instead, all he could do was watch in horror when the stranger stepped back. The last thing he remembered was a big black boot aimed at his head.

****

Bessie surfaced above the water. Tom squinted out at the lake and smiled as if he knew she was there. His smell was quite different from the other one. Bessie was puzzled. There were too many smells that surrounded Tom this time. Smells that drove her away. She went back under. She couldn't put this new smell to memory.

That's when she saw Tom take the blood stone from her man on the sand. That wasn't supposed to happen. Why would he do that? The magic of the blood stone faded. Bessie didn't like it and got ready to defend her man. Tom ran away. She settled herself down to slow her breathing and waited.

CHAPTER 2

"What do you think that was in the creek?" Jason asked, his voice an octave lower than last year.

"I don't know, maybe a whale." Troy glanced back toward the harbor; his voice sounding like a foghorn to him. They walked down Main Street, passed houses and shops and waved at Troy's mother, Rachel, through the window of the hair salon. She smiled and waved back over her customer's head. "Probably a big fish." Troy continued the conversation after they turned back down toward William Street. "She's too busy to ask. Let's go down to the beach." They crossed the steel bridge that spanned over Kettle Creek and headed south.

Jason shook his head. "Too big. I'll ask my dad tonight when he gets home from work."

The street curved to the left. The boys followed the sidewalk, passed the apartment building where the town's cop lived and walked on to the beach at the end.

Jason said, "I bet it was just a turtle or something."

"Maybe," Troy wasn't convinced. At the water's edge, they gave each other a nervous look. "What if it lives out there?" Troy scanned the horizon. "My dad is out there on a gas rig. I wonder if they ever see anything when they're working."

"He won't be home for a few days, will he?"

"Not till Thursday." Troy kicked at the sand. "Do you think it's ever killed anybody?"

"I think, if it did, we would have heard something by now."

Troy didn't say anything. Jason stepped closer. "I know, I worry too. My dad is out there fishing all day. Both of their jobs can be dangerous."

"Yeah, I know." Troy said sorrowfully as he looked out over the lake. "At least you get to see your old man every day. I only get to see mine after his eight-day shift."

"He's home for four days straight, right?"

"Yeah."

"And he does stuff with you, with us. My dad doesn't want to do anything after he unloads his catch for the day. My mom makes me cut the grass now because he won't anymore."

"And I cut our grass when my dad's gone." Troy's older brother, Dean, hadn't cut the grass since he'd moved into his own apartment three months ago.

They watched as Lake Erie lapped at their feet. It was calmer now, and not as angry looking.

"Want to go swimming?" Jason asked.

"Naw," Troy started walking along the shore. His buddy automatically fell into step beside him. They waved at school friends who were sunning themselves in the last days of June, getting a head start on their summer tans. Only two brave souls were bold enough to swim in the frigid waters, the creek wasn't as cold. The warm sun on their bare arms gave the boys a promise of warmer waters in the days ahead. After a long, chilly winter, they itched to go swimming every day and practice for the team at school.

"Oh no," Jason giggled. "Look who's coming."

Troy didn't need to look. He knew by Jason's reaction what was about to happen.

Hey, you two dipsticks, where are you going?" Dean marched up to the two boys. He was wearing gray shorts, a black T-shirt with a picture of the Beatles on it, and sandals. "You were spying on me the other night, weren't you?"

"No, we weren't, Dean. We were just walking by." Troy suppressed a giggle.

Dean scowled at them and pushed his long, blond hair out of his eyes. "What did you see?"

"Nothing."

"Why are you laughing?" Dean lifted his sunglasses onto the top of his head.

"I'm not laughing." Troy had sobered quickly.

"Your hair's standing straight up," Jason observed.

Dean turned on him. "What did you see, Jason?" He gave the young teen a playful jab in the arm.

"Nothing, honest."

The older boy pinched his eyebrows together and smirked. "I saw you through the car window, remember? You were watching us make out." Dean stepped closer to the boys. "If you tell anybody what you saw, you'll get the 'pants' right here. Got it?"

"Got it," Troy answered. He didn't want his pants pulled down, especially here where there were too many girls. Troy knew that Dean only acted like a bad ass in front of them.

Dean turned and walked toward three girls who sat on one blanket. After he was far enough away from him, Troy yelled, "She had nice tits, didn't she?"

Dean swung around and charged at them in a fury.

"Split!" Jason pulled Troy's arm. They scrambled along the shore past the last of the cottages. Dean chased them along the bottom of the cliffs that slowly took over the beach.

"We're going to be trapped," Jason puffed out as he dodged around some driftwood.

Troy glanced back. "He's gaining." He pumped his legs faster.

Not far ahead, the cliffs had given way. Large chunks of clay, filled with gravel spilled out into the lake. If they didn't go into the water Dean would be on them in minutes. Jason stopped and breathed heavily with his hands on his knees.

     Bessie — The Monster in Lake Erie by Deborah Tadema

"Hurry," Troy puffed as he ran by.

Dean was only a few feet away when Jason took off again and quickly outran the eighteen-year-old. He caught up to Troy who stopped so suddenly that Jason ran into him. "Look." Troy pointed to a man on the sand.

"You two are getting faster." Dean slid to a stop beside them to catch his breath. "What are you gawking at?"

Troy and Jason backed away, eyes glued to the body.

Dean stood, open-mouthed beside them. "Is he alive?"

"I don't know." Troy started to feel sick.

Dean gave the man a light kick with his foot. A soft moan answered their question. "Barely, I think." He rolled the man over onto his back. "Oh, damn."

Troy's voice cracked. "It's Uncle Mason." He glanced nervously at his brother.

"What's he doing back?" Dean walked around to the other side, didn't take his eyes off the man.

"Looks like his boat sank, dude." Jason pointed at the debris floating in the water.

"What do we do now?" Troy asked.

"I'm going to get Jack." Jason started to run back toward town.

Dean backed away from the man, turned and chased after Jason. "Typical," Troy thought as he watched them go. Dean always left him with the unpleasant part of anything.

Troy frowned at his uncle, wondering if he should do something. He started to shake and stepped away. Jason and Dean were halfway down the beach. Some of the debris from his uncle's boat had started to wash up on shore. Troy walked along the water's edge and looked for anything that his uncle might need. Nothing seemed very useful any more, so he stood and looked out at the water. The lake was rough even though there had been no massive storm. He wondered why his uncle's boat sank. Uncle Mason had sailed all his life, he knew what to do. Troy looked back at his uncle, watched his chest rise and fall. Mason groaned and moved a hand, which didn't do anything to ease Troy's nerves. He looked back out at the lake. At one point he thought he saw a pair of eyes watching him. When he looked closer the eyes were gone. He blamed it on the glare of the sun that bounced off a piece of metal. He sighed and walked back toward the body. The last thing he thought he'd be doing today was babysitting his dying uncle.

****

Bessie watched the cub pace nervously along the shore. He hugged himself around his middle, and talked to the man in a constant gibber. She was afraid he saw her. She didn't duck down fast enough. He wasn't supposed to know she was there. He splashed water on his face when he saw others run toward him. It disguised the tears, except his eyes were still red.

Bessie felt her man get weaker and feared for him. The pulse of the ring was gone; it faded after Tom took it. The cubs led several people to her man on the sand. A police officer cursed at Bessie's man and gave a female a wary look. She bent down and held the blond man's hand, the shock apparent in her eyes. The policeman tried to pull the female away. She refused to go. They argued until he was forced to order the growing crowd to step back.

The policeman asked the cubs a lot of questions and wrote on his little paper. The cubs called him Jack. While he did this, the female lightly ran her fingers on the blond man's cheeks. Bessie saw her push back tears. Several men lifted Bessie's man and carried him toward town. The female told them to be careful. The cubs followed as if in a daze.

The policeman held the female back. "How bad is he?" Bessie heard Jack ask.

"I'm not a doctor," she said through her tears. "I think he has a concussion, maybe a broken rib. We'll know better after they take x-rays. He probably nearly drowned."

"He going to make it?"

"He'll make it." The female pulled away from him. "Whether you want him to or not."

    Bessie — The Monster in Lake Erie by Deborah Tadema

She ran after the crowd. The man stood on the beach and called after her. "Well, Valerie, I never thought I'd see Mason Brooks back here again."

****

A nurse hovered over Mason when he woke up in a hospital room. "What happened?" he asked her groggily.

"Your boat sank, sir. Some kids found you on the beach." She continued to adjust the IV in his arm. Her warm smile didn't console him much. "You had a concussion and nearly drowned. Your ribs are bruised, but you'll be fit in a few days."

He rubbed the bandage on his head; the image of him fighting the lake slowly came into focus in his mind.

"Your doctor will be in shortly. I'll let you rest now." The nurse gave his hand a squeeze before she headed toward the door.

"Aw, who is my doctor?"

"Dr. Boyd," she called over her shoulder before she turned down the hall.

I thought he'd be retired by now, he thought. Old man Boyd had been his doctor for as long as he could remember, when he was in Port Stanley that was. Mason tried to ignore his headache as he looked around the room. His thoughts turned to the reason he hadn't been back home for so long. Valerie Hudson, and her long blond hair and blue eyes. She probably still hated him, especially after what he had done to her. He had walked out on her three days before their wedding. You don't do something like that to a favorite girl from a small town and get away with it. Mason was still in love with Valerie, thought about her constantly. If only he could make it up to her.

A candy-striper pushed in a lunch cart, giggled at him then left. He ate only half a sandwich with unidentified meat. Mason sat up against his pillows, as best he could with sore ribs. It took a few minutes for the pain to subside enough, so he could bare it. He'd clenched his teeth so hard that they hurt. After several shallow breaths he could breathe normally again. As he drank the bitter coffee, he tried to piece together the last few days. *How did I end up back here?* The last place he wanted to be. At least until he knew that the people in this town wouldn't throw him to the wolves.

He remembered he took his sailboat, the *Charisma*, out of the Port Rowan harbor where it had been dry-docked for the past four years. Yeah, it had been that long since he was home.

He had worked on his sailboat, got it seaworthy again. After he lived on it for the last two years, it was finally launched, and he took out to see how she would hold up. He remembered the cool breeze on his bare chest as he rounded Long Point. His face was turned up toward the sun, he breathed in the fresh air. Mason clenched his fist. He knew he had been set up. Someone had planted explosives on her. He set his cup down and pushed the tray away. No one from his hometown knew he was back in the area again, or did they? He had deliberately stayed in Port Rowan, an hour drive by car, contacting no one. His sister and his best friend didn't even know he was back.

Now he figured that all his plans would be screwed up. His plan was to sail around Lake Erie, hopefully, with his new wife. That's if he could convince the hometown beauty to marry him. And this time he wouldn't leave Valerie stranded at the altar. He would settle down, maybe do odd jobs for something to do and live a quiet life. Money wasn't an issue anymore. Between government jobs and the stock market, he had made over eight-hundred-thousand dollars, invested most of it and lived off the interest. No one knew about that either. It wasn't something he wanted to share now. Not when someone was out to kill him.

Mason dozed all afternoon. He dreamed of his sailboat blowing up over and over. Flames burst from down below. A huge puff of smoke filled the sky. He'd wake up in a cold sweat, and then doze again. He felt himself flying, landing hard and head first in the water. After that, he didn't remember anything until he found himself drifting in an angry lake at the base of the cliffs.

His whole body shivered. His eyes flew open in his dream and he swallowed several times to calm himself down. A tall, thin man dressed in black floated above him, sneering down at him, pulled out his IV.

"You upset her, didn't ya? You made Bessie mad." A big mouth with stained teeth and no body attached to it talked to him.

"Who the hell is Bessie?" his own voice asked.

The mouth disappeared to become the stranger's coal black eyes. They grew larger as they floated closer to him, glaring at him from only inches away. The face grew bigger and became distorted.

Mason screamed and bolted upright in bed, grabbed at the sheets and flung them wildly about. He saw several hazy forms run toward his bed. Several hands pushed him back down. Someone talked to him in a calm voice. Slowly he relaxed; the pain at his side becoming more apparent as the hospital room came into focus. The people seemed friendly as they cared for him, talked to him and smiled down at him. The people in this room were dressed in white.

****

Ernie Elliott swung his mop back and forth under Mason's bed. The janitor didn't care that it bounced off the legs, the wall, and the chair and side table. A whiff of stale booze floated toward Mason.

"Hey Ernie." Mason smiled at him. "How are things?"

"Mason," was all he got back for a greeting. "Fine." Ernie kept his head down, concentrating on swishing his mop around. After several strokes, he plunged it into the bucket and wrung it out. Too busy for idle chat, he chewed on his tobacco that Mason knew wasn't allowed in the hospital.

He watched quietly until the janitor took his mop and bucket to the next room. *That must have been record time.* Mason noticed scuff marks near the door. *Typical,* he thought. He and Ernie had never gotten along. Mason had stolen Valerie away from Ernie in high school. Ernie still held a grudge. Mason and Valerie had been an item ever since. That was until he'd done the unthinkable.

Police constable Jack Mullins walked into the room. Mason let out a groan.

"Hi to you, too." Jack pulled up a chair and sat. "Why are you back, Mason? I thought you'd never dare show your face back here again."

"I didn't know I was back here until I woke up."

Jack pulled out his pen and a small writing pad. "Tell me what happened."

"I was out on my sailboat. You remember the *Charisma*? You've been on her."

Jack nodded as he wrote. "You had some wild parties on her as I remember."

"I just got done fixing her up and was trying her out when..."

"And you fixed it up so good that it sank?" Jack said sarcastically.

"No. It was sound enough." For some reason, Mason held back and didn't tell the constable about his suspicions. He didn't yet know who he could trust.

Jack stopped, his pen poised in mid-air. "Is someone finally getting back at you?"

Mason scowled. "That's enough, Jack. You know as well as I do that you were just as wild as I was."

"Yeah, but I didn't leave town with someone waiting at the altar for me, without a word, sneaking off in the middle of the night."

"I told you why, for Christ sakes."

"Ah ha. Some secret deal with the government. Couldn't wait until after you married Valerie."

"Go to hell."

"What happened to the *Charisma*?"

"You won't believe me if I tell you."

"Try me."

"Forget it."

"I need it for my investigation, Mason. You want me to clear you of... say...going after insurance money, right? Or smuggling drugs or something. You can make this easy or hard. Frankly, I don't give a shit, Mason."

"Bessie." Mason watched Jack hold back a snicker. "That's the truth, Jack."

Jack stood and walked to the door. "I'll be back tomorrow. You rest your brain, Mason."

He heard Jack's laughter fade as he went down the hall. "Damn it." Mason punched the bed.

CHAPTER 3

Troy Jackson walked into the hospital room with his mother, Rachel. "Hey buddy," Mason called him, "I hear it was you who found me. Thanks."

Troy smiled a little nervously at his uncle. "Jason and I thought you were going to die." He watched his mother give her brother a hug. Mason looked groggy.

"You probably saved me from that." Mason said as his sister stepped back. "Why were you at the far end of the beach?"

"Dean chased us down there." Troy sat down on a hard-plastic chair. "We were just goofing off."

"How are you doing, Mason?" Rachel asked.

"Not bad sis, be out in a few days. How's Eddie?"

"Eddie's just fine. Still out on the gas rig." She looked at him with concern in her eyes. "Where were you all this time?"

"Niagara Falls."

Her face changed, her eyes became hard. "Have you apologized to Valerie, yet?"

Troy knew his mother was talking about Mason leaving Valerie before they were to be married. Rachel had called her brother all kinds of nasty names. Valerie had gone over to their place after Mason jilted her. Troy remembered her sitting at the kitchen table, crying while his mother comforted her. He himself had hated his uncle for a long time afterward, too. As the years had gone by Troy had begun to forgive Mason. And as he watched his uncle now, he could see remorse in his eyes.

"Haven't seen her yet," Mason answered.

Rachel studied her brother, eventually her face softened. "It took her a long time to get over that."

Mason nodded. "I know how devastated she must have been. And I am sorry."

"Are you going to run away again? Or are you home to stay this time?"

"I think I'll stay. Now that I am here."

Rachel still didn't seem ready to forgive Mason. After a bit she let out a sigh, and said. "Sorry about your sailboat." She sat on the side of the bed. "We didn't know you were back."

"I wasn't. I was trying to sort things out."

"Like what? You've only been away for four years. Plenty of time to sort things out."

Mason looked from his sister to Troy. "I fixed up the *Charisma* and was trying her out."

"It sank," Troy piped up. "Parts of it were floating all over Lake Erie."

Rachel stood up. "What's going on Mason?"

Mason watched Troy for a few seconds before he answered. "I don't know."

Troy said. "Someone said it was Bessie."

His mother scoffed as she walked toward the door. "Yeah, right." She turned and looked back at Troy. "You aren't coming?"

"Naw. I think I'll just hang out here for a bit." He had nothing better to do.

Rachel glanced at Mason then at her son. "You know what time supper is," she said before she left the room.

When she was out of sight, Mason turned to his nephew. "Did you see Bessie out there?"

Troy glimpsed at the empty doorway before facing Mason. "I thought I saw some big eyes watching me from out in the water."

"Do you believe in Bessie?"

"I don't know. Nobody's seen her for real." Troy shrugged. "There seems to be a lot of talk about her lately."

Mason glanced over at the door. A faraway look in his eyes. Troy shifted in his seat. Eventually, Mason faced Troy. "How is---"

"Valerie," Troy finished for him. Mason nodded. Troy saw his uncle hold his breath as if waiting for bad news. "She isn't married if that's what you want to know."

"Why not? Surely, she isn't waiting for me?"

Troy shrugged. "I don't know. You'll have to ask her."

****

The nauseating smell still emanated from Tom when Bessie found him in her den. He stood on the ledge and talked to her. Bessie's attention was on the sack next to him. Little by little, Tom had substituted her regular food with something new and delicious. Seaweed had become tasteless, leaving her unfulfilled. Bessie only ate that when she needed to, when Tom wasn't around.

She swam up to him in her little pond under the earth. It was dark; he shone a tiny sun in her eyes. Bessie closed her deep brown eyes and drifted to the edge, let him touch her face. When she opened her eyes, he smiled and called her his pet, whatever that meant.

Tom climbed up on Bessie's back and she gave him a ride around the inside of the cave. He seemed to enjoy it, laughing and petting her. After she set him back down, he threw big chunks of meat up at her. She caught them and chewed slowly with her double row of teeth. Juice ran down her long neck when she lifted her head to swallow. It was magnificent.

This time was different. Bessie started to feel weak. Dizzy. Her body felt light, her flippers felt heavy. She tried to fix her eyes on Tom who changed colors. Bessie's tongue grew thick and heavy. She couldn't bring it back inside her mouth, so it flopped around like a sail in the wind. High waves splashed around inside her.

He laughed.

What Bessie felt scared her. What did he do? Her movements became awkward and clumsy. The side of the cave got wet when she panicked and jumped around in fear.

He watched.

Her flippers grew numb. Bessie knew they were still there. They had grown feathers. She decided that she wanted to fly so she jumped and landed with a big splash.

He waited.

Bessie tried to bounce higher. This time her whole body lifted out of the water toward the fuzzy cloud. That was fun. One more time she soared up, and hit her head on the ceiling of the cave. Dirt cascaded down all over her. Bessie shook her head, and toppled over. Her foggy brain took its time to clear. She drifted toward him, nudged him for help.

He stood still.

Bessie's eyes rolled back, and darkness came.

****

"I think we should just stay out of the water," Troy told Jason, "at least for a while." They sat in the restaurant and looked out at the bridge that scanned Kettle Creek. They couldn't see the dock where they dove from two days ago; it was behind the building they were in. He thought of the shadow he saw and wondered about his uncle's sailboat.

"Even on really hot days? What if we just go in to get cooled off, come right back out again?"

"Maybe," Troy took a drink of his pop. "Something busted up Uncle Mason's boat."

"Yeah, I heard." Jason ate some of his fries. "If you were a sea monster, where would you hang out?"

Troy set his pop down on the table. "I think I'd hide in a cave or in a deep hole where no people could find me."

   Bessie — The Monster in Lake Erie by Deborah Tadema

"I was thinking of checking out that cave we found three summers ago."

"The one by Muddy Creek?" Troy sat up straighter. "I don't want to go up there by ourselves."

"Well, I don't think we could get any adults to go with us," Jason said. "Maybe we could ask Dean."

"Okay, I saw him down on the beach earlier." Troy finished his pop and stood to leave.

Jason grabbed the rest of his fries and followed his buddy out into the hot sun. When the boys reached the beach there was no sign of Dean, so they headed down the boardwalk.

"Hey, let's ask Shannon." Jason waited until Dean's girlfriend walked up to them.

"Do you know where Dean went?" Troy asked her.

"He said something about going home for something, why?"

Jason and Troy looked at each other before Jason answered. "We're just looking for him, that's all."

The boys found Dean later that afternoon in their driveway. He was working on his old Chevy; the hood was up, his arms coated in grease, his long hair tied back into a ponytail. Dean grinned at them when they walked up the driveway. "You guys here to help?"

"We want to ask you something," Troy told him as he looked at the engine and at the part that Dean held in his hands. His brother had left his car in the back of their driveway when he moved out. Occasionally he'd do some work on it, probably when he could afford the parts it needed.

"Do you want to come with us up on Picnic Hill?" asked Jason. "We know where there's a cave. We want to see if Bessie is in there."

Dean set the part on the ground and picked up a rag. He watched the two fourteen-year-old boys with a concentrated look as he wiped his hands. "You think she could be hiding in there?"

Troy shrugged. "I think she could be."

Dean glanced back at the car. "I can't leave this now. Why don't we go up there tomorrow?"

Justin looked over at Troy. "It's getting too late in the day, anyway."

Troy nodded. "We can meet here around one o'clock, okay?"

"That way, I'll have this all cleaned up," Dean told them. "I'll go with you. Bring a flashlight."

Justin walked up to the car. "What do you want us to do?"

****

That evening Dean had supper with his mother. Troy was eating at Jason's. Rachel made him spaghetti, one of his favorite meals. They listened to CHLO on the radio, the commentator reciting the hourly news. He watched her as he drank his coffee, knowing how much she missed his dad when he out on the gas rig. That was one reason he spent time with her, so she wouldn't fret so much. He kept telling her that they took every precaution out there that the crew followed all the safety rules. "It's mostly common sense," he told her, yet again. "And Dad's the best."

Rachel set her cup down on the table in front of her and studied her son. "You look so much like him." She let out a sigh. "I just wish his rotation wasn't so long."

Dean reached across the table and held her hand. After twenty years, she still wasn't used to being without her husband. And he knew too that his dad missed her just as much. "Just think," Dean said, "in twenty more years, he can retire."

Rachel pulled her hand back and wiped her eyes. "When do you go back out?"

Dean had started to apprentice under his dad last summer. Although his hours weren't as long. "When Dad goes back on his next rotation."

A knock on the back door sent Rachel to answer it. Seconds later, Jack Mullins walked around the corner and nodded at Dean. Jack was wearing civilian clothes, which told Dean that he wasn't on duty. Rachel asked him if he wanted a cup of coffee. Jack accepted as he found a seat at the table. Dean stood, shut off the radio.

After everyone was seated Jack said, "There's been a problem out on the rig. Seems three of the gas pipes near it have been punctured. And some of them are only four inches around." Rachel gave him a puzzled look. "They're supposed to be six inches in diameter," he explained.

"Oh."

"They're going to investigate." Jack shook his head. "If the drilling company skipped any corners when they made those pipes; well, I don't need to tell you about the trouble they're in."

"Are they still leaking?" Dean asked.

"No. They're shut off, for now. That will mean less production." Jack took a drink of coffee.

"Does that mean that Dean could get laid off?" Rachel gave him a sympathetic look.

Jack nodded. "Possibly."

"So, what's next?" Dean hoped not. He might have to give up his apartment, maybe have to move back home. He didn't want to move back into his old room, even though half of his stuff was still there. He'd lose his freedom, which he wasn't prepared to do.

"They're looking for a diver, to find out exactly where the pipes are leaking and why," Jack told them.

"There aren't many qualified divers around here," Rachel said. She looked at Dean; worry etched on her face. "It could take them a while to find somebody."

"This could turn into a big lawsuit," Jack said. "That also means that Eddie could be out of a job." Dean knew that Jack wasn't being callous. He was preparing them for the worst-case scenario.

Rachel's face paled. "I hope not," she said. "We can't afford that."

"Do you think the guys on the rig could be sued?" Dean hoped to steer the conversation in a new direction, so his mother had other things to think about. She was always worrying about money.

Jack watched Rachel, concern in his eyes. "I think that if the company used, say low-grade steel for the pipes; then no, the guys on the rig aren't responsible."

"Wow, what a mess this could turn into," Rachel said as she studied the inside of her cup.

"It's too bad," Dean said.

Jack frowned. "What?"

Dean answered. "That the best diver for this job is in the hospital."

****

Eddie Jackson hefted his duffel bag over his shoulder and stepped off the dock the next morning, his shift out on the gas rig over. He gave Troy a hug with his free arm. "Hey, you've grown an inch." Several men followed Eddie off the dock and greeted their own families.

"Hi Dad," Troy fell in step beside him. "How come you're all home a day early?"

"I'll tell you later. Your ma at work?" His forced jovial greeting didn't go unnoticed by his son. Worry lines etched deep around Eddie's eyes.

"Yep. She's taking the afternoon off, though. She'll be done in about an hour."

"Good. That'll give me time to have a shower. I'm starved; think you can rustle up some lunch while I get all pretty for your ma?"

"Sure."

Troy nearly skipped home as he walked down the street beside his father. "Hey, guess what?"

"And what does hay got to do with it?"

Troy playfully punched his father's arm.

"Oh, I'm bruised for life now."

"Dad," Troy tried to keep a straight face. "I got a hundred percent on my report card."

"Like I tell you, my son's a genius. Now, what did you really get?"

"Sixty-two percent."

"Seems to me you could do a little better than that, son. I hope you can pick up your grades next year." He stopped. "You don't want to end up like me, working twelve-hour days in the middle of the lake with the same eight faces day in and day out. Away from your family and friends all the time." They turned down the sidewalk toward their house. "The best thing you can do is get a good education, a decent job. Don't become a gas monkey like me. Or a dropout like your brother."

"I know, Dad." How many times had he heard that speech?

They walked up the porch steps. Troy opened the door and stepped back. His father passed through the threshold with a big smile. The duffel bag dropped to the floor with a thud. Troy watched as his father walked into each room and said, "It's good to be home."

This was his father's ritual after his eight days on the rig. Troy's ritual was to watch his father, glad to have him back. A sense of peace and love would wash over him when his father expressed such delight for a simple thing as coming home.

Troy went into the kitchen and made sandwiches. His father sang out of tune. "Everybody Loves Somebody" by Dean Martin, was drowned out when the shower started.

Coffee was ready when Eddie walked into the kitchen. "Nifty. Isn't that what they say, nowadays?"

Troy rolled his eyes.

Eddie ate two beef sandwiches while Troy only had one. "Any pie?"

"You know it, apple or blueberry?"

"Now, how am I supposed to choose?" Eddie eyed the pies that Troy pointed to on the counter as if ready to devour them both.

"Let's have the apple, it's already been started. Ice-cream?" Troy said.

"Certainly, my dear boy."

While Troy cut up the pie, his father poured himself another coffee. "So, what's new and exciting?" his father asked.

Troy set the plates down on the table. "Me, Jason and Dean found a man on the beach."

"Dead?"

"No. Nearly, I think." Troy watched the ice-cream slide off his pie and onto the plate. "It was Uncle Mason."

Eddie almost dropped his fork full of pie and ice-cream. "Mason? How did he get on the beach?"

"Something happened to his sailboat. Pieces of it were floating in the lake."

"Where is he now?"

"In the hospital. Mom and I have been up to see him. He'll be out in a few more days."

"When did this happen?"

"Three days ago, last Sunday."

Eddie shook his head. "I wonder what's going to become of this."

CHAPTER 4

Mason had just finished his breakfast when Jack strode in. "Two visits in two days. To what do I owe this pleasure?"

Jack ignored the sarcasm and pulled up a chair. His hat was gently set on the table by the bed. He reached into his pocket and handed Mason a couple of items.

"My driver's license, and," he flipped the other paper over, "a picture. Where did you get these?"

Jack glared at him. "You still carry a picture of Valerie in your wallet?"

Mason let out a whistle. Even though he vowed not to hurt Valerie, he was damned if he would cower before the likes of Jack. "She's a beauty, isn't she?"

"You leave her alone, you hear." Jack's nostrils flared. "She's my girl now."

Mason held up his hand. "Whoa, cowboy, give me some slack here. I didn't come here to steal my girl back," he lied.

"It wouldn't be the first time, Mason." They glared at each other. Neither one wanted to broach the subject that had put the dagger into the onetime friendship. Years ago, there had been three of them chasing after Valerie: Mason, Jack, and Ernie. Jack stood, paced up and down the room, passed a hand through his hair. "Someone broke into three cottages." He nodded at Mason's hand that held the papers. "Those were found near one of them."

"Well, I can tell you for certain unless I did some serious sleepwalking, it wasn't me."

"I know that." Jack sat back down. "How did you lose them?"

Mason studied the constable for a few seconds before he answered. "After I washed up on shore..."

Jack smirked, didn't say anything.

"I was ripped off."

"Robbed?"

"Yep."

Jack pulled out his pen and pad. "Describe this person."

Mason told him about the man all dressed in black. "He stank of booze and hadn't had a bath in a year." He waited until Jack caught up with his writing. "His big black boots had the name Tom engraved in them. He looked spaced out like he was on drugs."

"Anything else?"

"Those boots should have blood on them." Mason pointed to his bandaged head.

"Talk about kicking a man when he's down." Jack's pen scratched on the paper. "Is that when you passed out?"

"I guess."

"Is that it?" He flipped he pad shut.

"He was the one who told me that it was Bessie who sank my sailboat."

Jack's mouth popped open. "Have you ever heard of Bessie before?"

Mason shrugged. "I just thought she was a myth."

"And that's all she is. A figment of some drunk's imagination." Jack picked up his hat and walked to the door. "A couple of kids did see something in the water that morning you graced us on our shore."

Mason scowled at the cop's last remark.

Jack flipped his hat on. "I'll send in a sketch artist," he said before he turned and walked out.

****

Dean followed Jason and Troy up Picnic Hill and down a narrow path that led them to the bank of Muddy Creek. Each of them turned on their flashlights and pushed in behind a shrub.

Jason looked back nervously. "What if she's in here?"

"I thought that's what you wanted to find out?" Dean asked, a little perturbed. "Make up your mind." He gave Jason a push.

They entered through a small opening in the side of the huge hill and stayed to their right as they walked along a narrow ledge. To their left was a dark pond. It looked like black ink and was as still as glass. Dean squatted down on his haunches and scanned the pond with his flashlight. "I can see why you two might think Bessie is in here."

Troy crouched down beside him. "We've only been here once. That was three years ago. I didn't realize this pond was here."

"That's because we didn't have flashlights, and we didn't go in very far because it was too dark," Jason explained.

"I don't see any sign of Bessie," Dean told them before he stood up. He aimed his flashlight toward the ceiling. "This would be a perfect den for her."

"What do you want to do?" Jason asked as he searched around the inside of the cave with his flashlight. "She obviously isn't here now."

"We'll just have to keep coming back and checking," Troy said.

Dean headed toward the entrance. "What will you do if she does live here?" He called back over his shoulder.

"I don't know," Jason said. "We didn't think that far ahead."

The boys stopped outside the cave and watched the creek beside them. "She'd have to swim up here," Jason said. "It's moving fast."

"Spring runoff," Dean told them.

Troy walked along the small gravelly bank toward the lake. The other two went along with him. After a third of a mile, they had to stop because the cliffs blocked them. They turned and sauntered back toward the path that would lead them over the hill and back home.

"Have either of you seen Bessie?" Dean asked.

"No. I've heard rumors that she exists," Jason said.

"Who do you think smashed up Uncle Mason's sailboat?" Troy said. "How else could it end up like that?"

Dean said, "It could have been blown up."

Troy stopped in mid-step. "Who would want to blow up our uncle?"

Picnic Hill was on the west end of Port Stanley. For the most part, it stretched up a hundred feet, leveled off for a bit before a steep climb of another fifty feet. It was a wide hill and rolled three hundred yards before Muddy Creek cut it in half, flanked on both sides with tall cliffs. The path that led to the cave only reached a total height of fifty feet. It stretched across for fifty yards before it descended back down. A hundred yards to the left of that, a steep hill rose in two steps to a total of one-hundred-and-fifty feet from the creek. The boys stopped at the bottom and looked straight up the sand and clay cliff. At the top, trees and bushes swayed lightly in the breeze. Troy shivered with a sense of dread and felt that someone was watching them.

****

A gray-haired man in dark glasses led the way into Mason's room. His expensive designer suit and silk tie were copied by the younger version that followed him. Both had their hair slicked back with Brill Cream, making them look greasy. It looked ridiculous on the older, half bald man with a comb-over. Mason looked up from the newspaper in his hands and scowled, glad that he was no longer hooked up to an IV tube.

"Mr. Parsons. To what do I owe this unfortunate honor?"

Delroy Parsons faked a smile at the man who sat in the corner. His hand played with the change in his pants pocket. The clinking noise it made got on Mason's nerves within seconds. "You need to play pocket pool?" The hand whipped out.

"Mr. Brooks." Parsons stuck out the same hand; his shifty eyes darting around the room. Mason ignored it, taking his time folding the paper and setting it aside.

     Bessie — The Monster in Lake Erie by Deborah Tadema

"What do you want, Parsons?"

"Ah, this is Mr. T. Gillespie," he stammered and pointed to the younger version with a nervous twitch in his left eye.

Gillespie sat on Mason's bed as if he would catch some sort of disease if he touched too much. "We came to offer you a job, a very good paying job."

"Not interested." Mason took a sip of ginger ale from a plastic cup and then set it back on his side table.

Parsons stepped closer. "We're willing to pay whatever you want, Mason. Just name your price."

"I said no. I told you before; I'll never work for the likes of you ever again."

"Now, come on. I know we've had our minor differences before..."

"Minor? You threatened to dismember me, remember?"

"I know. I apologize, Mason. Forgotten all about it." He waved a hand as if dismissing the whole affair. "People say things they don't mean, sometimes, don't they?"

Gillespie agreed with a nod of his head. Mason noticed the worried look Parsons gave his protege.

"What happened? Something must have happened to bring you here. How did you know where to find me in the first place?"

"We had word," Parsons said quickly. His nervous glance reached the door as if that person might walk in any second.

Gillespie leaned forward. "We have a problem."

"No guff."

"Some of our pipes are leaking on number five rig."

Mason gave both men a dirty look. That was the rig his best friend worked on.

Gillespie squirmed. "We're hoping you could see for us how bad it is, so we can fix the problem in a timely fashion."

Mason wanted to hit the little weasel. He held himself back instead. "You mean that you want me to cover up for you. So, you can avoid a lawsuit for using second-rate material."

Mason stood, which made both men flinch, "You sons-of-bitches. Get out of here, now."

Parsons threw up his hands and started to plea. Gillespie ran to the door.

"I said, get out. Don't you ever come near me again.' Mason threw the glass of ginger ale which bounced off Parsons and rolled into the hallway. Parsons ran out of the door, looking at his suit in horror.

Mason grabbed at his side and sucked in his breath.

****

"Who was that?" Eddie asked as he entered the room after he saw the backs of two men run down the hall.

"Your boss." Mason gritted his teeth while he hugged his side.

"Still have your pitching arm, I see." Eddie laughed. "And your temper."

"Hey Ed, how's it going?"

"Fine," The men shook hands. "You look like hell."

"Finally, honesty. How's Rachel?"

"Worried about you as always. She's working, be up to see you again tomorrow." Eddie occupied the spot where Gillespie just scrambled from. "I never met them before, they from Calgary?"

"Yes. One of the co-owners, Mr. Delroy Parsons. The other clown is a Mr. T. Gillespie. Never met him before."

"What were they doing here?"

"Offering me a job."

Eddie sat up straight. "A job? Diving?"

"Yep. Seems they want me to fix the little problem of leaking pipes near your station."

"And they think the rest of what's happening out there will disappear? There's a lot more to it than that."

Mason furrowed a brow. "Like what?

"Too many accidents, inferior equipment, tools missing, one of the spuds buckling."

"What?"

"Our north spud is slowly buckling, about fifteen feet underwater. The rig is listing."

"Hasn't anyone looked at it?"

"The company did. Said everything was fine. All the officials split. Some of us have been trying to get the government to do something. Nothing has happened yet." Eddie took a big breath. "I can't afford to lose my job. Neither can most of the men out there."

"So, the company is ignoring it as usual." Mason felt the color drain from his face. "And they keep on drilling, don't they?"

"Oh, yeah. The spuds were monkey fixed. The hydraulics are screwed. We can't use that one side very well."

"What about the other two legs?"

"They seem fine."

"How many men hurt because of their lack of interest?"

"One man lost an arm. Two are off sick, I think they were exposed to chemicals they shouldn't have been. Another one fell off the derrick, landed on the deck, killed him. Three have gone overboard, one drowned. And that's only in the last two years." Eddie gave Mason a worried look. "Rachel doesn't know any of this."

Mason's eyes met his brother-in-law's. "I figured." After a few seconds, Eddie nodded. Mason asked. "Who's investigating all this?"

"The coast guard has been out. The Ministry of Transportation has been sticking its nose around."

"Your company still storing drilling rods in open wells?"

"Yep. Even after they've proved it a lot safer when they're closed in."

"What a mess." Mason shook his head.

"Our supply boat nearly overturned one time."

"That's not unusual in harsh weather."

"It was calm." Eddie walked to the window. Light rain washed down the glass. "You believe in Bessie?"

"I don't know, Ed. I'll tell you this, though. I did see something out there."

Eddie turned back around. "Some of the guys said they saw something out there, too. They blame Bessie for a lot of what's going on. She can't steal tools, can she? Or set fires, or mess with equipment."

Mason shook his head.

"I think it all has to do with the company. Someone wants us out of there." Eddie sat on the edge of the bed. "It's getting really bad."

****

The gas was leaking again, which gave Bessie another headache. It was worse over near the big steel thing the humans made, the one that looks like a giant spider. Someone had tried to kill it and made her sick in the process.

One man had punctured a hole in the pipe where it had started to rust. Another one watched as he held a weapon. When they were finished, they swam toward a small boat that bobbed on the surface. They checked behind them every so often. Bessie stayed out of sight and blended into the background, her eyesight far better than theirs.

They were near the boat when she decided to show herself. They panicked. The one with the weapon jumped into the boat and started the motor. Bessie cut the other one off before he reached it. He turned the other way and headed toward shore. She circled him, ever closer. He threw his weapon at her with little effect.

He surfaced, pushed off his mask, and yelled at his partner. His partner was long gone. Bessie heard him curse. His tank dropped and sank to the bottom. More junk.

She poked him with her nose. He yelled. The water around him got warm. His eyes widened. He swallowed a lot of water in his hysterical state and choked. Arms and legs that flailed around in a panic had gone slack, lifeless. He sank.

In six long strokes, Bessie caught up to the boat and surfaced in front of it. The man tried to steer away. There was no place for him to go, she was too big. He had no room, so he cut the engine. He realized his mistake and started to blubber. It wouldn't start again in his panicked state. Funny noises came from him as he looked up at her.

She nudged the boat. He screamed. Bessie waited, and watched. Her head still hurt.

The man jumped overboard and headed toward shore. She could have just let him go. Bessie knew he wouldn't make it; it was too far away for a human. She decided to play with him instead and followed far enough behind him, so he could just see her. He still had his tank on and ducked under. Bessie closed in.

He tried to hide behind some debris. She flicked it away with her flipper. He scurried out of there as Bessie drifted overhead. The man looked up at her, silent screams escaped through the bubbles. Bessie pushed him down with her flipper and held him on the bottom. When he didn't squirm anymore she let him go.

CHAPTER 5

"The government has seized control of the company," Eddie told Rachel when he arrived home after a big meeting in the high school gym. "It turns out they were listening to us goons after all. He hugged her. "I could lose my job, you know?"

"I know."

"I guess heads are going to fly. Mr. Parsons, one of the owners, is hiding. Mr. Gillespie is in the slammer. They're rounding up the head honchos in Calgary."

"And you think they'll go after you too?"

Eddie let his embrace go and studied his wife's eyes. "I don't know. There's going to be an inquiry" He passed a hand through his wavy brown hair; a hint of gray had crept in along the edges. "What a hell of a mess."

"Are they going to shut down all your company's rigs?"

"I don't think so. We'll have Union Gas on our ass. They won't let them break the contract. Not only that, gas prices will go sky-high because we'll be short."

"Your rig is scheduled to close up in a few years anyway."

"Yeah, it's getting harder to maintain. They'll just scrap her. That means I won't have another one to go to after that. They might just let me go, anyway."

"I'm sure you could get a job with a different outfit."

"I don't know. Look at my age; I'm starting to slow down." He gave her a weak smile. "I'm not the young pup I used to be."

"You have lots of experience, though."

Eddie became quiet.

Rachel hugged him. "I'm sure you'll get something."

He held her tight. "You know what I worry about the most?"

"What?"

"Losing you, and the boys."

"Oh, sweetheart," She kissed him, later said, "you won't lose any of us. I love you too much, and your sons adore you."

"Things can change in a hurry."

****

Dean thought about the cave and wondered if Troy and Jason had the right idea. Three days after they'd gone up the hill, he retraced their steps alone. He was sure he'd never find the well-hidden cave entrance if it hadn't been for them.

The flashlight flicked off when he reached the center of the cave. Dean leaned back against the hard clay and rock wall behind him and waited in the dark. He didn't know how long he was there and almost dozed off. Every sense in his body seemed to heighten suddenly; he could hear a muffled sound that seemed to come from within the hill itself. He pressed an ear to the wall and heard someone screaming.

There was no way he should hear something like that. The road to the old dump was at least a third of a mile away. The town was too far, on the other side of the hill. Was someone being tortured? Was Bessie eating somebody? Did someone fall off a cliff?

Dean turned on the flashlight and jumped. His heart felt like it slammed against his backbone. Bessie was mere inches away from him. Her huge head blocking his way out of the cave. She sniffed at him, made his clothes want to leave his body. His long blond hair stood straight up. He froze and held his breath.

Bessie backed up and studied him with one big brown eye. "Easy there, girl. I'm not going to hurt you." Dean talked to her softly and didn't make any sudden movements. She studied him for a long time, sniffed at him, watched him. Finally, Bessie backed away and snorted. Dean talked to her. She seemed nervous. He realized that she was no longer watching him, she was staring toward the entrance to the cave.

Dean walked toward it. He looked back at Bessie and saw that she had backed up to the other side of her little pond. She watched him intently and growled.

The screams came closer as Dean walked out of the cave. He realized that they weren't screams, it was someone calling. He ran along the creek bed and hid behind a big tree. The person he saw came down the path from the hill and entered the cave. That person was calling for Bessie.

****

Mason was up and about when Jack entered his room. "You might want to get back into bed," Jack told him.

Mason turned from the window with a raised eyebrow.

Jack stopped by the bed. "Everyone is in a panic for a diver."

Mason let out a snort. "Well, the company has already been here. It'll take the government a few more days to find me."

"How do you know?"

"Because the government is always slow."

"So, are you going to be diving for the company again?"

Mason scowled at Jack. "You know damn well the answer to that question."

Jack took a step back. "Yeah, I know, you fired them."

They faced each other for a few heartbeats.

"That's not why you're here, is it?" Mason watched Jack closely.

Jack reached into his shirt pocket. "Head's up," he said while he threw a set of keys at Mason.

Mason caught them and looked back at Jack. "Don't tell me, more break-ins?"

"No," Jack leaned on the bed frame, "worse."

Mason sat in the chair, his stomach in knots.

     Bessie — The Monster in Lake Erie by Deborah Tadema

"They were found in the dirt, not far from a house fire. A little girl died."

"Oh no."

Jack glanced over at the open door before he walked closer to Mason. "All of these items I'm giving you, I found. They weren't reported. No one else knows about them."

Mason looked up. "Why?"

Jack let out a huge sigh. "Because, I know you, Mason. You may be an ass, but you aren't a thief or an arsonist."

"Or a killer," Mason finished for him.

"Besides, you've been here all the time."

"Isn't that a cover-up?"

Jack checked the door again. "It's less paperwork." He handed Mason a piece of paper.

Mason unfolded it to the picture and write-up of his mystery man. "Black Tom? Where did you get that name?"

"From your description. It's all we have to go on for now."

Mason studied the picture and shivered. The likeness was uncanny. "The sketch artist did a hell of a job. She even captured those deadly eyes. Any leads?" He folded the paper and handed it back.

"Nothing. It sure looks to me that this man is behind all the break-ins, and now this fire."

"I hope you get him soon, Jack. He still has some of my stuff, like my watch."

"I know. No sign of your watch. You can kiss your cash goodbye."

"I didn't think I'd see that anyway." Mason tossed the keys on the table. "At least now I can get my truck."

"So, when do you get out of here?"

"Couple of days."

****

The smell of sewer reeked down there. Humans had put a pipe out into the lake. Their waste gushed out of it in big blobs that killed everything in its path. Fish died around it by the thousands. Bessie couldn't eat the food. She tried and got sick. She got dizzy and her insides wanted to explode.

There was another boat above her. Bessie bit a hole in its net before it was pulled up. It baffled her on how much a fishing boat can eat. They were the greediest. She liked to rescue the fish, they played with her afterward.

Tom was in her den when Bessie returned later that afternoon. He still wore the stone that was the color of the sky. Its pulse slowed her heartbeat, made her feel calm. She nudged him to open his sack for the food Bessie knew was in it. He climbed up on her back instead. She swam around the pond until he slapped her shoulder, the signal to put him down again.

Tom threw meat up at her. She caught it and spit it out. It tasted different, tough and stringy. After days without this food, Bessie changed her mind and gobbled it up. He seemed pleased and smiled up at her.

The sack was emptied too soon because she craved more. He scratched her head and talked to her. Bessie closed her eyes and nuzzled into him, feeling sleepy. Something sharp stung her neck, like a giant mosquito bite. Bessie opened her eyes in time to see him pull the offending object out of her. He captured it, put it into the sack, gave her a pat, walked away. Tom had protected her from its poison. Or, so she thought. Bessie had bad dreams after that.

****

Troy pointed to a clear area. "Let's camp over here." He stopped and looked around at the maple and spruce trees.

Eddie had led the boys up to the top of Picnic Hill, close to Lake Erie. "Looks good to me." He set down his gear and observed the lake between the trees. "What do you boys want for lunch; chicken sandwich or chicken sandwich?"

Both boys chuckled and reached into the cooler for the sandwiches.

Eddie watched them as they ate; his mind took him back to when they were born. Only a month separated them. How fast they had grown. Jason and Troy had always been best friends. Just like me and Mason, he thought. He hoped with all his heart that nothing would ever come between these too, as it almost did with him and his buddy.

It was when Mason and Valerie were together the last time. They had a big fight. Eddie couldn't remember what it was all about anymore. He had stumbled upon Valerie, upset and crying. All he did was console her. He had his arms around her when Mason found them. Boy, did he ever go into a rage. It seemed that every time Mason came back from a job diving, he and Valerie hooked up. The last time they'd gotten engaged.

Eddie tried to calm Mason down, told him that there was nothing between him and Valerie. Mason wouldn't believe him. A few days later, Mason up and left just days before they were to be married, left her brokenhearted and unsure of why he had abandoned her. It took her a long time to get over him that time.

Now he's back, again. Eddie didn't know if this was good or not. He did know that Mason hadn't gotten over her. He saw the way his face lit up whenever he mentioned Valerie's name. And he knew Mason, probably better than the man knew himself. He would go after Valerie, as usual. A guy like Mason couldn't help himself. He wondered if Mason would stay home from now on.

He watched the boys each devour Twinkies. Their voices had changed, he noticed. His son had fuzz on his chin. Jason had started to fill out; looking more like his old man every day. Yep, Frank had a good-looking kid. How many more camping trips would they go out on with him? Ed wondered. He dreaded the day when girls would be foremost on the boy's minds. Like they were on Dean's. They already talked about them. Melancholy set in, which he tried to shake off. Can't they stay kids forever?

The boys had set up their own little pup-tents. Eddie's way of teaching them the fine arts of camping. The fishing gear was already set out, ready for an early start tomorrow.

"So, when you wake up, Old Man." Troy teased. "We'll time you setting up your tent.

"We had ours up in eighteen minutes flat," Jason giggled.

"You're on.' Eddie jumped up and fumbled around with the poles. It took him twenty-three minutes. "Okay, I get cooking duty tonight."

"Let's go for a hike." Troy started down a new path he found. Jason grabbed a handful of chocolate bars and followed.

Eddie took his compass and a camera. They spent the afternoon exploring the same area they had camped in for the last five years. Although somewhat familiar with these hills, there was still a lot to discover. The boys delighted when they found a new creek or bird they had never seen before. Eddie took several pictures of the boys and of the scenery.

When they returned to their camp later that afternoon, it was torn apart. All the tents were down. The food was gone, the cooler included. The fishing poles and the tackle had disappeared.

The three stood in stunned disbelief. Only their families knew where they were. The boys inched closer to Eddie.

"One things for sure," Troy whispered, "a bear didn't do that."

****

"So, Jason followed you back to your car." Jack checked his notes later that day, as he sat back in his chair in the police station. Sun filtered through the window which showed the dust on top of his desk.

"And he stopped to tie his shoelace," Eddie told him. "That's when he saw a man."

"Who do you think it was?"

"Don't know."

"And your campsite? You sure it wasn't Dean?"

"No, it wasn't him." Eddie wished that the constable would lay off his oldest son. Sure, Dean had his scrapes with the law. It was minor stuff, like driving while drunk, speeding, and brawling in a public place. It was his kid's way of rebelling, of growing up without his father around, which made Eddie feel guilty for not being home to look after his boys properly.

"What makes you so sure? Seems to me it'd be something he'd pull."

Eddie sat forward in his seat. "Because Dean wouldn't cause that much damage. Sure, he'd eat some of our food. Maybe help himself to a fishing pole. He'd return it after a while and leave a fish dangling on the line." Eddie chuckled and sat back. "I've seen him make himself a meal, then sit back and wait for us to return. It wasn't him."

"You're sure he wouldn't knock down the tents?"

"Yep."

"And you'd let him join you after he's helped himself to your grub?"

"He's my son, for God's sake."

Jack was about to say something else when Eddie cut him off. "Aside from petty crimes, who has he hurt? Sure, he acts tough, gets into scrapes..."

"I know he likes to cause havoc. He just got another speeding ticket."

"Okay. What about the footprints we saw? They're too big for Dean."

"Is that the boy scout in you? You think they belong to the man Jason saw?"

"Who else?" Eddie stood to leave. "You going to talk to Jason?"

"Yes." Jack followed Eddie out of the station. "Then I'm going home and take the phone off

the hook."

Eddie found Rachel in the backyard, water hose in hand, aimed at her flowers. After he pecked her on the cheek, he headed toward the house. "You want a brew?"

"Sure."

Eddie grabbed a couple of bottles out of the fridge and sauntered back outside. Rachel rinsed the dirt off her hands, dropped the hose at her feet. She wiped her hands on her pants to dry before she took the bottle from her husband. They kissed and smiled at each other. He complimented her on how nice the garden looked. "Here's to the most beautiful chick in the world." Eddie saluted her before he took a drink.

"I love you too, Ed."

They sat on the patio and looked out into the yard. "You still want a pond over there?" Eddie pointed his bottle toward the red maple.

"I think that would be the best place for one. What do you think?"

"Sweetheart, it's your garden. If you want a pond there, just let me know so I can move that tree before it gets too big."

"Where are you going to put it?"

"I was thinking over in that corner." Eddie indicated toward the back of the garage. He looked over at Dean's Chevy that he'd been working on for the last two years and frowned. He wished that his oldest son wasn't so wild, and hoped that he'd settle down soon. And he vowed that he wouldn't let Troy end up the same way.

"That's what I was thinking, too."

Rachel's comment woke Eddie from his daydream. He sat back and took a drink, enjoying the day with his wife. After a few minutes, Eddie pulled out a piece of paper from his shirt pocket and unfolded it. He showed Rachel, who backed up instinctively. "Jack thinks that this is the man Jason saw today. He's gone over there now to talk to him about it."

"My God. He's evil looking, isn't he?"

"This is from the description Mason gave him as the man who robbed him. They're calling him Black Tom." By the way his wife looked at him, Eddie knew she was feeling the same thing as he did. Something dark and evil had been released.

CHAPTER 6

The rain came down at a horizontal slant. The wind pushed the waves into six-foot walls. Bessie tried to jump over them, but was pushed onto some small beach miles from her den. The hill behind her served to cut off some of the wind that blew into her face. She was stuck out there in the open, vulnerable to attack. If humans found her like this, Bessie knew they would kill her.

She tried to push out into the water with her flipper, except it was bent behind her. Bessie rocked back and forth to roll over onto her stomach. A big rock stopped her, so she squirmed on the sand to get away from it. This took a long time. She didn't move very well on land. She's too big and awkward.

****

"Mason. We need to talk," Valerie said as she walked into his room.

Mason's heart flipped as soon as he saw her. Man, she was gorgeous. She had the bluest eyes he had ever seen. Her wavy blonde hair reached to the center of her back. He itched to touch her smooth skin, to kiss those luscious lips. All he did was nod. "I agree. I've just been released. Will you take me to pick up my truck?"

She hesitated for a few seconds before she nodded.

Minutes later, Valerie was driving Mason to Port Rowan to pick up his truck. The hour-long drive proved to be a strain on them both.

"How long have you been going out with Jack?" Mason asked her as she drove along the lake shore.

"About two years."

"Are you two serious?" He held his breath until after she answered.

"Yes. He's asked me to marry him." She slowed the car to follow a farm tractor. Her knuckles turned white on the steering wheel. The tension stretched on in silence.

"What did you say?" Mason finally asked.

"I told him yes."

Mason watched her as she guided the car around the tractor feeling betrayed by his friend and his girl. "When?"

"We haven't set a date yet."

"I never thought you two would end up together."

"Why Mason? Who do I belong to? I'm getting too old to play games with you."

This wasn't the first time they'd had this conversation. "That's why I came back, to ask you to marry me." He watched her cheek turn red.

"And I'm supposed to just end it with Jack because you showed up, for how long this time, Mason?"

"I plan on staying home for good now." He turned in his seat to face her. "You know I've always loved you, Valerie."

"So, you tell me."

They were quiet after that. Mason watched the scenery go by and knew he had this coming. "I'm sorry," he told her after a while. "Eddie is right. I am a jerk."

She glanced at him then gave the road her full attention. "I never know what you're going to do next, Mason. You told me before you were home to stay."

"I know. The last job paid very well. I couldn't pass up an opportunity like that."

"You've asked me to marry you before, remember?"

He hung his head. "Yeah. Sorry for running out on you. The government wouldn't take no for an answer. It was a highly classified mission."

She glared at him. "So secretive that you couldn't say goodbye to your fiancée?"

He checked out the window. "Remember when Prime Minister Pearson sailed out of Niagara Falls on a navy ship? And Green Peace caused all that ruckus about polluting the Great Lakes?" Valerie nodded, and he continued. "I dove down several times to inspect the hull of that ship; to make sure Green Peace didn't stick a bomb on it."

She glanced at him as they made their way around a curve. "So, you were protecting our Prime Minister."

"Yes. And they didn't want me to tell anyone. Just in case the wrong people heard."

"What if they did? What would they have done?"

He shrugged, trying to downplay the danger. "They could have taken you hostage and used you as an incentive to make me see things their way. Maybe make me sabotage the ship our Prime Minister was on."

She shook her head. "Really, Mason?"

He gave her a serious look. "Yes. Really. They've done that kind of thing before."

"You were gone four years. Not a phone call; nothing."

"I'm sorry. I got caught up in another job after that."

Valerie dropped him off at his truck. Mason asked her if she wanted to go out for lunch, she declined.

"I have to get back to the drugstore," she told him before she drove back to Port Stanley. Valerie was the town's pharmacist.

He opened the cab door and let the heat escape. Mason got in and put the key in the ignition. He didn't turn it; instead, he laid his head back on the rest and closed his eyes. His side ached, his head ached, and he was tired. Mason slouched down in his seat to take a short nap.

He opened his eyes to the Port Rowan harbor after an hour. The dock where the *Charisma* had been, now housed another boat. He didn't tell anyone that he had cried the first night in the hospital. Not only for the loss of his boat, but for the two years he'd spent fixing it up.

And the explosion. Someone knew he was back, he had been targeted. And, from what he had learned so far, it had to do with the drilling company, the one that Eddie was still working for. Worrying about his friend had increased tenfold since the *Charisma* blew up. What if they go after him next? Who would ever want to harm a nice guy like Ed?

Mason thought hard about the people in his hometown, his friends and his enemies. Two people stood out as possible suspects, Black Tom, the mysterious man who showed up out of nowhere. And Ernie Elliott, who's been on edge ever since he had returned. He also thought of Jack Mullins and soon concluded that the constable was too much of a wuss. Mason was sure that Jack didn't know anything about explosives.

One way or another, he was going to find out who tried to kill him, with or without the help of the constable.

****

Eddie walked into the salon and watched Rachel set a customer's hair in big round curlers. After he greeted several people, he sat in the waiting area for her to finish. He pretended to glance through a magazine as he watched his wife at work. Her movements were graceful with an elegant flair. She laughed with the other woman, her beautiful face reflecting back at him from the huge mirror on the wall. She still took his breath away, even after all these years. Eddie considered himself the luckiest man on earth.

After she guided her customer to a big round green hairdryer, and made sure she was comfortable, Rachel approached her husband.

Eddie stood when she was a couple of feet away. "Are you busy? We need to talk."

"Just a minute." Rachel went over to her co-worker and said that she was going out for lunch. The lady smiled and waved at Eddie as they left the salon.

Rachel looked at him with concern. "What is it? Are the boys all right?"

"Yes, they're fine. Troy and Jason are on some spy mission or something." Eddie guided Rachel into the restaurant a few shops down.

They ordered coffee and a light lunch. While they waited for their sandwiches, Eddie told her what happened.

"I had visitors this morning, a Fed and a provincial guy. There was also someone from the Ministry of Transportation, the environment, and Union Gas."

"Wow." Rachel's eyes widened. "What did they all want?"

Eddie sipped his coffee that the waitress set in front of him. "They asked a lot of questions about the company. About how our rig is run, and all the accidents we've been having out there. Even asked me which men I trusted the most." He had told her some of the stuff going on out there, like the missing tools, and some of the minor injuries that had happened. There was no way he'd tell her about the horrible things. Like the man who fell to his death, or of the two men who were exposed to dangerous chemicals that burned their faces beyond recognition.

"I hope you told them the truth, Ed. Don't cover up for that company. It's not worth it."

Eddie snickered. "Oh, I told them exactly what I thought. Don't worry. I'm tired of their cover-ups and putting my crew in danger."

"I'm going back out there tomorrow with a skeleton crew," he told her after he finished his coffee. "Dean won't be coming with me this time, I need experienced men. We're going to help in the investigation, show them our concerns, give them proof that the company is at fault for a lot of violations."

"Does that mean you won't be working for the company anymore?"

"Pretty much." Eddie watched his wife's reaction. "I will be out of a job after this, and Dean is laid off. I think it's time to look for something else, anyway."

Rachel put her hand on his, their fingers curled together. "If we must dig into our savings, we will. It could be your opportunity to do what you've always wanted to do."

He smiled wistfully. "Yeah? You'd let me open a sporting goods store?"

"Yes. It's always been your dream." Rachel sipped her coffee. "How long do you think this investigation will take?"

"Well. They've already done a lot. We're scheduled to be out there for a week. I was told that it will depend on what we find."

Their sandwiches arrived. Rachel took a bite and chewed for a long time before she swallowed. A tear pooled in her left eye. "Be careful, Ed."

"I will." He set his cup down then stood. They held hands as they left the diner.

****

Troy and Jason had gone back up on Picnic Hill to explore some more. They walked up the same trail they had camped on a few days ago. Jason showed his friend where he saw the man he now knew as Black Tom.

"He had our fishing poles in his hand and was hiding behind this rock." Jason walked toward a huge boulder.

Troy scouted around the area. "No one knows who this guy is, or where he came from. If we can find his tracks, maybe we can trail him."

"You sure you want to? We could run into him, you know?"

"There are two of us against one. What can he do?" Troy picked up a stick. "We'll be ready for him."

Jason bent down to get his own weapon when he noticed something shiny in the dirt. "Look at this." He picked up a silver ring and studied it. "This looks familiar."

"Let's see." Troy took the ring and marveled at the brilliant dark red stone. "I know who this belongs to." He showed Jason the inscription on the inside. "This is Uncle Mason's ring."

"How did it get way out here?"

Jason and Troy both looked around nervously. Jason shivered in a sudden chill. Troy gulped and whispered. "I think that Black Tom left it here, maybe on purpose."

"Why do you say that?"

"Maybe he wanted us to blame Uncle Mason for ripping us off." They turned back down the way they had come. Halfway down a small hill Troy stopped. "I never saw this trail before, have you?"

Bessie — The Monster in Lake Erie by Deborah Tadema

"No."

Troy took a couple of steps on the new trail. "Want to find out where it goes?"

Jason looked back up from where they had just come from, then down at the path leading toward home. He followed Troy on the new one. They went up a steep hill, used rocks and tree branches to climb up. At the top, a sudden drop of fifty feet stopped them.

"Cool. Look at that." Jason gazed out over the landscape before him. A wide creek had carved its way through the clay hill. On the other side, across from the boys, the land stretched for miles. Farmer's fields turned from one crop to another before it rolled down and out of sight.

"That's Muddy Creek down there. Look how it winds around like a crazy snake."

The trees had thinned out on top of the hill the boys stood on. Wildflowers waved back and forth at their feet. Troy inhaled the fresh warm breeze that blew up from the creek below. An eagle floated on the air currents in the distance.

"Listen." Troy stepped to the edge and squinted down at the base of the cliff. A low rumble echoed up from something big and dark in the middle of the creek.

"That's it again," Jason whispered. "What I saw in the harbor."

***

Mason took his sister, Rachel, to the dance that night. The Stork Club was a popular dance hall that was on the beach. Big bands used to play there. Tonight, a rock and roll band played. They sat with Valerie and Jack along the wall. Mason watched the dancers in the center of the floor. The conversation turned to Eddie's return to the rig that morning.

"He's working for the government now, until the investigation is over, anyway," Rachel told them.

"I'm going out there on Monday," Mason informed them. "I ran into those same guys who hired Ed this afternoon."

"So, that's who you were talking to in the restaurant," Jack said, "I saw a bunch of suits through the window when I drove by."

"They ever find that Mr. Parsons, yet?" Rachel asked

"Not that I know of," Mason answered.

Jack asked Rachel to dance. Mason waited until they were on the floor before he moved next to Valerie. "Don't marry him, Val. Marry me." He gave her a look that he hoped melted her heart.

"Don't do this to me, Mason." She tried to sound harsh, he knew. She knew she failed when he saw her eyes tear up.

"He hasn't even given you a ring yet." He nodded at her hand that she held on to her glass with.

Valerie looked at it too and shrugged. "So, he'll get one."

"What kind of man asked a woman to marry him and not give her an engagement ring?"

Valerie sank into her chair. "I suppose you have one handy." She dared him.

"As a matter of fact, I do." He reached into his pocket and pulled out a gold band with a large diamond on it. Valerie gasped as the sight of it. "Give me your hand, Val. Please say you'll be my wife." He reached for her hand.

She pulled it back. "Mason, don't do this in here, like this."

"Do what?" Jack asked as he stood behind the seat that was once his. Mason glanced back behind him. "Ask the woman I love to marry me."

Jack looked from Mason to Valerie. "See, I told you he'd pull something."

Mason felt a hand wrap around his neck. Jack bent over and whispered in his ear, "Get the hell out of here, Mason. Val is my girlfriend, not yours. You are not going to steal her away from me again."

It was hard to breathe. Mason grabbed for the hand that tightened even more. Valerie jumped up out of her chair and tried to pull Jack off him. Rachel was on Jack's other side and pulled on his other arm. They both yelled at Jack to let go. Finally, he did and took Valerie by the arm.

"Who's it going to be, Val? Are you going to let him come between us?" Jack's deadly eyes left Mason and looked at her.

Valerie looked from one to the other, tears rushing down her cheeks. "Both of you back off. You're making me so confused I don't know what's what anymore."

Jack stepped closer to her and put his face inches away from hers. "I'm not going to compete with him, Val. You make up your mind once and for all." He waited for several seconds before he said, "Fine, have him, I'm out of here." He turned and walked out of the hall.

CHAPTER 7

Music came from the big building on the beach, drifting out over the lake. Bessie listened to the words. Some songs were sad. Most, though, were happy tunes. Bessie liked those. If she wasn't so clumsy on land, she would crawl up on the beach and dance. Her flippers would clap to the rhythmic sounds; her head would sway back and forth. Bessie could pound her tail on the ground to the beat like a drum. She liked the song about a bear, she knew what they were, she fought one once. The bear in the song loved a white dove. How can a bear love a dove?

It's out the question for her to sing. All she could do was growl or moan. Wouldn't it be something though if she could? What would she sing? Tom sang a song to her once. He called it "The Monster Mash." He danced on the ledge inside her den. That was a happy time.

****

Mason drove both women over to Rachel's where they sat in her kitchen with a cup of coffee. Valerie hadn't stopped crying since Jack walked out on her. He tried to comfort her. She pulled away from him.

"Leave her alone, Mason," Rachel scolded him. "She just broke up with Jack for heaven sakes." She looked over at Valerie. "Did you?"

Mason sat back in his chair and sighed. He tried to look sad for Valerie. Inside he was elated. He had accomplished his goal, break up Val and Jack. The ring was in his shirt pocket, ready for her.

Rachel stood up, "I'm going upstairs to check up on Troy. Be back in a minute."

Mason waited until his sister was out of the room before he leaned forward. "I love you, Val." He reached for her arm. "Never forget that."

This time she didn't pull away from him, leaned into him instead. He put his arm around her, kissed her cheek. Rachel came back in and glared at him. The look he gave her over Valerie's head told her to back off.

"Troy isn't here. Probably spending the night with Jason," Rachel said as she sat at the table.

The ringing of the phone startled them all. They looked at each other as if they expected more trouble from Jack. Rachel picked up the receiver and listened. The only word she said was, "No." Her face turned white, a shaky hand hung the receiver back up. Tears spilled onto her cheeks. Within seconds, Mason was out of his chair and holding her trembling body. His first thought was of Eddie.

"That was Frank. Troy and Jason went up Picnic Hill this morning. They're not back yet." Mason made her sit down. "They're always home before dark," she told them. "Even if they're late for supper. They're always at one place or the other."

"We'll find them, Rachel." Mason picked up the phone and dialed. A hesitant voice answered. "Jack," Mason said sternly. "Troy and Jason are missing."

Before dawn, Mason and Jack stood on top of the cliff and looked at the slide marks down its face. A chunk had broken off the edge, left a big U shape at the top. An uneasy truce formed between them as they looked for the boys. Frank Webster and a few others were looking elsewhere on the hill.

"Looks like they lost their footing here and went tumbling down," Jack backed up from the edge.

"Still afraid of heights, eh Jack?" Mason teased as he bent over to look at the bottom. "Can't see anything." He backed up, opened his canvas sack and pulled out a long rope.

"Good thing you brought that," Jack said as he pointed at Mason's supplies.

"It's called being prepared, Jack." Mason untangled the rope. "One of us will have to go down there." He handed the constable one end. "Tie this to that tree over there, or you can tie it around your damn neck."

Jack stopped and looked back at Mason. "Go to hell."

Jack stiffened as if bracing himself for Mason's temper to explode. Being built like a football player still intimidated the constable. Even as kids, Jack was afraid of him.

"Listen, about Val, I..."

"Cool it, Jack." Mason bellowed. "Or I'll throw you over the cliff."

They stood there for a few moments staring at each other and knew that whatever little comradely they had left had just died.

"You knew she was my girl. You nosed your way in there anyway," Jack hissed.

Mason rubbed his neck. The look of disgust on his face gave Jack the creeps, Mason knew by the way he shivered.

"You are the one who took off on her," Jack yelled. "How was I supposed to know you'd be back?"

Mason grit his teeth to calm himself down. "Let's find the boys," he whispered, and tried hard not to hit the man.

Jack tied one end of the rope around the tree, when pulled on, his knot came undone. Mason yanked the end of the rope out of his hands and retied it. "Can tell you're not a sailor," he barked.

Jack just backed away. Mason tied the other end around his waist and put on some gloves. "Wrap the rope around your middle and let me down, easy. Think you can do that much?"

Mason descended over the edge and glared at Jack as he went. Slowly, the rope was let out. He undid it after he reached the bottom and called the boys. He walked along the creek bank, following the footprints in the mud. After he pushed back some shrubbery, he found an entrance to a cave. He unhooked a flashlight from his belt and he went inside.

"Troy? Jason?" The echo of his voice bounced around in the darkness.

"Over here," a faint childlike voice answered.

Mason felt his way along a ledge toward the sound. He found them sitting in the dirt, backs against the wall. To his left, a dark pool of water glistened from the flashlight beam.

"You boys all right?" Mason asked when he reached them.

"Uncle Mason." Troy jumped up and hugged him.

"We're just cold, that's all," Jason's voice croaked, "and hungry."

"We saw her," Troy said, excited now, his fear forgotten. "We saw Bessie."

"Yeah. I think she lives in here." Jason smiled up at Mason. "She watched us for hours. And didn't hurt us or anything."

"Why didn't you go home? You aren't lost or hurt," Mason asked as they exited the cave.

"We were too afraid to move. Bessie was there all night," Jason said. "It got too dark to see, so we stayed put."

"I knew someone would come get us," Troy told him as he squinted into the sun.

"How did you get that far in there in the first place?" Mason helped Jason step through the bush.

"We heard a noise and went to investigate. Before we knew it, the sun was down." Jason said. "It shines through that hole there," he pointed, "until about five o'clock.

"Oh," Troy reached into his pocket and pulled out the ring. "I think this belongs to you."

Mason took his ring, slid it back on his finger. "Where did you get this?" The cold silver seemed to get warmer.

"We found it on the path where we were camping."

"Yeah," Jason said as he walked beside Mason along the bank of the creek. "I think Black Tom left it there."

****

Jack pulled the boys up the cliff face one at a time. Mason waited down below for the rope to fly over the edge once more. Behind him, low growls made every fiber on the back of his neck stiffen. Out of the corner of his eyes, a huge dark shape emerged from the creek. He gulped and turned slowly to face it.

Bessie lowered her head and sniffed at him. Mason looked right into her soft brown eyes, only inches away from his own. His fear dissipated as she tilted her head like a dog might.

"Hello, Bessie." He reached up and petted her. Her head dropped down and eyes closed as she nuzzled into him. He stroked her between the eyes, her skin, rough and wet, like an elephant's. Can a monster purr? Bessie startled, and then sank back into the creek. Mason stood where he was and wondered if he just had a dream. To touch a monster and still live was remarkable at best.

The flip of the rope made him jump into action. He tied it around his waist and tugged for Jack to pull him up. Troy and Jason helped him over the edge. Jack still pulled from ten feet away. Both boys looked at Mason in awe.

"You touched her." Jason's eyes bulged with wonder. "You touched Bessie."

"Okay, kids," Jack walked up to them, coiling the rope as he went. "Give Mason some room there."

Mason nudged Troy. "Bessie's down there, look."

Jack gave a quick glance before he stepped back.

Troy laughed. Jason stood there with his hands on his hips. "So? I'm afraid of spiders."

Troy sobered quickly, "Sorry," he said to Jack. "Thanks for looking for us."

Jack said, "Just glad you two are all right."

Jason placed his hand on the constable's arm. "Yea, thanks. Mason couldn't have done this without you." He walked up to Mason and whispered. "He did help you, you know. You don't have to be so mean."

Mason didn't know what to say. He leaned toward the youth and just said, "Sorry."

Mason helped Jack pack up the rope and hefted the sack over his shoulder. Jack led the way down the path to their cars. Frank hugged his son when he met them at the bottom of the hill. Both Mason and

Jack were given handshakes before he took Jason home. Jack got into his cruiser and left. Mason took Troy home, glad that he'd be in his sister's good graces again.

****

Bessie hadn't realized the human cubs were in her den when she returned for her sleep. When she rose above the water, she heard gasps and excited whispers. Bessie didn't get too close, for fear of scaring them. She only wanted to observe them as they watched her.

The sun's rays had passed the openings and left the cave pitch black. The cubs huddled closer together. Bessie slept because she knew they would not harm her. When the sun peeked through the holes again, the cubs were still there and yawning. Bessie ducked back under the water when she heard someone come inside the cave. She watched as a man herded the cubs back outside.

Bessie had recognized his scent and rejoiced. Her man was alive.

The cubs had climbed up a rope by the time Bessie swam out of the cave. She showed herself to the man. Slow and easy, so she didn't scare him. He wore the blood stone again. Her heart reverberated in her ears, as it pounded loudly. Bessie felt alive yet peaceful.

She lowered her head to listen to the ring's pulse. The man petted her with long soft strokes. His touch comforted her, she felt safe. Not like Tom, who had the sky ring. His touch made her feel warm yet anxious.

The rope twitched. Bessie sank back under the water then swam out into the lake. She would see her man again. This made her happy.

****

Sunday morning Troy was allowed to go over to Jason's. Jason, however, was grounded. He sulked in his room until his friend walked in. "Happy Birthday, Jason," Troy said. "Are you still having your party?"

Jason shrugged. "I don't know. My dad's really mad at me."

Troy sat on the bottom bunk beside Jason. The top one was the one he used when he stayed over, which was a lot. "I still can't believe that Uncle Mason touched Bessie."

"I know. This all seems like a dream. I mean, who would have thought that we'd have our very own monster."

"A tame one."

"Yeah. Were you scared when we were in the cave?"

Troy folded his hands in his lap. "I was at first. After a while, I got the feeling that Bessie trusted us not to hurt her."

Jason chuckled. "Maybe she likes us?"

Troy asked, "Did you see those two fighting yesterday?"

Jason nodded. "Yeah, I bet it had something to do with Valerie. I bet Mason took her away from Jack."

Troy snickered. "Well, Mason takes her away from anyone else that she dates."

"I think she should stay with Jack," Jason said. "At least he doesn't take off on her."

Troy gave him a dirty look. "Uncle Mason is a good man," he spat.

"So? He took off on her before. What makes you think he won't take off on her this time?"

Troy shrugged. "Maybe if they get married he won't."

"Are they? Do you think that Valerie will marry him?"

"I don't know." Troy looked down at the floor. "He's asked her. She won't give him an answer, though."

****

A federal investigator greeted Mason at the dock Monday morning. He threw his gear into the supply boat just before it left the harbor. Mason stood on the stern and watched the town shrink. The Fed, unused to choppy waters, retched over the side the whole five miles.

When they reached the rig, all the supplies were hoisted up onto the platform. Mason and the fed climbed up a steel ladder. The boat headed back toward shore. Strong arms helped lift the men onto the solid steel structure. Eddie stood there grinning at them as they tried to get their land-legs back.

"Let's get inside," Ed hollered over the wind that had picked up. The waves had started to roll over the platform, which made it slippery. He ordered his crew to haul the supplies inside. Mason and the fed hefted their duffel bags and followed Eddie.

The men were shown their bunks and storage lockers. "Looks like a glorified hallway in here," Mason complained. "I forgot how cramped these places are."

Eddie poured them a round of coffee as they sat at a long table in the galley. The fed introduced himself now that things had died down. Mr. Harback, a federal investigator from Ottawa, their new boss. Mason recognized him as one of the five that had surrounded him last week. Harback had stayed in the background while two other men did most of the talking.

"Good to have you back, Mason." Eddie tapped cups with him in a salute.

"I don't know how good this is going to be," Mason told them.

Harback cleared his throat. "Mason, I want you to go down tomorrow, weather permitting that is. Have a look around the spuds; see how the old legs are holding up."

"Wow," Eddie laughed, "this guy even knows the lingo out here."

"I was a roughneck for a while," Harback chuckled, "didn't last long, though."

"Good." Eddie winked at Mason. "At least we won't have to explain everything to you."

"What about the leaky pipes?" Mason was anxious to get started.

"That will come next. Right now, I want to know if this thing is in any danger of toppling over while we're on it. Eddie tells me the north spud doesn't have any hydraulics left."

"That's why we were getting wet out there. We can't lift the rig up anymore," Eddie told Mason.

"Okay." Harback finished the last of his coffee. "I'm going to have a look around. See what your five-man crew is up to."

After he had left, Mason noticed Eddie's strained look. "Don't worry, Ed. You're the best tool pusher this company has ever had. If anyone can find a loose screw, it's you."

"I'm glad someone has confidence in me."

"So, who do we have out here?"

"My motorman, of course, Rick Hall has been with me for about six years. He's checking the engine room, air compressors and such. Hal Johnson, a driller, came highly recommended, comes from another team."

"I thought we weren't going to do any drilling?"

"We aren't. He's doing a thorough investigation up on the monkey board and checking consoles, brakes, clutches and so forth. He's seeing if all their logs match up."

Mason pictured the men doing the different jobs that he remembered from when he worked for the same company many years ago.

"My electrician," Eddie said, "of course. Someone has to keep the generators going while we're here, keep the lights on. He's also checking all their logs. His name is Ken Hennessy." He chuckled. "My radio operator, a young man named John McIver, says he can cook. He'll be doing both jobs plus making sure the lifeboats are seaworthy, just in case."

Mason refilled the coffees. "Did I see a roughneck? There's a young kid out there."

"Yeah. And a very good one for a greenhorn. He knows a lot about cranes and heavy equipment. Says he grew up with them. He's also keeping us in supplies, including this delicious coffee."

"Who's my second?" Safety regulations forbade a diver to go down alone.

"Kevin Smith, our roughneck, has some diving experience. Plus, he knows how to run that damn camera."

"And you trust all these men?" Mason asked, suddenly feeling a little apprehensive.

"Very much so. Like I said, Hal Johnson is the only one I don't know personally. The other tool pusher, who I do trust, recommended him. Don't forget, we were all cleared by Harback."

"Good. Now all we have to do is nail this company."

     Bessie — The Monster in Lake Erie by Deborah Tadema

CHAPTER 8

It was Dean's last few hours of his community service he was obligated to fulfill, his punishment for getting too many speeding tickets. If he did this, Jack wouldn't charge him for the last time, which could have him end up in jail. Even though it was a few days late, Dean just wanted to get it over with, now that he had the time. It took him this long to get his car running again.

He flicked on the lights of the big dance floor in the Stork Club, smelled the stale booze as he headed toward the back room for the empty beer cases. Dean pushed chairs aside as he calculated in his mind the number of trips it would take to load up his car, probably seven. He smiled, knowing that Jack would let him keep the money for returning the empties to the beer store.

Pictures hung on the walls of the orchestras that once played there, some still did. Guy Lombardo, Glen Miller, Len Langley, and Johnny Downs, even Duke Ellington and Louis Armstrong played there, along with many others.

Country, rhythm and blues, and rock bands filled the stage on Saturday nights more often as the change of music demanded. He walked up to the stage and started to hum "The Stripper" by the David Rose Orchestra while he pictured a girl up there gyrating and teasing the room full of men.

He turned to his right and stopped in mid-step when he realized he wasn't alone. A man dressed in black hunched over one of the corner tables. After he backed up, Dean made his way to the door. He ran through backyards and crashed through the doors of the police station.

"Where's Jack?" he demanded. "I need to see Jack."

The clerk at the desk told him he'd just have to wait.

"I saw the man on the posters. The one they call Black Tom. I know where he is."

The clerk pushed a button on his radio and called Jack's car. All Dean could hear was static.

"He's coming in, Mr. Elliott," the clerk told him, "won't be long."

Dean paced until Jack's car pulled up. He ran out and slid into the passenger seat. "Black Tom is in the Stork Club," Dean spurted out.

Jack squealed the tires around the corner. Dean noticed that this was exactly what the constable charged him for. He was about to complain when Jack cut him off.

"What would he be doing in the Stork Club?"

"Free brew, cleaning up the dregs on the bottom of the bottles. Drink enough of them, you can get blitzed."

"You know this from experience?"

Dean smiled.

Jack quietly got out of the car after he parked next to Dean's black Chevy. He motioned to Dean to stay back. Of course, he didn't. The police revolver was pulled out, the two tip-toed into the Stork Club.

"It's him, all right," he whispered to Dean. "Be careful."

"Looks like he crashed here all night," Dean whispered back before he ducked down behind a table, peeking just above it, sucking on his top lip.

Jack made his way around tables and chairs then stopped a few feet away. He stood and aimed his weapon. "Tom put your hands up."

The man didn't move. Jack stepped closer, poked him in the back with his gun. Tom groaned and slowly lifted his head.

"Put your hands-on top of your head," Jack ordered as his other hand reached for the handcuffs.

Slowly, one hand rose. Suddenly a loud bang echoed through the building. Dean ducked. He heard someone fall, then nothing. His whole body began to shake. He inched his head up over the table, saw nothing so he eased his way toward the corner. Both men were sprawled out on the floor.

"Oh Shit," he said before he stood up straight. He used the phone by the bar to call for help. Dean barely remembered stumbling outside. He felt himself weave and saw the gravel come up to meet him.

****

The well was still locked, sealed and blocked off from when they shut the rig down. No gas was being pumped, a potential hazard for a diver. Mason lowered himself into the cool water, careful of his sore side, and gave his breathing apparatus a final check. He put his mask on before he submerged. Flashlight in hand, he inspected every inch of the north spud. A second diver, Kevin Smith, followed him with a camera, documenting Mason's every move. He took close-up shots at whatever Mason pointed at, usually something he didn't like. They swam over and did the same procedure to the other two legs. When their air supply was almost depleted, Mason gave the signal to surface.

The two divers changed then met Eddie in Harback's office. Harback asked Kevin to pop the tape into the machine. The four of them stood around the small television set to watch. Mason explained as the tape rolled. "See here? This is where it starts to buckle. The whole structure is corroding."

Harback landed hard in his chair and wrote frantically in his logbook. The camera followed down along one side that showed twisted steel. Mason pointed out several critical areas.

"That's not going to last long," Eddie told them. "No wonder the hydraulics aren't working anymore."

"What do the other two spuds look like?" Harback asked as he leaned his elbows on the desk.

"Not half as bad as that one. Just some rust. Nothing to worry about for now," Mason told them.

"Stop the tape a second," Harback ordered. "Look at that. It's twisting outward."

"So?" Kevin didn't see the significance in this.

"That means, it's not what we thought it was," Eddie watched Mason. "It means it wasn't Bessie. She can't fit between the spuds to push them out like that."

"No, it wasn't." Mason held out a metal object which Harback took.

"What's that?" Kevin leaned in for a closer look.

"That means that someone is sabotaging this rig," Mason explained. "That's part of an explosive device."

"Why small charges? Why not just blow the whole thing up at once?" Kevin asked. "I know that for a big bang, you needed more than what that tiny piece could do."

"Because," Eddie informed him, "one big explosion could devastate the lake. What if it followed the pipes into town? Whoever set these didn't want to blow themselves up, either."

"Who would want to do that?" Kevin's face twitched at the thought.

"That's why we're here." Harback set the object on the desk. "Start the tape."

Kevin started it again and watched Mason point to another twisted part of the spud. The camera zoomed toward a piece of wire that dangled on the side.

"That's another part of the explosive," he told Kevin.

The camera continued to record along the lake bottom where it showed Mason picking up the metal object that now sat on Harback's desk. Mason signaled, and the camera followed him to the second spud where he did a faster inspection. He was on his way to the third one when Eddie called for the tape to stop.

"Back it up."

Kevin re-wound the tape and played it again.

"See that?" Eddie asked, his eyes glued to the screen.

"What?" Kevin squinted.

"Stop," Mason yelled; making everyone jump.

Kevin hit the switch.

Behind Mason was a large, dark shadow.

"That could be anything." Kevin's voice was a little squeaky. "I didn't see that before."

"Back it up again. Watch it really close," Eddie told him.

"It's too bad we can't slow this down." Mason leaned in closer.

"Go a bit at a time," Eddie instructed. Kevin flipped the switch back and forth. The pictures flashed on the TV like a slideshow. "See, that shadow is following you, Mason," Eddie pointed out.

Kevin squinted at the TV. "Cool. That has to be Bessie."

****

When Dean came to, Frank Webster's face was hovering over him. The siren of the ambulance faded as it turned the corner. "Taking Jack to the hospital?" he asked.

"Yeah, you all right, Dean?"

"I have a mean headache."

Frank helped him to his feet. "Come over to my house, you can rest there, get your bearings." The young man leaned against his friend as they shuffled down the street. In the house, Dean sank down on the couch after Frank let go of his arm.

"Still feeling dizzy?"

"You're psychedelic."

"Are you stoned?" Frank asked, concerned.

"Don't do drugs, man. Not my scene." Dean swiped the hair out of his eyes.

Minutes later Jason and Troy walked in, slamming the back door behind them.

"I don't think we should tell anybody," Jason said when they walked into the living room.

"Tell anybody what?" Dean pulled himself into sitting position and waited until the people in front of him to stop waving around. He held his head and squinted.

"Nothing," Jason stopped so suddenly that Troy ran into him.

"Yeah, tell anybody what?" Frank came in and gave Dean a glass of water and two white pills. "You weren't at the Stork Club this morning, were you?"

Both boys shook their heads. "Good, because Black Tom attacked Jack." Frank sat on the arm of the couch. "Dean saw the whole thing."

Dean watched the teens reactions as he said, "With a big knife."

Jason's knees buckled. He grabbed the back of a chair and stayed upright. Troy sank into the same chair. Both had turned pale.

"Jack's gun went off," Frank told them. "Black Tom is in jail now."

"They took Jack to the hospital." Dean thought his brother was about to woof his cookies. "I don't know if he's going to make it, or not."

They looked at each other solemnly as if they didn't want to think that Jack might die. It was a few minutes before anyone spoke.

Troy piped up. "We saw Bessie."

"You fink," Jason screamed at him.

"What do you mean, you saw Bessie?" Frank asked.

"In the cave. There's a big pond in there." Jason slowly sat down. "She came out of the water. We thought she was going to eat us."

"She just looked at us for a while then went back under." Troy instinctively pulled his legs up.

"I went back to the cave," Dean told them. "Bessie was there."

Frank looked from one to the other. "You mean that Bessie is real?"

"She's real all right." Dean looked back at the boys. "What else did you find?" He needed to know how much these kids knew.

"Nothing," Jason said. "We just saw her, that's all."

"Did you see Black Tom there?"

"No, we didn't see anybody else," Troy said. "Why?"

"Because I think that's where he hangs out, up on Picnic Hill." Dean watched his brother closely. He was satisfied that he told him the truth and wondered if he should say anything about what else he had found up there.

Troy glanced at Justin before he told Dean. "Mason saw her too. He was talking to her."

Dean smirked. "I know. I saw him."

****

The pulse of the sky ring had gone out. It wasn't feeling the sunlight anymore. She felt weighted down. It was hard to breathe. At the same time, the blood stone called her. Bessie sensed danger around her man.

****

Dean knew who Black Tom was. After he found him in the Stork Club, he had to turn Tom in. The man was dangerous and not just to Jack. He had followed Tom to Bessie's cave, last week, stayed in the shadows. He saw Tom check behind him before he pushed the bush aside to enter the dark cave. Dean waited behind a tree on the shore beneath the cliff until the man disappeared, the same tree that Mason was near when he talked to Bessie.

He followed Tom through the blackness, waited until his eyes adjusted before he walked along the edge of the black pond. To his surprise, Tom pushed back a boulder and stepped into a low tunnel. Dean bent at the waist and silently felt his way to the other side. At the end, it opened to a decent size room. He stopped and watched as Tom lit a match to a single candle and set in on a table. Bunk beds along the back wall took Tom's long black coat after he took it off. It shocked Dean at how thin the man really was. The big coat had camouflaged the skinny man well. It was a wonder that Tom could stand up with such a fragile looking frame.

Tom had walked to a big wooden table in the middle of the room. Dean saw him pick up a small square white cube and put it into his mouth. The big black haunted eyes closed. Tom put his head back and smiled as he savored the taste of the cube. Dean knew immediately what Tom had done. He had taken LSD. The drug itself was odorless and colorless. It had a bitter taste that the sugar cube disguised.

Tom sank to the floor, sat against the table leg. Dean waited until the drug took over. He knew it would only be about an hour before Tom would start acting strange. Some of his friends were users. The man started to tremble, his arms dangling at his sides. A string of drool left his slack lips. Dean stepped into the room.

Tom started to babble. "Have you seen the white rabbit? Alice is still looking for the white rabbit." Tom's pupils had already diluted. He started to giggle. "Do you hear the color of black? I can. It sounds...hey, I'm the son of Satan, you know?"

Dean had ignored him, he knew that the man was hallucinating and wouldn't remember anything when he came down from his high. He checked around the room while Tom gibbered, laughed and stared blankly into space. They were in an old bomb shelter, built in the fifties when the nuclear threats made people panic. Shelters like this one had been built all over the place. Tom must have stumbled upon this one and moved in. His clothes were strewn on the top bunk. A pillow with no cover was on the unmade bottom one. A few cans of food stood on a shelf near it.

On the table were more sugar cubes, laced with LSD, Dean was sure. A pile of books and papers were scattered beside them. An oil lamp in the center remained unlit. Bottles and cans of powdery stuff lined the back wall on three shelves. Vials, measuring cups and spoons were on the shelf under the jars of what looked like Tom's own concoctions. Dean lit the lantern and took it over to read the labels. Most of them, he couldn't even decipher.

Tom started to scream. A horrible bone-rattling scream erupted that lasted until Tom saw Dean. Just as suddenly, it stopped. Tom crawled on his hands and knees toward the younger man. Dean backed up, uncertain of the man's intentions. The smell of urine reached him as he blew out the lantern and carefully made his way toward the tunnel.

He knew the instant he had turned to look back that he had made a mistake. Tom was on the floor. His legs pumping the air as if he was kicking something away. His hollowed-out stomach reminded Dean of a skeleton. He could see the rib cage and imagined Tom's heart pounding on it, trying to escape its confines of weak flesh. The hollowed-out cheeks and sunken eyes made him think of a living corpse. The flicker of the candlelight sent ghosts around the tiny room. One of them brushed his cheek. Tom's elbows bounced off the floor, his hands flat against the empty space above him, pushing up, to throw off the demon that only he could see. He screamed again.

Dean ran down the narrow tunnel, bouncing off the walls. The song "Paint It Black" playing in his head. It's a dark song by the Rolling Stones that could have been written about Black Tom. A howl that curdled Dean's blood chased him. It sounded more animalistic than human. Like that of a wolf; maybe a werewolf. It seemed to come from the bowels of the earth as it echoed down the tunnel. His blood felt icy even though sweat poured down his face. Dean stopped at the end and pushed the boulder back over the entrance and wondered how a man that frail could have moved it in the first place.

A whimper came from behind him. He had felt Bessie there before he turned around to face her. Big, frightened eyes stared back at him. He knew she wasn't afraid of him, but of the horror that came from behind the big rock. She trembled so badly that waves splashed up onto the narrow ledge, making his escape slippery and dangerous.

CHAPTER 9

Dean got drunk on his nineteenth birthday. His buddies had taken him to a friend's place where they partied well into the night. He woke up the next morning with a hangover. "What did you guys do to me last night?" he complained and held his head in his hands.

"What's the matter, can't handle your booze?" Ryan Cooper snickered.

Dean sat up on the threadbare couch he was on and held his head. "What kind of screech was that?"

"It's my old man's own concoction."

"Well, don't ever let me drink any more of that stuff."

"You remember the dare?"

"What dare?"

"We dared you last night that you wouldn't steal Jack's speedboat."

Dean glared at his friend. "Did I agree to that?"

"Yes. You even bragged that you would take it out to the gas rig and visit your dad out there."

"We're not allowed on the rig. I'm not working there anymore." Dean slouched back down into the couch. "Mom will kill me." He did remember some of what Ryan was talking about. The apartment they were in was Ryan's, one of five in an old house. Ryan was two years older than Dean, his friend since public school. Ryan didn't have that much education and it showed by the low paying job he had, in a shoe store. Except now Dean was out of a job. He looked around the room at all the second-hand furniture. His own apartment wasn't much of an improvement. He swore to himself that he'd do better, he wanted nice stuff.

"And I'm going with you to make sure you do it, too."

"When am I supposed to do that?"

"As soon as you sober up."

Dean sat up straight. "Okay, let's go."

"You sure? You don't look so great."

Dean forced himself to his feet. "I'm good."

Ryan followed him out of the house. "You sure we won't get caught?"

The two young men walked down toward the dock. "Jack's in the hospital. What better time to steal his boat?"

"What about your father?"

Dean huffed. "My dad won't do anything."

They stomped down the dock and looked at the boat. "Do you know how to run one of these things?" Ryan asked.

Dean snickered. "It wouldn't be the first time I've taken this boat."

****

Mason dove down again that morning. Kevin followed with the camera. This time, they swam out away from the rig and along the lake bottom. Mason followed several pipes, checking them closely as he went. He stopped at one and pointed down. Kevin zoomed in with the camera and waited until Mason flagged it. They moved along to another pipe. When they were done, Mason signaled that it was time to surface.

They were near the rig when Mason was grabbed from behind and yanked backward. He tried to push the arm away that was wrapped around his neck. His mouthpiece was pulled out. Mason twisted and broke free. The man cut his air hose. Mason seized the knife, the man knocked out of his hand. The two men fought, rolling in the water, sinking. Mason tried to pull his assailant's mouthpiece out to get at the air. His lungs threatened to burst after holding his breath for so long. He felt himself getting weaker. His chest hurt. The man held him until he lost consciousness.

Mason woke up on the deck. Kevin was still in his diving suit, dripping on the platform. Mason coughed and spit out a ton of water. He had to hold his sore ribs that hadn't fully healed yet. Eddie's face told him a lot. They were in danger and that he himself almost met his maker.

They waited until Mason told them he could walk then helped him to his feet. Eddie and Mr. Harback each took an arm and half-carried him inside.

"Sure, you're okay?" Eddie asked him for the tenth time.

"Yeah."

"All I can say," Harback helped him into his office, "is that it's a damn good thing you're so well trained."

"And in such good shape," Eddie said. "A lesser man wouldn't have made it."

Kevin crashed through the door and handed Eddie a pile of Mason's clothes.

"We'll help you get out of that wet stuff." Eddie started to undress his friend. "Before you get sick on us."

"How did I get back here? The last thing I remember, someone was attacking me." Mason's teeth started to chatter. His throat felt like someone was sitting on it. Shallow breaths were all he could manage. He stood in the middle of the room and let his friends peel off his wetsuit.

Eddie toweled the now nude diver. Harback helped Mason step into dry jeans.

"I brought you up." Kevin said as he handed Eddie a T-shirt. Eddie dropped the towel and helped Mason slide his arms into the short sleeves. Harback wrapped a blanket around him and sat him down on his leather chair.

Eddie nodded for Kevin to insert the tape into the machine.

     Bessie — The Monster in Lake Erie by Deborah Tadema

"You're not going to believe this," Kevin said as the tape rolled. "Something made me turn around. I heard a muffle or something. Anyway, you weren't there." He nodded at Mason. "So, I went back down looking for you. I turned the camera on again."

The television showed Mason as he swam along inspecting the pipes. They were on their way back when the screen went black for a couple of seconds. It showed the fight between the two men. Kevin had gotten there just before Mason lost consciousness.

The assailant dropped Mason and swam away. A giant mouth reached down and crushed the man within seconds. Blood floated out from the body that Bessie dropped before she disappeared in the murky water.

****

The call of the blood stone was hard to ignore. Bessie headed out toward the big spider thing that sucks up the gas from the earth. Someone was trying to kill her man. She caught his assailant in her mouth and bit him in half. She hid, in case they came after her.

****

"Where are you going? Jason asked.

Dean spun around and swore when Troy and Jason walked up to him. "What do you guys want?" he asked perturbed.

Troy looked down at the boat. "We want to go with you."

"No," Ryan told them. "We're on a mission. You aren't allowed."

Dean walked up to the boys. "We're going out to the rig."

"Good," said Troy, "I want to see where Dad works."

"Get out of here." Dean pushed the boys back up the dock toward shore.

Troy stepped on Jason's foot who yelped. Jason stopped and refused to move any further. "If you don't let us go, we'll tell everyone who you were with the day before we found Mason on the beach."

Dean stopped. Anger filled his eyes. "You wouldn't dare." They would tell his girlfriend, Shannon McCurdy that he was in the back seat of his car with this hippie girl called Rain. Troy and Jason walked past the car just after he had gotten Rain's top off. She wore no bra, she never did. He had been with her several times. Rain was a free spirit and did only what she wanted to and when. Dean also knew that she was only here for the summer.

Shannon was a nice girl. She teased him to no end. He wasn't allowed to feel her below the waist. She wanted to save herself for marriage. It only made Dean worked up and frustrated. That's when he'd take Shannon home and seek out Rain. She was free and easy and always available to him.

He thought he should let Shannon go, but didn't really want to. He liked the fact that she wanted to save herself. He was in the prime of his life. What did she expect from him? Shannon was the type of girl he wanted to marry someday. Right now, he wasn't ready for that.

"Like I said," Troy snickered, "she has nice tits."

Dean looked back at the boat. "They can come with us."

Ryan jumped into the boat. "No, they can't. Get in Dean."

"Hurry," Dean whispered to Troy. "Jump in the back."

Troy and Jason jumped into the back while Dean got into the front. He reached down under the console and pulled out a key. The engine was started. Troy and Ryan undid the ropes from the dock and the boat floated out into Kettle Creek. Ryan glared at Dean as they went toward the lake.

As soon as they cleared the pier, Dean opened the throttle and the boat skipped across the waves. He let out a whoop; his long hair flying out behind him. He smiled at Ryan who grinned back at him.

Ryan hollered over the sounds of the engine and the waves. "Now I know why you like stealing this thing."

Dean glanced at the boys in the back seat. Both Troy and Jason had big smiles on their faces. "We'll be there in about a half an hour," he yelled. Ryan tapped his arm. Dean looked over to where his friend pointed. Frank's fishing boat was way off to their left. Dean called back to Jason and showed him.

"Think he can see us?" Jason asked nervously. "He'll kill me for joyriding."

"He can probably see the boat, but not who is in it," Ryan told him. "Maybe he'll think it's the supply boat going out."

"This doesn't look like the supply boat," Troy said as he watched the other boat. "He's turning the other way."

Dean saw that Frank's boat was heading eastward and sighed in relief. He looked back over at Ryan. "Remember, we're just going to get up close, and then head back in, right?" Ryan nodded before he faced forward.

They got three-quarters of the way there when the engine started to sputter. Dean looked down at the gauge in horror. "We're almost out of gas."

****

Mr. Harback had scheduled Mason for another dive the next morning, canceled it. His diver was in no shape to go back down there. All the men sipped coffee in the galley after a meeting. Reports had come in that were very damaging to the company. The first one to leave was Hal Johnson, the driller. Ten minutes later, the motorman, Rick Hall went out to check the air compressor that was acting up. Twenty minutes later, he ran back in.

"The driller's dead!" he shouted through the door.

Everybody exploded from the table and rushed up top to see Hal Johnson's crumpled body on the platform. Eddie checked for a pulse then shook his head. Mason glanced up at the derrick where the man would have fallen from. Part of the steel rail had given way. Drilling fluid sprayed in the wind and on the men below. Eddie sent Ken and Rick up top to stop the leak. Mason covered the body with a tarp. Harback went to his office to notify the authorities and phone for the supply boat. He came back and motioned for Mason and Eddie to follow him. Back in his office, Harback shut the door.

"There will be no boat to pick him up. The phones are all dead." Harback shook his head.

"What about the radio?" Mason gave Eddie a worried glance.

"Dead too." Harback paced the tiny room. "I think it's time we got out of here." He stopped in front of Eddie. "Start closing down. We'll take the lifeboats."

Both men started toward the door. Eddie stumbled backward when Kevin burst in. "Look at this." He handed Eddie a lighter. "Ken found it up on the monkey board. Even I know these aren't allowed on a rig."

"Thanks, Kevin." Eddie handed the lighter to Harback.

"The drill pipes were rolling around loose up there," Kevin reported. "Ken said that some of them have gone overboard."

"They fastened them down?" Harback asked.

"Yeah, now we don't have to worry about getting conked on the head."

"Thanks, Kevin. Tell the crew that we're shipping out in an hour."

Kevin nodded then left.

Mason stood beside his friend. "Didn't you leave the big crane over by the control room?"

"Yes. Why?" Eddie pinched the top of his nose. "That's the usual spot."

"It was over on the west side of the platform."

Eddie sat in the nearest chair. "What's going on here? All the crew's accounted for."

"I don't think it has anything to do with your crew, Ed," Harback told him. "I think there's someone else on board, hiding out."

"That will explain all the communication going out at the same time. And the oil spill Kevin cleaned up this morning." Mason took a seat.

"And there are the missing tools and the drilling fluid," Eddie added. "And the little fire in the motor room two days ago."

"One thing for sure," Harback put in, "if there is someone hiding on this rig, he won't be leaving with us."

"And he'll be stuck out here." Mason smiled.

****

Bessie heard the squeak of the winch as it hoisted up the net. She rose above the waves in time to see a man run back to help a three-man crew dump the catch into the hold. It was a good haul, this time, mostly trout and perch. The men grumbled when the captain told them he wanted to take one more run. A short one, while they still had daylight.

The sun already tickled the horizon. The sky to the west was now a deep purple. He turned the boat toward the setting sun. Bessie swam beside it just under the surface. They stretched the net out behind the boat, it sank as it unwound from the winch.

Bessie gave the boat a nudge; a warning not to take too much fish from the lake. It listed starboard. The captain swung the steering wheel to the left to compensate. He must have felt the drag of the net as it pulled them back. The boat finally righted itself.

A loud noise came from the hull as Bessie scraped along it. The boat tipped to the port side. A man's scream suddenly stopped when he hit the water. Bessie ignored him. The boat up-righted and bounced in its own waves. The motor died.

Bessie rose up from the deep, a gray mountain that blocked the sun, putting the boat in dark shadow. She looked down at the men, her roar muffling their screams. One man emptied his stomach on the deck. The remaining crew of two ducked in behind the captain, who stood paralyzed with a vice-like grip on the wheel. Bessie rammed into the boat. So much water rushed in that this time, it couldn't upright itself. The hatch door flew open; letting the day's catch out. Bessie watched the captain slide down into the water.

****

Mason, Eddie, Rick and Kevin sat in one lifeboat with most of their gear. Harback, Ken and John were in the other one with Hal Johnson in a body bag.

A couple of miles inland, debris from Frank's fishing boat stretched over a mile across the lake. The men in the lifeboats searched for the fishermen well into the night. Harback's boat carried two more bodies toward shore, dangerously overloaded. Eddie's lifeboat stayed out and searched back and forth for the other two men they knew were on the capsized boat. Eddie dug out a flashlight from a sack. Kevin found a box of cookies and chewed on them absent-mindedly while he kept his eyes peeled in front of him. Rick took a handful that he choked on then gave up. Neither Mason nor Eddie ate anything, their stomachs in knots as they worried for their friend.

Lightning flashed in the distance. Thunder rolled faintly from the east. The lake got rough, spraying the men as they turned once again in another direction, in a wider circle. They had a red sunset, it wasn't supposed to rain. And there it was, a dark cloud rushing toward them, covering the sky.

The rain came, sudden and furious. Lightning streaked across the sky, thunder boomed overhead. The lake answered with angry waves. Mason pulled on a raincoat. Rick pointed to their left. Eddie swung the flashlight in that direction. Another body floated in among the debris. As they stopped beside the man, Mason knew it was Frank. He and Eddie pulled him inside the boat. Kevin started CPR while they raced toward shore. Mason had found a faint pulse.

It was midnight when the lifeboat pulled up to the dock. The storm had eased off to an irritating sprinkle. Harback was there with an army of rescue workers he had called three hours earlier. Three hours he told them that he had paced up and down on the gravel in the dark.

They rushed Frank away in the ambulance still unconscious. They had passed the Coast Guard on the way out to help them. They were still looking for the fourth man. The men from the second boat looked beyond exhaustion, stood upright out of pure will.

"You guys go home, get some rest." Harback shook each man's hand as they staggered slowly toward their vehicles. Mason was barely aware that Harback left in his car. Kevin yawned beside him then hitched a ride with Rick. All Mason knew was that the longer he stayed down there, the more it smelled of dead fish and oil.

"Come on, Eddie. I'll give you a lift."

Mason watched his feet carry him to his truck. Eddie slid in beside him. They sat there, watching the rain and the lightning streak across the sky over the lake.

CHAPTER 10

They picked up the dead from the fishing boat. Bessie sensed sadness in her man. The pulse of the blood stone quickened when they lifted the man from the water. He must have been another den mate, just like the one that sat next to him in the boat. Whenever he was near someone he loved, the stone would sing.

The cubs were not safe. Their boat was drifting in the storm. They are the cubs that have been in her den. Bessie like these youngsters. They must get away from the spider, there was evil on it.

****

Troy opened his eyes to a dark sky, glad that he was still in the boat. Slowly, he pulled himself up into sitting position and coughed. It felt like he had swallowed half the lake. He shook Jason who lay on the floor in front of him, head on a life jacket, and heard him groan. Finally, Jason got up and sat beside him. Both boys pulled their feet up and out of the water that lay in the bottom of the boat. Dean was gone. In the front, Ryan sprawled across the seat, a huge gash across his face, eyes wide open. He wasn't breathing.

"He's dead," Jason whispered. "What do we do now?"

Troy got sick over the side of the boat. When he was done, he leaned into Jason and wiped his mouth on the back of his hand. "I think the first thing we have to do is find Dean." Troy looked out over the black water.

The boys clung on to each other. Their boat bobbed in the water, the worse of the storm well off to the west. "We can't go anywhere, the gas is all gone," Jason said. "We'll just have to stay here until they come looking for us."

"Nobody knows where we are. We could be here for days or weeks even." Troy's throat constricted.

"We shouldn't have come with these guys. We should have just stayed home."

"We're here now and there isn't anything we can do except wait. Now is there?"

"What if we just float on this lake for the rest of our lives? What if Bessie comes and eats us?"

Troy wiped his eyes with his shirttail. "Everything is soaking wet. We're going to get pneumonia."

"I'm hungry." Jason didn't move.

"How can you think of eating now?" Troy looked at Ryan. "Especially when he's like that. His eyes are giving me the creeps."

"Close them." Jason inched back.

"You close them. I'm not touching him."

"Don't look at him."

Troy punched Jason in the stomach. "He's right in front of us. How can I not see that?"

"Maybe we should throw him overboard."

"What will that do?"

"I don't know," Jason said. "Maybe you'll stop whining."

****

The back of the boat bounced hard off something, jarring the boys awake. Troy screamed and sat up. Jason looked behind them and let out a big expanse of air. They had drifted into the rig. The big steel structure loomed like a giant monster above them. Moonlight shone on it which made the rig look like it could be haunted. Troy tried to wrap his arms around a steel leg, couldn't, it was too big. The winds had died down to a warm breeze; the rolling of the little boat made the boys sick to their stomachs. It took all their might to keep the boat from getting sucked underneath the giant.

"We have to go around to that side, so we can climb up the ladder." Jason pointed under the platform to their left. "Then we can get your dad."

The two of them hand paddled and pulled their way around the rig toward the steel ladder. If they went under it, they'd be killed. The waves would have lifted them up to the underside of the platform and crush the boat. When they reached the ladder, they tied the speedboat to it and rested. They climbed up one at a time.

They stood on top the platform and looked around. It was still too dark to see anything clearly, so they inched their way toward the biggest building and jumped at every new noise they heard. A chain banged against a structure to their left. A loose board flopped back, and forth which sounded like knocking. Water sprayed them with each wave. The wind whipped around them like giant fingers trying to pull them into the lake. Shadows moved. Some kind of tool rolled off a table and clattered to the floor. A machine started up behind them.

Bright lights suddenly blinded them. Troy put his arm up to shield his eyes and tried to see what it was. The machine came right at them. He screamed and dove behind a small shed. The machine roared past him. He heard Jason yell. The machine backed up and raced past him again, to the other end of the platform. It shut off and sat there silently. After a few seconds, the lights went out.

A light touch on his arm made Troy jump. Jason stood beside him, fear in his eyes. They both watched the machine, afraid to move. It seemed harmless now that it sat still. Troy started to second guess himself. "Did that thing try to run us over?"

Jason nodded. "All by itself." The boys jumped again when they heard something come up behind them.

"Hey, you two," Dean said as he walked up to them. "I'm glad… what's wrong?"

Troy pointed. "That machine just tried to kill us."

Dean looked from the younger boys to the machine. "I hate to tell you guys this. We're the only ones here."

Troy and Jason looked at Dean in astonishment. "Where did they all go?" Jason finally asked.

"I don't know. Maybe they ran away because of the storm." Dean seemed perturbed. "Where's Ryan?"

Jason's bloodshot eyes looked at Dean. "He's dead. Something hit him on the head."

"He's still in the boat," Troy said.

Dean looked from one to the other as tears formed in his eyes. He headed toward the building behind them. "You guys need to dry off. And I know where there is food," he yelled back at the boys.

****

Jason and Troy didn't move. They watched the machine unsure what to do next. "Come on," they heard Dean's yell. As they turned to follow their friend, a shadow moved away from the machine. The form of a huge man came toward them carrying a steel bar in his right hand. That bar hit on every surface the man passed. The thuds and pings it made sent chills down Troy's back. He grabbed Jason's arm and ran past a crane. They ducked down behind a row of oil drums. The pings and thuds came closer. Suddenly all went silent except for the wind. Troy looked over at Jason, his heart thumping loudly in his chest. "Do you see him?"

Jason shook his head, keeping his eyes glued in front of him. "Maybe he went after Dean."

Troy inched up to look over a drum. The steel pipe flew past his head. He ducked and crawled further away. It took all his nerve to peek over the crate he was behind. He saw his friend inch between the drums ahead of him and headed that way.

A hand grabbed Jason by the back of the neck and lifted him up. The boy screamed and tried to fight off his assailant. The man only laughed and pushed Jason toward the edge of the platform. Troy looked around for a weapon. He spotted a hatchet that hung on the wall of a shed and

        Bessie — The Monster in Lake Erie by Deborah Tadema

ran for it. He broke the glass in front of it and lifted it off the hooks. He slipped and fell, pulled himself up and went after their enemy.

Troy darted behind machines, drums, tools and sheds as stealthy as he could until he was just behind the man. He lifted the hatchet above his head and struck. As he did this, he slipped. The hatchet didn't hurt the man as much as he intended. The man landed on his knees with the hatchet still in his back, about an inch or so. He reached behind him, trying to get hold of the hatchet, swearing at them. Jason streaked past him toward his friend.

They ran into the building that Dean had gone into and shut every door behind them. There were no locks on them. They thought it would slow the man down. They could hear the man's screams as they went. Dean walked out of the door at the end of the hall. The boys pushed him back inside the galley and shut the door. Jason pushed a chair under the knob and backed up from it.

Troy sank into a chair and rubbed his neck. Dean looked from one to the other; fear suddenly took over by the look on his face. They listened for the man, heard nothing for a long time. Troy felt like he could get sick any minute. "Maybe he's dead now," he said hopefully.

****

Mason drove Eddie home and went in with him. Rachel greeted them at the door even though it was well past midnight. Wind whipped into the house, Ed shut the door and locked it. Rachel pulled her sweater closed. "Troy and Jason are missing," she told them, as tears ran down her face.

"Again?" Mason gave Eddie a sympathetic look, whose face had drained of color. "Where do you think they went?"

"All I know is that Jack's boat is missing, so is Dean." She sniffled. "I called the Coast Guard; they were already out looking for someone else."

"Yes," Eddie told her. "Franks fishing boat sank. He's in the hospital. Two of his crew are dead. They're looking for the other one."

"He hasn't come to, yet," Mason said. "There's one hell of a storm out there."

"Oh no," Rachel cried.

Eddie hugged her. "We'll find the boys, sweetheart."

Mason's stomach clenched as he drove them down to the dock. "We can borrow this one," Eddie said. "A friend of mine owns it." They climbed aboard a homemade pontoon boat. "It isn't the fastest thing, but it's all I can come up with right now."

"It's fine Ed. It's faster than anything I have now."

"Are you going to get another sailboat?" Eddie eased out into the lake.

"Yeah. I've just started to look around."

"Where do you think we should look?" Eddie scanned the lake ahead of him. "I have no idea where to start."

"Me either." Mason looked over the vast expanse of the lake, glad that the storm had eased up. The moon lit their way. "Why don't we go back to the rig, maybe they headed out that way." A sense of hopelessness engulfed him.

"That's the best idea I've heard so far." Eddie turned the boat to the right. "I think I'm going to tie both my boys up when we get them back home."

"I feel sorry for Sherry. Just think, Frank is in the hospital and now Jason is missing. All in the same night."

They fell silent for a while. Each man thought of their own horrors of what this night could still bring them. They caught up with the Coast Guard who gave up the search for the lost man and changed their itinerary to find the boys. Mason told them where they were heading. The Coast Guard turned westward to check along the shoreline.

****

The boys found some food and made sandwiches for their empty bellies. "Where did everybody go?" Jason asked before he took a bite.

"I don't know. They must have left in a hurry," Dean said. "They forgot all this food. You guys want a beer?"

"Yeah," Jason walked up behind Dean.

"Forget it. They don't have beer out here. Just kidding," Dean chuckled. It was a hollow laugh. He was grieving for his friend.

"I don't think they allow booze out here," Jason said, "too dangerous."

"I don't like being here if Dad isn't," Troy said.

"Well, in the meantime...," Dean started. Something banged against the galley door. He ran over, pushed the chair away and tried the knob. It wouldn't open. "I hear something," he whispered, fear in his eyes.

Jason and Troy helped him push on the door, it wouldn't budge. "See," Jason told Dean. "Someone else is here, too."

"Why would he lock us up in here?" Troy asked with a shaky voice.

The boys pounded on the door and yelled at whoever was on the other side of it. Dean stopped when his voice became hoarse and went back to the table. He dropped down into a chair and took a drink of water. Whoever it was had just left them there.

"Now what?" Troy asked. "What if it's the same guy?" He looked into Jason's big eyes.

"I think he's dead. How long can you walk around with a hatchet stuck in your back?"

There was no sound after that. A half hour later they started to breathe normally again. "What do you think we should do now?" Troy asked his eyes still on the door.

"Get drunk and pass out," Jason said. "That's what I feel like doing."

"Don't pass out anywhere unless you know your surroundings," Dean advised. "I think it would be..."

"I smell gas," Troy interrupted and looked around.

"Look!" Jason pointed toward the door. Smoke filtered under it into the galley.

"Holey shit! We're going to die!" Troy ran to the far side of the room. The others followed, and they huddled in the corner.

****

Bessie rose up out of the murky water beside the pontoon boat. Eddie jumped "I just had a heart attack," he said as he put his hand on his chest. "Man, she's huge."

"I wonder what she's doing." Mason watched her swim toward the rig, then back toward them. She repeated this move several times. "I think she wants us to follow her."

"Seems like it, doesn't it?" Eddie didn't appear to believe this. He followed her anyway. They reached the rig and found Jack's boat. Ryan was still inside and started to smell. "This can't be good."

The men went up top and looked around. Nothing seemed amiss, at first. "Look," Mason pointed to the main building. "Something is going on over there."

The men hurried closer. When they were a few feet away, they smelled smoke. "It's on fire," Eddie yelled. "I bet the boys are in there."

"If they are, they're trapped." Mason found a fire extinguisher and pulled the pin.

Eddie went for another one. "This one is missing," he called back. He went to another station and this time found one. Eddie joined his friend and they sprayed the flames that whooshed out at them from the open doorway.

Flames burst through the roof of the building which sent the men backward. "Troy! Jason! Dean! Where are you?" Mason yelled.

Eddie headed into the building. A long board fell, just missing him. "Troy! Dean!" Mason pulled him back. All they could do now was watch.

****

Part of the roof collapsed, which exposed the three boys in the far corner. They coughed from the smoke and squinted at the flames that crept closer. Bessie lowered her huge head through the gaping hole and nudged Dean. He looked at the other two, "I think she wants to save us." He climbed up onto her nose, then sat on top of her head. Jason was right behind him. Troy followed only after part of the wall caved in beside him.

Bessie backed up, swam around to the other side of the rig. She let the boys climb back down to the platform. Dean turned around and petted her. "Thank you, girl."

Troy ran up to his father. Eddie hugged his son tight, tears running down his face. "Let's get out of here." His other arm went around Jason.

They ran toward the boats, the fire licking at their heels. Mason was the last one to climb down the ladder. He reached for the rail. Strong arms pulled him backward. He landed on the platform and rolled. His assailant jumped on top of him. Mason's fist connected with the guy's face. The man punched him in the chest. They rolled. Mason felt a blow to the side of his head.

The man straddled him, lifted his arm, ready for another hard hit. Dean plowed into him, knocking the man sideways; his fists balled up and pummeled the man until he passed out. He helped Mason to his feet. They climbed down the ladder and onto the pontoon boat.

Eddie had the steering wheel of the speedboat tied so it wouldn't turn, ready to be towed. The motor of the pontoon was running. He stood at the helm with his son on one side and Jason on the other. As soon as Mason and Dean stepped aboard, he sped out of there as fast as he could.

Bessie swam alongside, like an escort. She disappeared when the Coast Guard came up beside them. Eddie slowed the boat and they all turned to watch the rig burn up. Fire reached high into the night sky. Thick black smoke blew toward the town. Several explosions split through the night air. It wobbled on two of its spuds. It squealed and groaned as metal twisted, listing onto its side. Oil, grease, sewage, hydraulic fluid and several other toxins floated to the surface. The smell was making them sick. A high-pitched squeal erupted when the north spud folded in on itself, pulling the rig over. The fire went out. Steam mixed in with the smoke and the water boiled. The last thing they saw was the monkey deck as it sank into the black muck. Small fires spread out all over the place.

Eddie gasped. Suddenly, the rig he had worked on for so many years seemed to lie down and die. "Now I know how a captain feels after his ship sinks; nauseous."

"Let's go, boys." Mason broke the spell. He sat on the bench and hugged his ribs. Dean sat next to him as if he didn't want to leave him alone. The Coast Guard led the way toward shore.

CHAPTER 11

The big man-made spider died. It burnt to death. It no longer sucked the gas from the earth. Bessie watched it fall over, spilling its guts. Awful stuff leaked out of its belly. It cried as it drowned, squealed and groaned as it snapped apart. Now it lay on the bottom of the lake crumpled and broken and still, the parts that didn't burn.

What would happen when the gas was all gone? Would humans take the life blood from the earth? Would the world die?

Bessie's man was there. She saw him, felt the pulse of the blood stone. The herd of men escaped in the boat. They have left one behind. Why? She watched as this man caught on fire. A big beam fell on top of him, crushing the life out of him. The others didn't seem to care. She was glad that the cubs were okay, she liked them.

She felt listless. The sky ring was still not seeing the sun. Tom had not been outside for a long time.

****

No one was home at the Webster's place when Mason took Jason home. "Sherry must be at the hospital." He looked around the kitchen and felt the emptiness of the building. Nothing breathed within those walls, making him even more despondent.

Jason hadn't stopped crying since Eddie told him about his father. "I don't want to stay here by myself." Imploring eyes looked up at Mason.

"If you want, I'll take you to the hospital."

Jason nodded and then followed Mason out into his truck. They drove slowly through the streets; Mason trying hard not to nod off. A bright orange sun peeked through the trees on top of the hill on the east end of town. The streetlights went out. Mason parked the truck in the parking lot and sighed. Beside him, Jason had fallen asleep.

"Were here," Mason nudged him. Jason sat up and yawned. The two of them walked into the building. Bright lights made them squint as they walked up to the nurse's station. She directed them down to the lower floor.

Sherry sat in the hall, her head bobbing on her chest. She jumped up and enfolded her son in her arms, "Oh Jason, they found you." She looked ragged and exhausted. Mason felt worse.

Mason pulled her down onto the chair and sat beside her. "How is he?"

"He's in a coma," she wiped her eyes. "They don't know when he'll come out of it."

A doctor walked around the corner an hour later. He shook Mason's had before he addressed them. "There's no change in Frank." Sympathetic eyes watched Sherry. "You can go in and see him now."

Mason went in with Sherry and Jason. Frank lay on the bed, motionless except for the slight rise and fall of his chest. A needle was stuck in the back of his hand; a tube ran up to a plastic bag that hung on a pole. A clear liquid dripped down inside the tube. No one asked what it was. Mason rubbed his own hand. It wasn't that long ago that an IV tube was in his arm. A machine stood beside Frank and back by the wall, it puffed and hummed and gave Frank oxygen through a tube stuck down his throat. Mason fought back the urge to gag.

He walked out of the room a half an hour later and felt lonely and scared. Two of his friends were in this hospital. One, he knew would recuperate. He hoped with all his being that Frank would open his eyes within the next few days. Mason knew he wouldn't get any sleep now, so he went up two floors to visit Jack.

****

Eddie was on his second cup of coffee when Rachel walked into the kitchen. He looked up from the empty plate that once held his toast and gave her a weak smile. "You get any sleep at all last night?"

"Not much." She gave him a kiss before she poured a cup of coffee for herself. "Troy's sleeping, at least. I wish Dean took you up on your offer and stayed here last night." Two pieces of bread went into the toaster. "We should go to the hospital today."

Eddie nodded. "Yes, we'll go as soon as you're ready." He looked down at his half empty cup. "I'm out of a job now."

"You'll get something else," Rachel said this as if there was no doubt in her mind.

"I don't even know where to begin to look." He took a sip.

"You wanted to get a new job, anyway," she reminded him. "I know you wanted to plan things out better. Now is your chance."

Troy came, plopped down in a chair. An ashen face looked from one parent to the other. "That man died out there, didn't he?"

"Yes son, he did," Eddie told Rachel how a man hid out on the rig and caused a lot of problems for his crew. He even told her how that man set the rig on fire, how the boys ended up trapped and how Bessie saved them. Rachel didn't say anything. He knew she didn't believe in Bessie.

"He attacked Troy and Mason." Eddie shook his head to clear his mind. Everything was like a bad dream. "We didn't have time to save that man before the whole rig burst into flames. We had to get out of there before it exploded."

"And Dean saved Uncle Mason," Troy told his mother. "He whipped that guy."

Eddie wondered how Dean was making out at that moment. He was by himself in his apartment, all alone, with no one to talk to. He should have come home last night.

Troy refused the offer of toast for breakfast. He did have a glass of milk. Eddie stood up and stretched after his coffee was gone. "Well, let's go." He motioned for Troy to go with them. Troy sighed then fol-

    Bessie — The Monster in Lake Erie by Deborah Tadema

lowed his parents out to the car. Eddie wasn't going to let him out of his sight for a while.

****

Mason walked into the police station three days later, a narrow cubical next to the bakery. The clerk nodded to him as he walked up to the desk. He didn't know what drove him there, except he was curious about this strange man. Mason nodded toward the back. "I would like to see Black Tom."

"You're not going to believe this. Wait till you get your eyes on this guy," the clerk told him while he selected the right keys and lead Mason down the long musty hall. Mason waited while the clerk unlocked two sets of doors before he sent him down between a row of cells.

"He's down there, at the end." The clerk pointed to their right. Mason stopped at the last cell.

The smell of body odor and stale booze didn't throw him off-balance this time. Mason noticed that Tom was clean-shaven, still had long black hair to his shoulders. His eyes were a dark blue, almost navy. It was hard to tell in the dimly lit room. Tom was slightly taller than Mason with a slender, wiry build, almost too thin for his height.

"Hey, Mason," the low baritone voice defied its owner.

"You know me?"

"Known you all my life." A sly smile showed stained, even teeth, and two rather long eye teeth that reminded Mason of fangs.

"Who are you?"

"Your brother."

Mason took a step back. "I don't have any brothers."

"Well, your father had two boys. That makes us brothers." The man didn't laugh. He gave Mason a serious look that said, "I'm not kidding, jackass."

"Explain." Mason's fingers tightened around the bars.

"You have your ring?"

Mason showed Tom the garnet. "Yeah, so?"

"Remember the inscription on the inside? *My pulse, my blood, carries the heavy load of my life.*"

Mason felt himself weave. "How do you know?" It wasn't as if he showed off his ring. Very few people knew about the mysterious inscription. "And you stole it. You could have read it."

Tom looked at the big door then at the drunk a few cells down. He pulled a silver band out of his pocket. The stone was the same shape and size, except it was bluish-green.

"Yours is garnet," Tom explained. "Mine is aquamarine." He handed Mason his ring.

"They have a similar inscription." Mason held it up to the light. *My air, by breath, carries the light load of my life through your being.*

"See how the silver bands have the same scroll work? Notice how all the letters slant backward?"

"What does this all mean?"

"I'm three years younger than you are, brother."

Mason's mouth flew open.

"You lived in Port with dad and your mother, Betty, right? My mother and I lived in Eagle." A small hamlet near Lake Erie to the west of them. Tom waited until this sunk in.

"I never knew," Mason said. "Why did you try to kill me on the beach?" His hands clenched at his sides.

Tom shrugged. "When I rolled you over and saw that it was you, all the memories came flooding back. You had everything, Mason. You were spoiled, so was our sister, Rachel. You had all the vacations, new clothes, popularity. Hell, you even got a car when you turned eighteen." Tom walked in a circle before he stopped at the bars again. Mason nodded; he knew all of this was true.

"My mother was dirt poor, living on the leftovers our father handed her," Tom continued. "I had nothing, Mason. Dad treated me like an afterthought. All those years I wanted to be just like you, you know? And when he died, I was glad because I thought my mother would get on with her life. Instead of waiting for him to show up. You know what? She loved him."

     Bessie — The Monster in Lake Erie by Deborah Tadema

Tears filled Tom's eyes as he tried to control himself. "You have to get me out of here, Mason."

"And why would I do that?" He wasn't buying a word this man said.

"Because we have to protect her, before it's too late."

"Protect who?"

"Bessie."

****

Dean didn't know what to do with himself, so he hung out with Troy and Jason. Shannon had gone on vacation with her parents for two weeks. He only saw Rain at night and met her on the beach before they'd find a place to make out. The boys had gone to the hospital to visit Frank and Jack. Jack told jokes and even got Jason to laugh. Their mood turned somber when they stepped into Frank's room. There still wasn't any change; he remained pale and deathly looking.

An hour later, they sauntered uptown and bought Cokes at the restaurant. Jason picked a table near the back where Dean slipped a nickel into the jukebox. He selected a song, tapping his fingers on the table to the beat. It did nothing to lighten the mood they were still in.

It seemed that the bond between these boys had gotten even stronger. Ryan's death had hit them hard. They looked at each other, sharing guilt so powerful that they couldn't even talk about it. It was like they belonged to a mob and had just done a hit.

Your dad will get a job soon," Jason told Troy. "It wasn't us who set the rig on fire."

"I know. It's just that he's been miserable since then." Troy looked sadly at Jason. "It doesn't help that his best friends are in the hospital, either."

"I hope they get out soon." Dean nodded to three guys that stood just outside the window. "They're dealing drugs. We need Jack back."

"How do you know?" Troy strained to see.

Dean smiled at him. "I know those guys. The one with the bandanna on his head is the dealer named Jay. The other two are junkies."

"Have you ever tried drugs?" Jason asked Dean.

Dean shook his head. "No, and I don't want to hear that either of you have. It's not something you want to get involved in."

Dean sat back and closed his eyes. He remembered the day he followed Black Tom into the bomb shelter. Black Tom's face waved above him in a haze. Dean shivered. That day with Tom, still so real that he could smell the urine, and his own fear. The worst thing about it though, was that he knew he was destined to go back there.

****

Later that afternoon, Jason and Troy strolled down the beach and spread out their towels on the sand.

"It sure is getting hot," Troy said as he eyed the water. "I'm going in." He stood, took off is shorts and shirt, dropping them beside the towel. Jason joined him. They ran into the lake. This time they wore matching blue bathing trunks. They came out a half hour later and sunbathed on their towels for another hour. Troy, getting sunburned, said, "Want to go for another swim?"

Jason shook his head. "No, once a day is enough." They gathered up their stuff and walked across the sand. A group of men in a heated debate on the far side of the parking lot drew their attention.

Ernie Elliott stood in the middle of it, talking loudly at the crowd. "There's a ten-thousand-dollar reward for whoever can bring her in alive. A man in London wrote in the newspaper. He wants her captured."

Some people roared with laughter while others cheered Ernie on.

"How do you propose to do that?" someone yelled.

"By setting a trap."

"Yeah, like the nets she keeps destroying?"

"No," Ernie addressed the doubter, "we can make a bigger, stronger cage; like out of steel or something."

"I say we just shoot the beast and be done with it once and for all," another man yelled. "I'm going to get my shotgun."

Most of the crowd headed toward their vehicles. Ernie tried to call them back, to no avail. His audience had dispersed. The parking lot was near empty when he looked over at the kids and frowned.

"It's murder," Troy told him.

"We have to do something about that monster." Ernie spat back at him before he jumped into his car and sped away.

They ran to Troy's house and burst into the back door just as Eddie was taking out the garbage. "Whoa there, troop, where's the fire?" He laughed while he danced around the kids.

"They're going to shoot Bessie," Troy and Jason said at once.

"What do you mean, kill Bessie?" The trash hit the bottom of the metal pail with a clunk. Eddie slammed the lid on top.

"Ernie Elliott talked a bunch of guys into shooting Bessie," Troy told him between breaths.

"We heard them all leaving the harbor a few minutes ago," Jason said. "A lot of boats went out."

"Holy crap," was all Eddie could muster.

****

"Sounds like a lot of boats heading out suddenly," Mason said to Tom. They had just gotten into Mason's truck after he bailed Tom out of jail.

"Then it's started." Tom closed his eyes and faced the sun. "They're going after Bessie."

"Tell me, why is it so important that we save that beast? She sank my boat, remember?" Mason knew this wasn't so, it was what Tom had told him.

"Yeah, I lied," Tom chuckled. "It wasn't her. I wanted to see your reaction."

Mason gave his passenger a dirty look.

"She was too far away," Tom continued. "It exploded, big brother. That's why I went down to the beach to investigate."

"So, who wants me dead, besides you?"

"I don't want you dead, Mason. I just wanted to hurt you. Pent up anger, you know."

"You still haven't told me why we should save Bessie."

Tom faced his brother. "Because if we don't, the ecosystem in the lake will collapse. She eats the seaweed that forms, mostly on the west end. She keeps it from spreading too far. If it grows unchecked, it will take all the oxygen out of the water. It will snuff out the fish and everything else that lives in the lake. The lake will die. She helps to regulate it, keeps it balanced."

"So, you're saying that Bessie is good for the lake?" Mason let out a whistle. "What about her killing people? What about Frank Webster? Did she do that?"

Tom shrugged. "She hates fishing boats. I think she destroys them because they take all the fish away. She plays with them."

Mason turned the key in his truck and revved the engine. "You're saying it was Bessie that sank Frank's boat?" Tom just grinned at him. Mason shrugged then turned toward Eddie's house. "We can't do this alone."

****

Bessie could breathe easier. The sky ring saw the sunlight. Soon, it would happen again.

She was near the rig watching emergency crews clean up. A boom circled the area, capturing oil, hydraulic fluid and other toxic substances that floated on the water. She'd heard Eddie comment the other day as he drove the pontoon boat back to shore, "Good thing the gas wasn't on."

CHAPTER 12

Tom followed Mason into the bustle of teenagers who were all talking at once. Troy was begging Eddie to save a forty-foot sea-monster. Jason wanted Bessie dead because of what she did to his father. At the sight of Tom everything went silent. Eddie gave Mason a look that said, 'what in hell did you get yourself into now?' Black Tom was supposed to be in jail because he attacked a cop. Jason turned green and left the room.

Mason told Eddie that he bailed Tom out because he knew how to save Bessie. He explained how fragile the ecosystem was and how Bessie kept it balanced.

"I have an idea." Tom made himself at home and sat at the kitchen table.

Eddie leaned against the counter, arms folded in front of him and scowled at his unwanted guest.

Tom continued, ignoring his host. "We have to get her into her cave." He gave Troy a look which made him squirm in the seat he just took.

Mason exchanged glances with Eddie to ease his friend's mind.

"Explain." Eddie uncrossed his arms and hung on to the edge of the counter behind him.

Tom lifted Mason's hand and showed them his own. "She will recognize these rings. Somehow, they give off a high-pitch frequency that only she can hear. She will protect any man wearing these."

Mason pulled his hand back. "Yeah, right."

"It's true," Tom turned to Mason. "She pushed you on to the beach that day, Mason."

Jason gasped as he quietly walked back into the room.

"And she killed that man who attacked me when I was diving. Remember Ed?" said Mason.

"I remember," Eddie said.

"Wow," Troy said. "She saved us, too." He looked over at his father. "Why did she sink Frank's boat?"

Tom smiled at the boy. "You look so much like your father, you know?" He paused for effect. "I think she just wanted to stop him from over-fishing. She does that. She was only trying to keep her world from being destroyed."

"How do you know so much about Bessie?" Jason finally found his voice.

Tom gave him a pleased smile. "I'm her keeper."

****

Jason turned green again and rushed out of the room. This time, Troy ran after him, chasing him into the bathroom. Troy shut the door behind them. Jason turned around, haunted-looking eyes stared at him. "That's the devil." He turned and emptied his stomach into the toilet. He didn't look any better afterward. He washed out his mouth then brushed his teeth. "That's the devil," he repeated after he wiped his face on a towel. Afterward, Jason leaned against the sink.

"You all right now?" Troy asked. He looked into the mirror and saw that his own face had turned as white as Jason's.

"What's he doing here?" Jason asked. "He's supposed to be in jail."

Troy shrugged. He didn't have an answer to that.

"I'm going to kill Mason for letting him out." Jason put the lid down on the toilet and sat on it.

"He looks like the devil, doesn't he?" Troy said as he leaned against the sink. "I sure wouldn't trust him. He's creepy."

   Bessie — The Monster in Lake Erie by Deborah Tadema

"Why would Mason bring him here? Doesn't he know?"

"He must have a good reason to; why else would he get a man like that out of jail?"

Jason thought about it for a few seconds. "Think we should get back in there?"

"We'll be able to find out if we do. In here, we won't." Troy opened the door and stepped out.

The boys waited a bit before they got up the nerve. They finally entered the kitchen and stood as far away from Tom as they could. Mason saw them and led them into the living room.

"You look like you want to choke me to death," he said, watching both boys intently.

"How could you bring the devil in here?" Jason said, angrily.

"He's not the devil. And he has something to say that I think you all should hear."

Jason shook. "That's the guy who ripped off our fishing poles and wreaked our campsite."

"I know. He promised me he'll return all that stuff."

"So, how could you bail him out, Mason?" Troy asked. "He should be shot. Look what he did to Jack."

Mason gave them a beseeching look. "I'll be responsible for him. I promise you that he won't hurt anybody else."

"I don't trust him," Troy said. "I bet nobody else does, either."

"Do you trust me?"

"Yes." Troy didn't hesitate. He always had loved this man. Mason had never given him any reason not to trust him.

"Good. All I ask is that you trust me now. Can you do that, Troy? Jason?"

Troy watched Mason's face for signs of betrayal. He saw nothing except the love in the man's eyes. Mason would always be there for him. He nodded.

****

Tom called this thing a pier before. It's a long stone structure that humans can walk out onto the lake on. At the end was a building with a sun that twirled around and around. If Bessie did that all day she would get dizzy. Sometimes she would swim along it near the bottom to scoop up algae that grew there. This was a delicacy for her which she didn't get a chance to eat very often.

Sometimes it's impossible to avoid humans. Yesterday, as she ate some of this alga, some cubs saw her. Bessie heard them yelling as they ran up and down on the pier. Before she could turn around in the shallow end, where she found herself, they threw rocks at her. One hit her in the eye. Bessie had to dig out some of the sandy bottom in to get past the cubs. By the time she got out into the open water, her eye was swollen.

That's when she heard a loud roar of many boats come out of the lake at once. This scared her. Bessie swam out into the middle and lay on the bottom. She waited until they went over her head before she slowly swam toward her den.

****

It seemed that everyone in town turned up for all the funerals. They buried Ryan the day after all the fishermen and Hal Johnson. Mr. Harback stayed to investigate all the deaths from that night. The Department of Transport sent another guy to help him. His name was Lyle Trudell. They asked everyone that was out on the lake the day of the storm a lot of questions. Before they got to the boys, though, they had fine-tuned their story.

The three of them were in Jason's bedroom. He and Dean sat on the bottom bunk while Troy sat in a chair. The open window behind him let in a warm breeze. The boys were too solemn to enjoy the beautiful day. Sherry brought them a tall glass of lemon-aide and left without a word. Jason looked down at the floor after she left. "She hasn't stopped crying ever since that day."

"I don't think my mom has either," Troy told them.

"Remember," Jason said after a bit. "It was Ryan who stole Jack's boat, not Dean. We don't want him to go to jail."

Bessie — The Monster in Lake Erie by Deborah Tadema

"My dad and Uncle Mason agree that we should leave Bessie out of this," Troy said. "We're supposed to say that we crawled out of the building and that they helped us."

"Yeah," Dean said. "There is no way they can check that out."

"What do you think they'll do to Bessie?"

"I hope they don't kill her," Dean said as he watched Jason. "We don't know if it was her that sank your dad's boat, not for sure. What if they got caught in the storm too?"

"She might just as well have killed my dad," Jason shot at him. "I hope they get her."

"Black Tom said she didn't mean to hurt him, right?" Dean asked Troy.

"He did," Troy answered. "Ernie wants to kill her."

"He's nuts. Nobody will listen to him." Dean shifted in his seat. "They think he's just the town's drunk, anyway."

"What if that detective asks us if we know Bessie?" Troy asked. His face scrunched up when the doorbell rang from downstairs.

"I don't know," Jason said as nervous eyes looked toward his bedroom door. "Nobody told us what to say about that."

****

Three days later, Mason had taken Tom back over to his sister's. Eddie stepped into the doorway to block Tom before he could enter his house. Mason pulled him back. "He has something to tell Rachel, Ed. I think you should both listen to what he has to say."

Eddie willed his nerves to calm down. He had been ready to explode as soon as he saw Jason's devil. He relaxed his contorted face and backed away from the door, giving Mason a dirty look before he said, "This better be good."

Mason hung on to his arm, sadness in his eyes. "Believe me, this is very important."

Eddie nodded slightly and turned to Tom, who had already made himself at home. "Who the hell are you?"

"I am the man known as Black Tom. I am Bessie's keeper. I am..."

"Oh my God," the female voice startled them all. Rachel stood in the doorway to the hall and turned pale at the sight of Tom. Eddie told her Mason was on his way over. He knew she wasn't prepared to meet Tom in her kitchen and he hadn't had time to warn her. He gave Mason the dirtiest look he could.

"I'm sorry." Mason looked ashamed at what he had just done to his sister.

Tom stood and looked over at Mason and shrugged his shoulders. "I am the brother to Mason and Rachel."

Eddie was inches away from Tom in seconds. His big bulk made the skinny man cower into the corner. Mean eyes glared at Tom. Eddie's fists were ready to pound him into mush. "You're a liar," Eddie yelled. "They don't have a brother."

"Easy, Ed." Mason pulled him back. "I'm going to consider this."

Rachel sat down with a stunned look on her face. She turned from Tom to Mason and said, "I don't see any resemblance between you two. I don't believe you either, Tom."

"I don't blame you," Tom told her from behind her bear-like husband. "Look into it. I am telling you the truth."

Eddie heard the skinny man's sigh of relief when he backed off and leaned against the counter. He held on to the edge as if his life depended on it.

"We have different mothers, you two and I." Tom straightened himself up. "We have the same father, you know. Gary Jackson was my dad, too."

"Dad didn't. He couldn't have..." Rachel was near tears.

"He's told me things." Mason gave his sister a hug. "Things that only you and I should know. I'm going to check this out very thoroughly, sis." He sat down beside her, squeezed her hand in his. "Dean is helping me. He's going to Eagle to ask questions and show the picture around."

All went quiet for a few minutes before Eddie piped up. "So, why didn't you go after those guys when they chased Bessie the other day, to stop them?" He still eyed Tom suspiciously, noticing that he was breathing normally again.

"Because," Tom told him, "they wouldn't have found her. With all the noise they were making, she just hid from them. "But she's not out of danger. Those guys won't give up that easily. They will go after her again when they get the muster up. That's why we have to get her into the cave when the time is right." Tom sighed, keeping his eyes on Eddie. "First, they'll run out like a bunch of cowboys at a roundup, guns at the ready. When they get tired and hungry, after spending all day looking for her, some of them will feel cheated out of a good kill. That's what they did. Now the meetings will start; the planning. They'll come up with ingenious ways of capturing her or killing her. Somehow, we have to find a way to stop them."

"So, if we get her to the cave, then what?" Mason broke the silence that followed Tom's speech.

Tom studied the floor in front of him. "We have to send her away." He looked at each face in turn. "We have to send her into the future."

No one said a word.

Tom looked warily at Eddie before he walked around the room. "History tells us that the sightings are helter-skelter. You see her for a while, and then she vanishes for long periods of time."

Mason nodded. "According to all the write-ups, she's seen by several people for a few years."

"I get it," Rachel said, "is that when someone sends her into the future?"

"Yep," Tom smiled for the first time.

Eddie asked. "Why?"

"To save her life," Tom told them. "If that gang does kill her, the legend will also die. She has to die a natural death."

****

She swam up the creek toward her den, stopped to eat some grass that grew along the edge. That's when Bessie found herself surrounded by coyotes. They bit her flippers and tail. She crushed one with her teeth, the yelps it made echoed down the valley. One swam out into the water, chomped at her side. She hit it with her flipper. It flew into the trees.

The third one followed along the bank, snapping and growling. It took chunks of skin off Bessie's back. She dove through the cave entrance with the coyote on her back. Its teeth piercing deep into her neck, its claws dug into her like sharp knives. Bessie stayed under water until it let go. He swam toward the ledge where Tom usually stood. The coyote climbed up. She crunched down on his tail and pulled him under. Bessie let him go when he didn't squirm anymore and watched him float to the surface. She pushed his body out of her den satisfied that she was safe once more.

****

It felt very good. Tom hadn't given her meat in weeks. Bessie didn't go into a frenzy anymore, and she didn't kill. There was plenty of new seaweed growth at the west end of the lake. Her stomach felt better even though she was troubled. Bessie worried that something was about to happen. The two stones were at odds, pulling against each other. She could only wait to see what would happen next.

****

"What do you mean you're Bessie's keeper?" Eddie asked Tom through gritted teeth. He looked down at two canoes they had tied to the dock.

The pale, skinny man showed his ring. "This ring represents the air Bessie breathes. The more it sees the sunlight, the better her lungs work. The better she feels. When it doesn't get exposure from the sun, she gets sick."

Mason lifted his hand, looked apprehensively at the ring.

"Yours," Tom continued, "represents her life blood. Her heartbeat, as it were. Your ring needs to touch the water she lives in. It sends her a life-pulse." He chuckled. "You have never been too far from Lake Erie, have you, Mason?"

Mason shook his head. "Come to think about it, no. Not for long, anyway."

Tom stood in front of Mason. "You are also a keeper. Even though you don't know it. You've been keeping her alive all these years, too."

"How," Eddie wondered, "did you get those rings? Why Mason?"

"Our father," Tom answered. "While you two were living the good life, I was being taught how to care for a monster." He addressed Mason. "Put that in your essay for school on 'how I spent my summer vacation.' How many times do I have to explain this to you guys?"

"How are two canoes going to outrun a bunch of boats?" Eddie ignored Tom's question as he and Mason lowered their gear into one.

Tom threw in another sack. "We aren't. We'll be waiting for them to come to us."

Mason gave Eddie a look that said, "this guy is nuts."

Tom saw and faced his brother. "You have something to say to me, Mason? Get it out now. If we are going to do this thing, we have to be on the same team. Got it?"

Eddie had turned back to get more gear out of Mason's truck. Out of the corner of his eyes, he saw the two men face each other, both trying to stare the other down like moose in a rut. Mason took a step forward. Tom's eyes widen, showing his fear. Or was he high? He was suspicious that Tom took drugs.

"And if I don't. What are you going to do, send me back to jail?" Tom yelled

"Yeah, and throw away the key," Mason hammered back.

The punch in his stomach sent Mason backwards a few feet. He flew at Tom, swinging blindly, connecting each shot. Eddie ran toward them yelling for them to stop. Tom tackled Mason, sending them over the end of the dock and into the water with a huge splash.

Eddie stood topside, arms crossed over his chest and waited for the two men to run out of steam. They surfaced and still went at each other. Tom was already spent, his punches weak. Eddie reached down and helped him out before Mason killed him. Tom bent over at the waist, gasping for air. Eddie helped Mason climb up the side of the dock.

"You two cooled off yet?" Eddie blocked their access to the shore. "If not, I'm going to throw you both back in and leave you there."

Mason and Tom looked sheepishly at Eddie.

"You're a wiry little bugger." Mason held out a stiff hand.

"And you are a raging bull." Tom gave it a limp shake. "I'm done," he told Eddie.

Eddie watched as Tom's lip started to swell.

"I'm done," Mason said before he pushed past Tom and his friend. He walked off the dock and onto the gravel.

"Well, that might happen anyway, after the trial. Assaulting a cop is going to do just that. Exactly what you want, isn't it, big brother?" Tom yelled at Mason's back.

"Don't call me your brother." Mason stopped and turned around. "I don't know that you are. How do I know you're not making this whole harebrained scheme up?"

"You don't. I don't know how else to convince you. All I know is that our father passed down the responsibility of looking after Bessie to me. And I was to get your help if things got bad for her. We are responsible for her now, you know. Whether you like it or not."

CHAPTER 13

Mason jumped in, slammed the door to his truck and hit the gas, left Eddie and Tom surrounded in a cloud of dust. "Bessie be damned," he yelled at Eddie in the rearview mirror. All he knew was that he had to get away from Tom.

He burned rubber when he hit the pavement, the stench seeping into the cab. Mason didn't stop until he was at his apartment where he changed into dry clothes. The hospital was his next destination. He felt like an irritated zombie as he walked down the hall to his friend's room. Sherry stood when he entered, he gave her a hug. Jason gave him look that begged him to fix this. *I'd bring your father back to you if only I could.* The kid's sad eyes made him want to take him in his arms and protect Jason from the hurt he was feeling. Mason sniffled and walked closer to the bed.

"You smell fishy," Jason told him.

"Just went swimming in the creek." Mason realized that his legs were still damp and began to itch, making him feel uncomfortable. He hadn't towel down enough.

He went into Jack's room next and sat on the chair beside the bed. Jack was sitting up with a bowl of cereal on the tray in front of him. "That stuff will kill you," he chuckled.

"A slow death for sure," Jack answered. He set the empty bowl on the tray and pushed it aside. "Mr. Harback and Mr. Trudell were just here. Sounds like you have a lot to answer for."

Mason tried to look calm, unconcerned. "We didn't do anything illegal, Jack. All we did was protect ourselves."

"Did you kill that guy on the rig, the one who attacked the boys?"

"No. We just couldn't get at him to rescue him in time." *Not that we wanted to,* Mason thought.

"Well, all I can say is just be careful, old friend. Those guys are out for blood."

"Will do," Mason said as he stood to leave. He looked down at the constable and wondered if he should say what was really on his mind. Maybe he should do as Valerie asked, let her tell him that they were seeing each other again.

****

Mason drove back to the dock. Both Eddie and Tom had left long ago. The canoes bounced up and down in the water, heavy tarps covered them in preparation for the morning. A bright moon shone silver streaks across the black creek. A fish jumped, breaking the silence with a soft splash. Footsteps approached from behind. He knew who it was before he turned to greet the young man.

"You're wondering about Black Tom, aren't you?" Dean asked as he stopped beside the older man.

Mason nodded, feeling tired and run down.

"Seems he is your brother, Mason. Sorry." He made a face. "Yuck. Him for an uncle."

Mason turned toward the lighthouse, watched the light on top blink six times, and said nothing. He had also checked and tried to deny it, until now.

Dean continued, "I checked birth records and asked a lot of questions. The dates and his description all matched up. He told you the truth. People in Eagle said that Gary Jackson was Tom Brennan's father, even though he wasn't married to his mother." Dean shrugged. "Although some of them said that the picture I showed them didn't do him justice. Some weren't even sure it was him."

"That's what I found, too." Mason clenched his teeth. "So, my old man was living a double life."

"Gary married your mother instead. I figured he went where the money was, from what I hear."

"She did have some money. He used it all up on her. That's why we fought all the time. That leech." He faced Dean. "And she couldn't see it."

They both turned to watch seagulls fly out toward the lake. Dean shuffled his feet in the gravel. "Your father was Bessie's keeper before he handed it down to Tom. He made sure she was fed, kept her pad clean and patched her up when she got hurt. When Tom took over he started to experiment with drugs."

"You're saying Tom's been drugging Bessie? No wonder her moods have been altering. You know that until recently, she never attacked or killed anyone? I bet Tom's poisoning her."

"She's been doing damage lately, hasn't she?"

"I think that Bessie gets blamed for a lot of things she's not responsible for."

"You know the cave where you found Troy and Jason? Well, that's Bessie's pad. There's a tunnel at the far end that leads to an old bomb shelter. It was abandoned until Tom found it. He lives there now and that's where he has been doing his experiments. He has all kinds of chemicals and potions down there."

"How do you know this?"

"I followed him. I saw him feed Bessie meat."

"Meat? I thought she was a vegetarian?"

"She is. That's another one of his experiments. Something tells me he's been giving her LSD. I saw him take it. He had some wicked trip, man."

"Really? He's that bad?"

Dean nodded. "I think it's going to snuff him out someday."

"Isn't he supposed to be protecting Bessie? How can he do that if he's high all the time? He's treating her like a lab rat." Mason watched a dead fish float under the dock. "What will that do to her?"

"I don't know, man. That's a bummer."

After several seconds of silence, Mason thanked Dean and flipped him a couple of twenty-dollar bills. "I don't know how this town would survive without you, kid."

"What are you going to do now?" Dean beamed at his uncle.

"I guess I better tell Rachel she has another brother." After Dean turned to leave, Mason gave himself a shake before he called, "Hey, get a haircut."

"You're a real gone cat, Mason. Later." Dean walked away.

****

Bessie watched as the pilot brought the small plane around and swooped down for another pass. Chemicals sprayed over the farmer's field below as he skirted the top of the crop. Over Port he flew in a large circle, low as he followed Kettle Creek then up over Picnic Hill, touching the treetops. The side window opened, and a tiny package dropped out onto a small clearing and landed not far from the man dressed in black. Bessie saw Tom pick it up and wave at the plane. The plane made a large circle before it flew out over the lake.

Bessie didn't duck down fast enough; the pilot saw her and flew closer. This time, as he swooped over she jumped out of the water. She heard him scream and looked right at him. He must have known that he was a goner. He had to tip the wings of the plane to miss her. A long flipper shot up at him, flipped the plane. He screamed again as his plane spiraled down into the lake.

****

That night was the most glorious Mason had ever experienced. He had made love to Valerie. Her skin was so soft, so smooth. She fit into his arms perfectly. He took his time and savored every moment with her. God, he had missed her.

Dread engulfed him when the time came to leave her. He had to go and save Bessie. "I'll be back as soon as I can," he said between kisses. "Just promise me that you'll tell Jack about us today."

"I will."

He studied her eyes for a few seconds. "Are you sure? I know how you feel about him, too."

"I will," she repeated. "It's you I'm in love with, Mason."

He had once looked down on Jack Mullins. Ever since he could remember, he scared the smaller guy. He knew that Jack was afraid of him; heaven knows he had punched Jack before. They had their fights, they had their handshakes. Deep down, Mason did like the guy, he finally admitted to himself. Jack wasn't a bad man, just someone he could bully.

It did surprise him that Valerie took up with him. After he thought about it, he saw that they made a nice couple. He watched her head to the bathroom; her naked body still stirred him. He sighed and sat up in bed. The next item in his grand scheme of things was to move in with her.

****

The morning was hot and humid when the men met at the dock. Mason watched as Mr. Harback stepped into the Coast Guard cutter and headed out toward the lake. Both he and Eddie waved at the man who was too far away to speak to.

"I wonder if they know what's going on," Eddie said as the cutter skipped over the waves when it reached open water.

"C'mon guys, we don't have a lot of time to waste." Tom clomped up the dock as if he forgot all about yesterday, and handed each man a life jacket. They threw them into the canoes. None of the power boats had left yet. Tom told them he was certain that they would leave in a few short hours.

"So, how many days will it take us to paddle to the mouth of Muddy Creek?" Mason asked as he settled into the canoe. He watched his brother closely for any signs that Tom was under the influence of drugs. So far, he seemed sober. Tom settled in the lead canoe with most of the gear. Mason and Eddie followed in the second one.

"We're not going out into the lake," Tom answered while he turned upstream. "I know another way; shorter, where Muddy and Kettle Creeks come close together."

Mason looked back at Eddie who seemed to be enjoying the ride. Eddie was watching the scenery as they glided over the murky water.

"You love this, don't you?" Mason felt better after he'd convinced Eddie to do this thing. His friend still glared at Tom but didn't threaten him anymore.

"Relax, man," Eddie yelled at Mason who squirmed in his seat. "You're perfectly safe in a canoe if you don't tip us over."

Mason settled himself down and concentrated on paddling. His bare arms glistened with sweat as he took long deep strokes. He looked back again, noticed that Eddie seemed a little too relaxed. "This isn't too bad, once you get used to it," Mason laughed.

"Just look at how peaceful and quiet it is. It wouldn't be the first time I fell asleep in a canoe."

"Did you tip over?" Tom asked.

"No. Luckily I didn't." Eddie let out a roar. After he settled down he said, "Just like when a guy falls off his chair without spilling his beer."

Tom and Mason both let out deep laughs as they steered around a bend.

A half hour later, Tom pulled up beside a steep bank. "We have to portage to the other creek from here."

They emptied the canoes then flipped them overhead. Tom and Mason carried one while Eddie followed with the other one, each man with a sack on his back. Tom led them up a hill and twisted and turned through the thicket. When they reached the other creek, they lowered the canoes into the water and re-loaded them. This time they headed downstream toward the lake.

Mason recognized the cave entrance where he found the boys. He looked up at the sides of the cliffs; saw that the opening couldn't be seen from up top. He showed them where the boys slid down the cliff face and where he propelled down from.

Tom nodded thoughtfully as he scanned upward to the top of the cliff. Mason knew he remembered the place where he planted his ring for the boys to find. Tom looked down at his brother. When their eyes met, Tom paddled faster.

****

Her heart pounded loudly. The stones pulsed in a steady rhythm. Bessie didn't know what to do, so she swam back and forth. She felt jumpy and didn't know why.

Yes, she did. The others were on their way to get her.

****

Troy and Jason climbed up Picnic Hill, went along the narrow path to the top of the cliff. "Look at how much the side's caved in," Troy said as he pointed down the embankment. "I can't believe we slid all the way down there."

"Yeah. And there's the tree where Mason talked to Bessie," Jason said as if in awe of the man.

Troy saw something in the creek and suddenly pulled Jason back. "Someone's down there."

Jason lifted his head enough to peer over the edge. "Two canoes. Hey, what are they doing with Black Tom?"

"Dean told me that he's our uncle," Troy said with distaste. "He's mom's brother, too."

"How can they have a brother they didn't know about?" Jason asked.

"They all have the same father. Grandpa Jackson had a chick on the side."

"Tom's sure not like your Uncle Mason, is he?"

"No."

"Hey. Let's follow them." Jason jumped up after the canoes left their sight. The boys glanced at each other. Jason pointed to the edge. "There's only one way that I know of."

Troy walked to the edge, gave a wave and yelled "Geronimo," before he jumped down the gravel packed bank. He slid and rolled and bounced until he stopped suddenly and spit out a mouthful of grit. He stood, brushed himself off and looked up at Jason. "See, nothing to it.

Jason tucked his arms in close to his body and slid off the edge. He was over to the left too far and Todd saw him hit a boulder on the way down. He cringed at the thought of his friend being hurt.

Jason stopped beside Troy, his face screwed up in agony. He writhed on the ground and grabbed his at his leg. "I think I broke my ankle."

Troy dropped to his knees and brushed the sand from Jason's leg. "It's swelling up."

****

They waited at the mouth of the creek, the three men sat on a sandy hill mixed with clay and gravel. It reminded Mason of the place where he almost drowned. Eddie searched across the lake. "Nobody, so far."

"They're coming." Tom took a set of binoculars out of a sack and carefully checked all around. "Hang on to these." He gave them to Mason and took out another pair for himself and hung them around his neck. He lifted Mason's hand and pointed to the ring. "When you see them coming, point this at me across the creek. When I give the order, turn this clockwise." He twisted the stone.

"I didn't know it turned." Mason studied his ring closer. "What will that do?"

"I will do the same with my ring and point it toward you. This will call Bessie in."

"Aw, won't that be awful loud? We'll all go deaf." Eddie looked at them nervously.

Tom shook his head. "No, we won't hear it. It's too high of a frequency."

Eddie said, "You're forgetting something there, chief. That's a bit too narrow for her to fit through, don't you think?"

"That's all we need is a stuck monster," Mason said while he looked the mouth of the creek over.

"She won't get stuck," Tom told them in a huff. "There's a channel under there. It helps to hide her. That's how she gets to her cave almost undetected. Who would expect her to swim up this creek?"

Both Mason and Eddie nodded at the logic of Tom's explanation.

"I need for you to set up over here." Tom led Eddie down the bank. "Pull the canoes over by that cedar and hold them ready. We're going to have to paddle like mad after she goes through the gate."

Eddie nodded then headed down to move the canoes into place.

Tom went back up by Mason and took several bundles of dynamite out of a sack.

"What are you going to do with those?" Mason balked.

"Just close the gate, that's all, so none of their power boats can get through." Tom showed him. "I'm only going to plant these near the center. You'll be sprayed a little. I'll be over there on that rock," he pointed, "and light the fuses from there."

"You've played with matches before, I take it?" The explosion of the *Charisma* flashed before Mason. Could it have been Tom? Could he have set a timer, or used a remote switch to set off the explosion?

Tom grinned back at him.

Mason looked down at the dynamite Tom held and wished he was still at home in bed. Better yet, in Valerie's bed. Sweat glistened on Tom's hands. Was it the heat, the excitement? Or was he in need of his drugs?

"Why can't you just do this by yourself?" Mason wanted to back out suddenly.

"Because we need the power of both rings. They'll feed off each other. Bessie will know when she hears them."

"Why wait until the entire world is on top of her?"

"Timing, dear brother. We have to do this just right, or it won't work."

"Then what?"

"We send her into the future. She must go through the gate first. Got it?"

"They're coming," Eddie yelled while he braced himself. The canoes drifted downstream pulling on the rope he held.

Tom swam across to the other side of the creek, stopped only long enough to plant the dynamite. Mason waited until Tom was sitting on the rock and pointing his ring at him. He pointed his at Tom. They waited.

CHAPTER 14

The roar of a dozen boats came from the east. Gunshots echoed across the lake. The Coast Guard cut across the bow of one boat, stopping in front of it. Mason saw someone hop over and several pairs of hands reach up in surrender. Now he knew why Harback was there that morning, to stop this illegal hunt. Not to mention, to confiscate all the illegal weapons. Several shots rang out. Boats skipped across the water in all directions. They all turned at once, heading back out toward the old gas rig that lay broken on the bottom of the lake.

The boats turned again and headed toward shore. More shots rang out. The Coast Guard chased back and forth in a futile attempt to stop them. Harback hollered through the blow horn. Another boat surrendered.

Bessie rose up, high above the water, which made one boat fly through the air. Another one turned and headed back home. The rest kept after her while the Coast Guard remained too busy as they picked up men out of the water. She dove again and surfaced a quarter-mile away from the gate and headed back out.

"Now," Tom yelled. "Now Mason."

Mason turned the stone, still aimed at Tom. A sudden jolt made him jump as if he was just electrocuted. He looked across the creek, Tom had done the same. There was a hazy yellow light arching between the two rings. Bessie turned, plowed past three boats as she headed straight for them. He could hear them yelling in triumph because they thought they had her trapped. More shots fired. Bessie faltered. He knew she had been hit and watched as the four remaining boats gained on her.

"Come on Bessie. You can make it, girl."

Out of the corner of his eye, Mason saw a speed boat skipping across the waves toward them. It cut off the fleet from its prey. "Looks like Jack's boat," he muttered. Jack was still in the hospital. He lifted his binoculars with his free hand, careful to keep the ring pointed at Tom. Dean let out a whoop as he made a pass in front of Mason; his long blond hair flying behind him. Several men didn't shoot anymore, afraid they might hit a kid. Ernie Elliott, however, still fired his shotgun and yelled at Dean to get out-of-the-way. Several passes later, Dean headed back home.

Bessie had enough time to dive deep and swim through the gate. When she surfaced beside Eddie, Tom set off the dynamite. The ear-splitting explosion sent rock and sand straight up in the air. It land-ed into the mouth of the creek, blocking it off completely.

One boat, unable to stop in time, ran into the debris and crashed. The rest pulled up before they too were destroyed. Tom yelled at Mason to run. They skirted down the bank toward Eddie who had the canoes pushed out into the water. All three jumped in and paddled like mad. Mason looked behind them to see if anyone was following, seeing no one. Bessie swam slowly after them.

With arms that ached and near exhaustion, their willpower alone kept them going. The creek got narrower, the trees thicker on the banks. The cliffs grew higher. Bessie laid down, unable to move any further. The men tried not to get squished under her weight when her big bulk landed across the creek. They raced around the last bend. Troy stood on the narrow shore near the cave waving frantically at them.

****

She knew they were going to come today. They chased her, again. Bessie couldn't stand the noise they made. Her head pounded. They pointed their weapons at her. She had seen these things in the past.

That's when she felt a sharp pain, like before. Bessie found it hard to move, her strength leaving her body.

The stones had come together. The pulse had intensified. Bessie needed to answer the call. She'd fought a few more boats and dove deep. She was able to get through the gate just in time before she could rest. Those men were her life.

****

Dean guided Jack's boat back into its slip after his joyride and cut the motor, exhilarated after the excitement he just had. "Bitch'in," he yelled, heady that he had ripped off the cop's boat again. He jumped out, walked up the dock and hummed a peppy tune. Bessie was safe now. He rounded the corner of the fish shanty and ran into his Ernie Elliott and a couple of his goons.

"You," Ernie yelled, "Get back here."

The men chased Dean across the parking lot and down the street; he ducked between houses and jumped a fence. Under a porch, he slid and waited while he caught his breath. The men stopped on the other side of the skirting and leaned on the rail just inches from the terrified young man.

"You have to do something about that kid," one man threatened, "he's going to ruin everything."

"What do you want me to do," Ernie's angry voice shot back, "shoot him?"

"You did aim at him," one of them snickered. "Are you sorry you missed?"

"Shut up." Ernie's angry voice made Dean crouch back in fear. "We can't afford any more mistakes," Ernie said. "Mr. Parsons will have our hides."

"It was bad enough we started the wrong house on fire. I didn't want to kill a little girl." A third man said.

"Where is that damn hippie?" The first man walked away.

"At least we did our bit with the rig, eh?" the second man said. His voice faded as he went.

"Shut up," Ernie warned. "We have to figure out how to pin this all on Black Tom, remember?"

Dean's whole body shook as he listened. It was unbelievable that Ernie shot at him. What had gotten into him? He had never seen Ernie like this before.

****

Between Eddie and Mason, they had Jason seated comfortably in one of the canoes. Eddie eased in behind him and paddled toward town. Mason and Tom argued over whom was going to stay and look after Bessie. Tom didn't have strength or stamina to win against his over-powering brother. Mason pushed Tom and Todd off in the second canoe and watched them float away.

Mason walked along the creek bed below the cliff. Every now and then he'd try to climb up, only to turn back. He chose a place covered with trees that wasn't too steep, pulled himself up by roots and branches, finally making it to the top. After he caught his breath he headed toward the path that led home.

A half an hour later, Mason was at his sister's explaining to her where her husband and son were. She went with him to Valerie's. He asked her to help him.

Valerie shook her head. "I'm not a physician, Mason. I've never done that sort of thing before."

He held up his hands, beseechingly. "You're the only one I trust, Val. And none of us have done this sort of thing before."

Valerie looked over at Rachel. Rachel shrugged. "Let's see if this monster is for real."

Mason led the two women up the hill. As they approached the top he could hear Bessie. A sickening roar echoed from down below. Mason looked over the edge and watched Bessie try to get her head unstuck from between two trees. She was on her side, half in the water. Her long neck stretched across a patch of gravel and into the woods. Behind her, the cliff expanded a good hundred feet straight up.

Bessie herself was as big as a two-story house. Her long tail reached across the creek, back to where Mason stood. One long flipper waved high in the air. Blood ran down her side from her shoulder. Mason glanced down at his ring. It was the same color, dark red, almost black.

"She's hurt," Valerie whispered beside him.

"She's been shot." Mason gasped as Bessie freed her head, lifted it high above the trees and looked right at him.

"Her head's bigger than my car." Rachel instinctively stepped back. "I didn't realize how huge she really was. And she's real."

A low rumble filled the little valley below them as Bessie laid her head back down. Mason unhitched Valerie's nails from his arm and turned to her. "Think you can help her?"

Valerie looked down at the beast. "Is it safe?"

"She won't hurt you," he told her calmly, "you're with me." He could feel her body shaking and gave her a little squeeze. "I promise," he told her. "Remember, how many times she's saved my life?"

"How do we get down there?" she finally asked.

****

The popping of Troy's nerves was hard to keep in check. The devil sat behind him in the canoe. At that moment, he hated his Uncle Mason for putting him in this position, with all his heart. Black Tom's breath raked the back of his neck. Troy's whole body shook as he paddled hard and fast to catch up to his dad.

"It's kept in the family, you know," Tom said.

"What?" Troy willed the canoe to break in half, so he could get away from this man.

Tom spoke louder. "I said, the role of the keeper; it stays within the family. It's our curse."

Troy shook his head. "Not me, man. If that's what you're thinking. Don't get me involved with this."

"You already are, Troy. So is Dean. The rings have to stay in the family. You're the next in line for one of them."

Eddie's back showed after they rounded a bend. *Slow down, Dad.* He knew that his father was trying to get Jason help for his ankle. He wouldn't slow down just because his son was a little afraid. Hell, he was scared out of his wits.

It comforted him, just a little, to know that he could shout at his father. "Forget it," he yelled back at Tom.

"Can't. You need training. Someone needs to show you what to do."

"Nobody showed Uncle Mason. He didn't even know he was a keeper."

"I know. That is unfortunate, isn't it? Now he has to learn as he goes along, the hard way."

"So? Just keep me out of it."

"He would have been a big help if he knew," Tom kept on. "Maybe I wouldn't have gotten all screwed up if I had help."

"Why don't you teach him?"

"Dad should have taught him when he was younger. By the time I took over; well I just couldn't handle that, too."

His father's canoe was pulled up on the shore, they stopped beside it and he jumped out. Troy let Tom pull the canoe up onto the grass. He ran to catch up to his father, his wet shoes sliding in the mud as he tried to get up a hill. He caught up to his dad, out of breath and sore from paddling.

Eddie carried Jason in his arms, making his way through the trees. Troy stayed close behind, checking behind him for the devil to swoop down on him and devour him. Tom had fallen back, out of sight.

Eddie turned toward town when he reached the road. Troy stepped up beside him. Jason had passed out. "That's good," he told Troy. "He won't go into shock."

A blue and white Ford slowed to a stop beside them. An older lady asked if she could help. Troy opened the back door, so Joe could slide Jason in.

"We need to get him to the hospital," Eddie told her as he shut the door behind him, Jason's head cradled in his lap.

Troy sat in the front seat, next to the kind lady. "Thank you," he told her. To himself, he mouthed, "for saving my life." He laid his

    Bessie — The Monster in Lake Erie by Deborah Tadema

head back against the seat, closed his eyes and forced Tom out of his mind.

****

Dean waited until dark before he crawled out from under the porch, a good two hours. After he brushed himself off, he ran two more blocks. Into a back door of a familiar house, he flew and locked the door behind him. He called out. No one answered. Dean wondered where Sherry was. Probably at the hospital. He found his way into the kitchen, opened a bottle of pop he found in the fridge. A fried egg sandwich helped ease the hunger in his belly. A bag of potato chips did for dessert. He left the dishes in the sink and went into the living room, picked up the phone and dialed as he stood in the dark. On the third ring, Eddie's voice sounded through the receiver like a security blanket.

"Dad," he whispered even though he knew he was alone. "Ernie's after me. Mr. Parsons hired him and a couple of other dudes to do his dirty work."

"Where are you, Dean? I'll come and get you."

"I'm in Frank's house."

"Smart boy. I don't think they'll look there. I'll be right over, you hang tight."

Dean didn't get a chance to respond. The phone went dead, left him feeling more vulnerable. He blew out a sigh and checked out the front window. The big clock on the wall chimed. Dean jumped, knocking over a lamp. He set it right, didn't check to see if it was broken. Eddie's car pulled into the driveway a few minutes later. The car lights flicked twice. Dean ran out and jumped into the passenger side. Eddie took Dean home, sneaked him in the back door then locked it behind them.

Troy greeted them with a nod and checked out the downstairs windows. "Someone's coming. Backdoor."

Eddie told Troy and Dean to hide while he checked out the kitchen window. "It's Tom," he said as he unlocked the door and let the man in. Tom stepped inside. Eddie locked the door again. The boys stepped back into the kitchen looking warily at Tom.

"We need to get you to a safe house, Dean. It'll only be a matter of time before they come here looking for you," Eddie said.

"They killed that little girl." Dean was shaking. "Ernie destroyed your rig, Dad. Mr. Parsons hired him, so he could collect insurance money. I think he knows where to find Mr. Parsons."

"What a bummer," Troy said to Dean while he stood as far away from Black Tom as possible.

"I know where he can hold up." Tom placed a hand on Dean's shoulder which made him squirm. "Don't worry, you'll be safe until we can get this all sorted out."

Dean nodded; he knew where Tom had in mind, Bessie's den and the old bomb shelter. Ernie would never find him there. Tom's bad trip on LSD still haunted him. None of his friends had ever gone harry like that. He wondered why it had hit Tom so hard.

Eddie walked around to the other side of the table. "You stole Jack's boat. I'm betting that wasn't the first time either, was it? Was it really Ryan who stole it last week, or was that you?"

"That was genius," Tom laughed. "You helped us get Bessie through the gate. I for one thank you." He looked seriously at Dean. "Want me to go with you?"

Dean didn't want Tom to know that he had been inside the bomb shelter. At the same time, he didn't want Tom there with him. He nodded.

Tom slapped Dean's shoulder. "I'll show you the way, then I have unfinished business to attend to."

****

They had to camp overnight. Rachel found berries for supper. Mason also had a few biscuits left over in his sack. They built a small fire and dozed throughout the night. In the morning, Mason guided them down to the creek. They swam across to the other side and knew that the hot sun would dry their clothes before too long. Valerie was trembling when Mason walked up to her. He held her until she gave him a weak smile. Bessie's double row of teeth showed when she yawned.

 Bessie — The Monster in Lake Erie by Deborah Tadema

"You think she's smiling?" Rachel asked. "They say dogs do."

"Maybe." Mason put his hand on his sister's shoulder, hoping to ease her fears. "We better get started." He watched Bessie blink as if she too was nervous.

"How do I get way up there?" Valerie asked.

"Climb up," Rachel told her. "Use her neck like a bridge."

"Come." Mason shouldered Valerie's little black bag she had brought. "I'll help you."

Mason climbed up on Bessie's nose then reached down and pulled Valerie up. Together, they scaled her head and walked up her neck to the shoulder, dodging the flipper that waved overhead. Valerie positioned herself near the wound and examined it. Mason set her bag within easy reach and sat down beside her. "You can do this, I know you can." He encouraged her to concentrate on the task at hand and not who her patient was. Within minutes, she wasn't shaking anymore.

Valerie might not be a physician, but she had been a nurse a long time ago. She decided to become a pharmacist instead. Mason knew that she still did a little nursing occasionally.

After she dug for a bit, Valerie clamped down on the bullet and pulled it out. She dropped into a plastic bag that Mason held open for her. A whole bottle of antiseptic was poured on the wound before she bandaged it.

"That's all I can do," she told Mason who planted a kiss on her lips to thank her.

He helped Valerie stand and let her slide down the neck first. They climbed over Bessie's head, slid down then flew off the end of her nose. Rachel caught Valerie when she landed to prevent her from going head first into a tree. Bessie opened her eyes and grunted. Mason landed beside them.

"I think she winked at me." Rachel let out a nervous laugh.

"I bet she did, too," Mason said. "She knows you as a friend now." He turned to look up at Bessie.

Rachel gave Valerie's arm a squeeze. "I'll be right back. I have to tin-kle." She looked at her brother as she made her way through the trees. Mason grinned and looked back up at Bessie.

"Ain't that touching?" Ernie Elliott walked into the clearing and held a shotgun on Mason. Another man followed close behind and aimed his rifles at Valerie. Bessie stayed still.

One of the men nudged Ernie. "Look at that beast. Looks like you didn't kill her, after all."

"Yes, now I can get that reward."

"You mean us, don't you?" Both men gave Ernie a dirty look.

"Yes. That's what I mean." Ernie grinned up at his catch.

The two men pushed Mason and Valerie to one side. One reached into his pocket and pulled out a rope. He sneered at Mason while he laid his rifle on the ground. The other man cocked his rifle and aimed it at him.

Bessie raised her head and clutched the man with the rifle in her huge jaws. Mason heard bones cracking as she shook him. There wasn't enough time for the man to scream. He landed in a heap on the other side of the creek. Bessie flipped the man with the rope high into the air with her nose. He crashed into the trees a hundred feet away.

Ernie ran through the woods blindly. Rachel waited behind a tree for him then tripped him with her foot. Ernie landed face first in the dirt. Rachel picked up the shotgun and aimed it at the man until Mason took it from her. Valerie ran up with the rope and tied Ernie's hands together behind his back.

CHAPTER 15

The stone, the color of the sky, no longer pulled. Bessie felt only the faint pulse as it weakened. She knew she would not see Tom again as her keeper. She sensed that he also knew. There was a quiet sadness about him the last time she saw him. Bessie didn't worry; the stone would be passed on to another, to someone who was worthy to wear it.

The blood stone, however, was close. Bessie had waited for her man while she lay there, too weak to get to her den where she must go to sleep. She couldn't move her flipper on that side; too much blood had been lost. The magic of the stone wasn't where it needed to be. Bessie couldn't keep it inside her to run through her heart and body. She had laid her head down on the ground and waited.

The rustling of leaves woke her early the next morning. Her man stood in front of her. She sniffed him just to make sure her mind wasn't playing tricks on her. The females were next. At once, she realized that one of them was her man's mate. Bessie decided to trust her as she did him. Soon, she would be whole again. She would let go of this time and place herself in another. Soon.

****

Eddie and Tom met them just as they stepped out of the bush. Eddie hugged his wife. "I got your note. I still worried like hell anyway." His tired eyes found Valerie. "Jason's home. He'll be fine in a few days. Just sprained his ankle"

"Good, I'll look in on him later."

Ernie was locked up in the tiny jail. Everyone gave their statements to the temporary officer and left.

"We have to go back," Mason told them after the women went home.

"Yes," Tom said, "we have to open up the creek again before it starts flooding everything."

Eddie nodded. "I know. What if we borrowed Jack's boat. He's out of the hospital now. I'm going up to his apartment."

"Well I'm not going," Tom told them. "He's likely to throw me off his balcony. I'll see you guys later." He walked away.

"Thanks. That got rid of him," Mason said after Tom was out of earshot.

"I thought you'd like that. Frankly, I still don't trust the guy." Eddie watched Tom cross the street.

They took the elevator up to the fourth floor and knocked on the constable's door. Jack opened it in his housecoat, tightly belted around his waist. Mason saw him wince when he sat down on his couch. "We came to ask if we can borrow your boat."

"Well, 'hi' to you, too. I heard what happened. And I know that someone stole my boat yesterday. Why don't you just get Dean to take you?"

"Because, I'm asking you to come with us." Mason saw the look Eddie gave him. He ignored it.

"What do you want me to do, chaperon?" Jack asked.

"We need you to steer the boat. Eddie and I are going to blow the dam before the creek backs up too far and starts flooding homes. You in or not?"

"What dam?"

"I thought you said you knew what happened?" Eddie asked.

"I heard that someone shot your monster, that's all. And that Dean tried to stop them by getting my boat full of buckshot."

"Your boat's fine," Eddie huffed. "We only need it for about a half an hour. We better get a move on."

"Okay," Jack pulled himself up, "let me get dressed. Don't you two have any patience?"

The two men waited until Jack came back. Mason was relieved, Valerie hadn't told Jack about them yet. He could hide it for a little while longer. They went over to Mason's apartment to get his sack. Mason drove his truck to the docks, helped Jack settle into his boat and jumped in behind him. Jack started the motor and drove toward the lake at a fast idle.

At the mouth of Muddy Creek, Mason and Eddie planted the dynamite. Mason dragged the fuse along the ground and over behind a huge chunk of earth. Eddie jumped in behind him. Jack had taken the boat out further in the lake, away from the blast zone and waited. The fuse was lit, the dam blew. Water gushed out into the lake in a tidal wave. The men waited until everything settled before they climbed down to the water's edge. Jack brought the boat up for them to step aboard. They drove home in silence.

****

A light blanket covered Valerie as she dozed on her couch. Mason had let himself into her apartment, smiled down at her. Knowing it had been the first time she spent the night in the wilderness and how exhausted she was from being up all night. She had jumped at every little sound, worried at what might be out there, besides sea monsters. She hadn't been able to get comfortable, even in his arms. She had become more nervous of the coyotes then the thought of Bessie not too far away.

Mason's hand brushed lightly over her face. Valerie opened her eyes at Mason as he knelt next to her. "Have I told you lately how beautiful you are?" He caressed her face and arm. She kissed his fingers when he teased her lips.

He lifted her in his arms and carried her into her bedroom. Mason put her down gently on top of the bed and settled down beside her. Her kiss was like the taste of honey, sweet, easy to become addicted to. He took his time, but Valerie didn't want to wait. She rolled over on top of him and vanquished him with kisses, tore off his clothes as she traveled down his body with light kisses.

At last, they made love. When it was over, he cradled her in his arms. They slept. And when they woke, the sun was still out. The birds were singing. Still, they didn't move.

"Hungry?" Mason asked.

"Starving."

"I'll make us some bacon and eggs."

"Fine. I'm going to take a shower."

They cuddled closer. "We should get up, you know?"

"Yeah, I know."

It was six o'clock when they stumbled out of her bedroom. Mason fried up some bacon while Valerie had her shower. Supper was there for her when she entered the kitchen. Mason laughed and teased her while they ate. They took their coffee out to the balcony where they sat on her patio chairs. A bright orange sun lay half sunk over the lake to their west. Mason could hear the quiet lapping of the waves, inhaled the fresh breeze that drifted off the water. Valerie closed her eyes and relinquished a sigh. When she opened them again, Mason was on his knees in front of her. He lifted her hand and kissed it.

"Marry me, Val," he pleaded.

Tears swelled up in her eyes. "Give me time to get used to this, Mason. You've only just returned," she told him.

****

Mason left her shortly after that and felt down and out of sorts. He knew she was right, he expected too much too soon. Somehow, he had to get Valerie to trust him again. He won't run off on her this time. It felt as if he had waited for her all his life. Now that he decided to settle down and start a family, she wasn't ready. Give her time. Let her break it off with Jack first.

He headed to the local hotel and sat at the bar. The place seemed empty without Ernie Elliott to occupy a seat. His trial was coming up soon. Charges against him were as long as Mason's arm. Weapons infractions, endangering wildlife, sabotaging the rig, attempted murder, insurance fraud to name the ones he could remember.

He looked at himself in the mirror behind the bar and scowled. Man, he looked a mess. His eyes were bloodshot, and not because of booze. He was worried, hadn't slept in days. Please Frank, get better. Please Tom, go hide under a rock.

****

Early that morning Tom pushed the rock aside and walked into the bomb shelter. He smiled at Dean. "You can come out now. Ernie's been arrested."

Dean scrambled past Tom and made his way home.

"We should at least change the locks on the doors," Dean pleaded to his mother.

Rachel looked toward the back door and set her coffee cup on the counter. "You're probably right." She turned to look at him. "I'll get Eddie to, as soon as possible."

Dean put his arm around her waist. "With any luck, Ernie won't be coming out of jail. Just in case, get those locks changed."

She kissed him on the cheek. "You've always been my rock, you know that? I can always count on you."

Dean moved away from his mother. He didn't want to be her rock. His dad should be looking after her. Ever since he was old enough his mother leaned on him when his dad was out on the rig. He was glad that his dad wasn't working now. Maybe his mother would lean on him from now on.

A tear slipped down her cheek. "You're growing up too fast." She pulled a chair away from the table and sat down. "Just remember what I always tell you."

"I know, Mom. Be a better man than my father."

Mary sighed. "That's all I ask of you, son."

Dean looked out at the backyard through the dirty window and noticed that his dad had dug the hole for the pond his mother wanted. A pile of dirt was behind it with a shovel stuck in it as if waiting for Eddie to return. He let his mind wander. He pictured Ernie lying in the gutter, him spitting at the drunk as he walked by. What drove a man to want to live in oblivion? He thought of Black Tom. Here was another man who left this world to travel in his own. What was the difference? Only the weapon they chose. Ernie used alcohol, Tom used drugs.

Dean sat down at the kitchen table. The use of drugs hit a person hard. He still had bad dreams of Black Tom's trip. That was the most frightening experience he had ever had, except when he was behind a wall of fire with no way out. Sure, he liked to party and drink one beer after another; he had passed out on a friend's couch. Did that lead to dependence? What harm would a few drinks do once in a while?

Rachel put her hand on his arm. "Don't worry so much, Dean. We'll be all right. I still have my job."

He gave her a weak grin. "Sure Mom. We'll be fine." He reached over and gave her a hug.

****

Bessie didn't die after she was shot. All the signs were right. Both of her rings had come together in a unified goal. What happened? Why was she still there?

****

Tom overdosed. After days in intensive care, he teetered toward death. They moved him to the third floor, his situation...critical. Mason visited him in the hospital, wondering if he was there to say good-bye to the brother he never knew---if he was his brother--- to a man he would never choose as a friend. Yet, something drew him to see Tom and he didn't know why. Or why this man had such an effect on him.

If possible, he looked worse. Tom's eyes were drawn into their sockets. Yellowish-gray skin hugged his bones. His arm was black and blue, almost transparent where an IV entered his skin. Mason watched a vein pulse in Tom's neck. He looked more like a shrunken old man, almost hidden in the bed. Tom spoke just above a whisper. "Hey, brother. We did good, you and me."

"I thought Bessie was going into the future. Why is she still around?

"I don't rightly know. Something must not have added up right." Tom coughed. "It's all in the books. Read the books." His breath came out haggard. "I was the one who blew up the *Charisma;* I couldn't let you leave again."

"I wasn't going to leave Lake Erie. I was only going to the other end and back."

"I couldn't take that chance; the time was too near."

"You set it off by remote control?"

"Yes."

"You tried to kill me?"

"No. I waited until you were topside. I knew you wouldn't be killed."

"You said you didn't know it was me until you were on the beach."

"Yeah, I lied."

"I almost drowned." Mason's eyebrow lifted. How many times had Tom lied to him?

"Bessie was there. She wouldn't let you drown."

"You're so sure of yourself, aren't you?"

"I know Bessie."

"You're an ass."

"Yep." Tom coughed up phlegm. Mason wiped his mouth with a tissue. "You need to do one more thing, for Bessie." Tom's breath got shallower.

"What?"

"Take my ring." Tom pulled off the aquamarine that dangled on his finger and handed it over. "Give it to Dean."

"Dean?" Mason's eyebrow lifted again.

"He's my successor, and will know what to do. He's been watching me, learning. It's all by design, you know." Tom's words came out raspy. "Promise me, Mason."

"Yeah, sure."

"Say it."

"I promise." A tear slipped down Mason's face in spite of himself. "Who will I give my ring to?"

"You will know when the time is right. Someone always comes around when they are needed."

Mason looked at Tom's ring, cold in his hand. "What about when you get out of here?"

"It's up to Dean, now. He's the next generation. The ring won't do anything for me, even if I do get out of here."

****

The lake was angry again. The waves were high and fierce. A strong wind blew across the top. Bessie stayed near the bottom where it was safe. There was a big boat above her, tossing around like a stick on a fast river. Lightning illuminated it. The night got dark. The muffled thunder above sounded like drums underwater. If she surfaced, it would have hurt her ears. This was the first time she'd been out in the lake since she'd been shot. Her shoulder was still sore and stiff. Bessie would be forever grateful to the female who helped her.

Bessie did not know why she was still there. She had prepared herself to die. There must have been more she needed to do before that day would come. It was close, she could feel it.

The wind shifted suddenly. The boat tipped over. All kinds of crates spilled over into the water. Some broke open. Bessie found what looked like food and tasted it, spit it out again.

Oil spread across the surface, spreading further out with each wave. The boat cried. She heard its wail as it was grieving its own death. It's a sound they all made just before they sank. Its eyes went dark. Everything was in blackness.

Humans screamed. Every boat had some. Some jumped into the water. A man clutched to a flat piece of tree. He floated along until struck by lightning. That was the first time Bessie saw a human burn like that. Which reminded her of the time she watched hundreds of trees along the shore burn. The smoke had made her eyes water, made her cough.

More humans were in the water and tried to swim far away from the boat before it sank and pulled them down with it. There were females, too. Most boats only had males. Bessie wondered why that was?

 Bessie — The Monster in Lake Erie by Deborah Tadema

It was nice to see females once in a while. They weren't as much of a threat to her as the males were.

Small boats raced away. They picked up the humans in the water, the ones that didn't die. The big boat cracked and snapped loudly as it broke in half. The steel twisted and groaned. It settled on the bottom, kicked up sand. It turned quiet, except for the storm.

****

"Uncle Tom is in the hospital," Troy told Jason. "He overdosed on LSD. Uncle Mason says he could die." Troy opened Jason's fridge and took out two Cokes. He opened one and handed it to Jason, who sat at his kitchen table.

"Will you be sorry if he does?" Jason asked.

Troy sat at the table, shook his head. "No. I don't like him. He's too creepy."

"I'd be sad if your Uncle Mason died, though."

"Yeah, me too," Troy thought about how his uncle played with him when he was small. He rode on Mason's back as a kid, his uncle down on all fours. Mason played baseball with them and sometimes camped with them. He also blamed Mason because he brought Black Tom into their lives. Jason called Tom the devil, he knew why. That man was the scariest he had ever seen.

"Dean saw Tom take a bad trip on drugs," Troy said. "I don't think I'd want to try LSD if it did that to you. And I know you hate it when your dad gets drunk."

"Yeah." Justin looked down at his bottle of Coke. "I'd give anything to have him home, so he could get drunk." After a few heartbeats, he said, "I talk to him when I visit him."

Troy nodded. "Dr. Boyd says he can hear you." He took a drink then said, "I saw Uncle Mason talking to him. He said that your dad moved his finger."

Jason looked at him. "He did? Does that mean he'll wake up soon?"

Troy shrugged. "I don't know. That's what Uncle Mason told me this morning."

Jason gazed off into the distance. "I wish I could go see him."

"I'm going up to see him in about an hour," Troy said. "I'll tell him that you're hobbling along on crutches." Jason nodded.

CHAPTER 16

Dean led the others to Tom's pad from an old gravel road that was hardly used. Tom had shown him the way that made it easier to get to. A long path wound around, through the bush that led them to a hidden door behind a large rock. They pushed it open and walked into a twelve by twelve cement bunker. An oil lamp was lit that sat it in the middle of the table. Dean picked up several sugar cubes and showed them to Mason and Eddie. "This is where the LSD is. They hide it in these to take the bitter taste away. Parents don't realize that a powerful drug is in here, and they're easy to hide." After that, he didn't know what to do with them, so he handed them to Mason. Mason handed them to Eddie.

"I don't want these," Eddie protested. "I have a teenager at home. He's not getting his hands on drugs if I can help it." He squinted at his oldest son. Dean caught his eye, shook his head. Eddie sighed as if relieved then handed the cubes back to Mason.

Mason took them and slid them into his pocket. "I'll flush them down the toilet."

"Don't do that." It shocked Dean. "You know how much those are worth?"

"Do we care?" Mason asked. Dean didn't answer.

"So, this is the old bomb shelter." Eddie was looking around at all the bottles and books, his face lit up as if it amazed him.

Papers Tom had written on were scattered in loose piles on the table. A steel bunk bed stood against one wall. The top bunk served as Tom's dresser. It held piles of clothes and other personal items. Two shelves were on the wall beside the headboard. His comb and shaving stuff were there with other small items like matches and candles. A camp stove was on the floor next to the bed, cans of food on the shelves above it.

"Over there," Dean pointed to a hole in the cement wall at the back of the room, "is the tunnel that leads to Bessie's den."

"What are we going to do with all this stuff?" Eddie picked up a book and blew the dust off. "This looks like Greek to me." The medical book he held told about diseases and unorthodox treatments. It was set back down.

"What was he trying to do down here?" Mason studied some of the bottles whose labels he couldn't decipher, "besides getting high."

"I think," Dean stood beside Mason, the sky ring now on his hand, "that he started out as a cool head, and went all queer. He told me he was trying new cures for diseases Bessie's prone to. He also wanted to improve her diet." Dean huffed. "And the water quality. That sort of thing. Then, he started giving her meat. He knew it made her go harry."

"Yes, and he kept doing it," Mason spurted.

"So, what was his goal?" Eddie said while he searched through Tom's notes.

"I really don't know." Dean peeked over Eddie's arm. "I think somebody needs to study those."

"Yeah, let's take these back with us." Eddie picked up one pile. "Before someone else gets a hold of this stuff."

"What about this?" Dean wrinkled his nose as he stood near the corner. "This stuff is raunchy."

"We need to destroy all of this," Mason said as he turned back to a label he was still trying to pronounce.

"How? We can't just close this off. It's the secret way to Bessie's den. It's the shortcut from town." Dean watched as Eddie picked up a vile and peered into it.

"Maybe we should get Valerie. She'll tell us what bottles here are dangerous and how to dispose of these things." Mason tried to say a long title. His tongue got all twisted.

"Good idea," Eddie said. "We should hang on to all those books. Maybe it'll help us; or you Dean, in how to look after Bessie properly."

"Yeah," Dean said as he eyed all the books, "lucky me."

****

Harback showed up at Eddie's early one morning. Lyle Trudell from the Department of Transport followed him into the kitchen. Harback reminisced about life on the gas rig and told Lyle funny stories about Eddie until Mason arrived.

"What about Ernie Elliott?" Mason asked after he took a seat at the table. Eddie gave him a cup of coffee.

"Along with theft, murder, attempted murder, endangering wildlife, firearms infractions, illegal discharge of a weapon, sabotage, and whatever else we decide to throw at him; he's not coming out," Lyle said.

Harback shook his head. "Mr. Gillespie told quite the story about how Parsons and his goons were working. Gillespie will be getting off pretty easy, considering."

Lyle added, "They've charged five others from their Calgary office, too."

"What about Parsons?" Eddie asked, "Haven't you caught up with him, yet?"

"No," said Harback, "he's still hiding. It wouldn't surprise me if he shows up here."

"Why do you say that?" Eddie ran his hand through his hair.

"Because, my theory is that he will blame you two especially, for what went wrong with his operation. You were the ones who brought Ernie Elliott in. You were the ones who shut him down. Don't be surprised if he comes looking for revenge."

Mason gave Eddie a nervous look. "You think he might go after our families?"

"I'd keep an eye out, just in case," Lyle told him. "That's why we came here, to warn you. If you do run into him, call Harback immediately."

"We will." Eddie stood and paced the room.

"The company has been sold to an outfit out of Toronto," Harback said. "They're going to run the remaining rigs. We have all the records from your old company. More people could be rounded up." He sipped on his coffee.

"Are you done with your investigation?" Eddie asked.

"Yes, I think so," Lyle told him. "You two and all the boys have been cleared of any wrongdoing." He leaned forward in his chair. "I still had to investigate, even though I thought all along that everything was on the up and up."

"Good," Mason smiled, satisfied. "That sums it all up then."

"Not quite." Harback turned to Mason. "We also found out what you were doing for the past few years."

Eddie leaned in closer. Mason wouldn't tell him when he asked.

"And?" Mason shifted in his seat, his eyebrow twitching.

"It had nothing to do with us," Harback teased. "He got rich from his last adventure." His eyes clouded over as he studied Mason.

"Which was what?" Eddie asked.

"It seems that our man here was ripping off treasure from sunken ships. Just outside of Canadian waters."

Eddie furrowed a brow. "Stealing?"

"No," Mason said.

"I bet the Yanks don't even know what you've done," Harback smirked.

"So, that's why you're not busting your ass trying to find another job." Eddie glared at his brother-in-law. "And here I've been out beating the pavement every day."

"I didn't get all that rich." Mason sat back in his seat. "I am comfortable though."

"Yeah, sure," Harback laughed. "I hear you made over a million dollars."

"Not that much. A few hundred thousand, enough to buy a house."

"Shit, Mason," Eddie said. "Next time take me with you."

****

Troy climbed up Picnic Hill and followed the path that led him to the cliff where they fell off. *"It looks steeper,"* he said to himself as he looked over the edge. He dropped a stone down and watched it tumble and roll. "If I go down there, Dad will kill me." After some more thought, he added, "so will Mason." Letting out a long sigh, Troy looked up at the sun and wished that Jason was with him. At least Jason was able to hobble around the house. His ankle was healing too slow for Troy. He wanted his best friend to climb the hill with him, to go swimming and camping.

"I'm going to the cave." Troy willed himself out of his somber mood. "I want to see if Bessie is healed up."

He retraced his steps until he came across the path and ended right beside the entrance to the cave. He ducked into the darkness and followed along the ledge. Troy pulled a small flashlight out of his pocket and turned it on. Bessie floated toward him. "Hi, Bessie," he said as she sniffed at his T-shirt. She snorted and backed up. The flashlight made a narrow swath across the pond. Troy found the big rock Dean told him about. He wanted to see the bomb shelter. "You think I should go in there?" he asked Bessie. He answered his own question. "Why not? Tom won't be there."

Troy set his flashlight on the ledge then pushed on the boulder. He couldn't budge it. He backed up, ready to go home. Bessie eased forward and slowly pushed the boulder to the side with her huge head. Troy smiled and said, "Thanks, Bessie." He picked up his flashlight. "I wonder how Tom and Dean can move it by themselves." Troy headed down the tunnel.

He found a lantern on a big table and lit it with the matches that were next to it. He looked in wonder at the room. "This would make a neat fort, wouldn't it?" He walked around the room and saw the stuff Dean talked about. The books, papers and shelves of bottles with liquids in them showed him just how much Tom was into this science stuff.

Troy moved a stack of papers and noticed something underneath; he picked up a sugar cube and held it to the light. He smirked, remembering the lectures he got from Dean about taking drugs. Not knowing why, he shoved it in his pocket and headed back out.

Bessie was gone when he made his way out of the cave. Troy decided to show Jason what he found. Jason was walking back and forth in his kitchen, working his foot to strengthen his ankle. He wasn't limping as much as he was and smiled at Troy when he walked in.

They sat at the table and Troy told him about his visit in the cave. He took the sugar cube out of his pocket. "Look at this." He held it out.

Jason's eyes bugged out. "Want to try it?"

Troy shook his head. "Not on your life. I don't want to end up like Black Tom."

Jason plucked it from Troy's hand and studied it. "What if we cut it in half, one for each of us? We won't get the full dose."

Troy looked from the cube into Jason's eyes. "You're serious, aren't you?"

Jason shrugged. "Just this once. Nobody will find out."

"Why do you want to do this?"

"Maybe I want to forget that my dad is in a coma and may never come out of it, to not see my mother crying all day. I want to forget about that guy on the rig who tried to kill us." His hand shook.

"It would be one way to find out what all the fuss is about," Troy said after a bit.

"Well," Jason looked around. "Help me find something to cut this in half with." They both stood, looking at the cupboards.

****

Dean staggered into the apartment and landed in the nearest chair. Mason could smell the booze on his breath from the other side of his couch.

"That old man tried to kill me," Dean spurted.

"He had a lot of issues." Mason had always told Dean exactly how he felt. He figured it was the reason they had always been friends.

Dean, he knew, did the same for him. They were alike that way, showing their emotions on their sleeves. Ernie's betrayal played heavily on the kid's mind. He was convicted of seven serious charges, now serving a twenty-year prison sentence. The trial was still fresh on their minds and played havoc on Dean's.

"What kind of man would try to kill a kid?" Dean had asked Mason several times since.

Mason didn't tell Dean that he was considered a man now. "Someone that is either sick or too greedy. I think he was only thinking of the reward money if he captured Bessie." Mason sat on the arm of the couch, facing Dean's red eyes. "Don't forget, Mr. Parsons was blackmailing him, or so he said. Ernie shouldn't have tried to sabotage the gas rig. He was lucky that he wasn't the one who attacked me out there, or it would have been him that Bessie killed."

"I know. Those two other dudes talked him into doing things that I don't think he would have, too." Dean made a face. "That Gillespie guy sure knew a lot of what Ernie did, didn't he?"

"Remember, they haven't found Parsons yet. Ernie could face even more charges."

"I know. I hope they find that dude soon. My mom thinks he'll come after us, especially after the testimony I gave."

Mason worried about the same thing. "I'll do what I can to keep you safe, Dean. And Jack will be back at work soon."

He watched as Dean's head slowly dropped to his chin and then he tipped sideways in the chair. *Pass out, Dean. Forget things for a while.* Mason did what he had wanted to for years. He knelt in front of the chair and kissed Dean on the forehead. He pulled the boy to him and held him close.

****

Troy reached over and snatched the sugar cube from Jason. "I don't want to get hooked," he said, "neither do you."

Jason grabbed for it. Troy pulled his hand back. "Give it to me," he hissed between his teeth. "If you want to be a coward then be one. Let me have it." He grabbed for it again.

Troy swung sideways and dropped the cube down the front of his shorts. "You won't reach in there for it, will you?"

"Try me." Jason chased Troy around the table, limping with his bad ankle.

"Jason, what's gotten into you?" Troy yelled. "You're obsessed." He stopped to catch his breath. Jason stopped across from him.

"I just want to try it."

"You promised Dean that you wouldn't do drugs."

"So?"

"So, why don't we sell it instead? I bet we could get at least fifty bucks for it."

Jason considered this for a few seconds. "Who could we sell it to?"

"That guy with the bandanna on his head." Troy said. "Look. We sell it and buy a case of beer. I'd rather do that then take this." He pointed to where the cube was stuck in his underwear.

Jason scrunched up his nose. "I don't want that now. Not after it's been down there."

Troy smiled. "I thought you'd see it my way."

****

The next day, Bessie lowered her massive head and sniffed at her new keeper. The sky ring he wore seemed to hum. She never experienced this with any of her keepers before. "I won't hurt you, girl," he told her. "I'm not like Tom."

She recognized this young man as one that she had rescued from the big spider that sank in the lake. He was also the one who blocked the screams that came from the tunnel. He had pushed back the rock and locked Tom inside there when he went mad. Except that Tom had gone mad a few times since then. Bessie hoped that this keeper wouldn't do that.

He told her his name was Dean. She liked it, it was easy to remember. Bessie also liked his long mane. This was how she could find him when he was far away. This man was suited to wear the sky ring, she just knew it.

****

"What should we do with this now?" Jason asked as he held the sugar cube in his hand. He had made Troy wipe it off after he hid it in his underwear.

"Find a place to hide it until we can sell it." Troy gave his bedroom door a quick glance and decided to close it.

Jason extended his hand out for his friend to take it. Troy backed up. "I don't want it. You keep it."

"This was your idea, you have to hide it." Jason dropped it in Troy's pocket. "Besides, you have to make sure I won't decide to take it, right?"

"Okay," Troy patted the pocket. "We better find that guy soon, or I'll just flush this down the toilet. My dad will kill me if he finds this."

Jason smiled. "Yeah, my dad, too."

"I'm glad he's awake, Jason. When is he going home?"

"In a few days. He has to get his strength back first." Jason sat on the bed. "He sure was weak when we were up there this morning. His legs shook when he stood up. He had to lean on me."

"Yours would be weak too if you were in bed for a month."

"You know what I'm going to do when we sell that thing? I'm going to buy my dad a case of beer."

"He'd like that." Troy sat beside his friend. "Where do we look for that guy?"

"He usually hangs out on the boardwalk at night. We could go down there after supper."

Troy nodded. "Yeah. The sooner we get rid of this, the better I'll feel."

CHAPTER 17

Valerie directed the traffic that went out of the old bomb shelter. As the men loaded boxes with all the chemicals and potions, she labeled and sorted so they knew which vehicle to put them in. It reinforced to Eddie in how smart Valerie was.

Valerie checked the vials carefully, told the men what each did and what it contained. It gave them a better sense of whom Tom was and what he was up to down there. One vial caught her attention. "He's taking wolf hormones." The rest of them gawked at her as if she had three heads. "He's been injecting it and LSD."

"What a soup that would be to the system," Dean said.

"A lethal combination for sure," she confirmed. "Plus, with those needles over there," she nodded to the shelf by the bed, "he's also taking heroin."

"How can he take all those drugs and still live?" Eddie shook his head. "No wonder the guy's nuts."

Mason filled his truck with the stuff that was to go to Dean's, things that could be used to keep Bessie healthy. The stuff that was safe to handle, plus all the books and papers. The jars of concoctions that Tom mixed went into Eddie's car to go to a hazardous disposal dump, along with the used needles. Eddie also took the lethal and poisonous bottles and vials. It took them three hours.

Dean tried on Tom's long black coat he found on the top bunk. It was too small, so he packed it along with the other clothing that reeked. Tom would get those back if he got better. Regular garbage was to go to the dump six miles further from town than they were now. They filled big plastic bags and put them in Dean's car. By the time they finished the path that took them to the old gravel road had turned into a well-worn trail. After the last box was loaded, Dean and Eddie locked the cement room up and disguised the trail as much as they could with branches and rocks. They shook hands and departed to their destinations.

Mason and Valerie coughed in the dust that swirled up around them. Dean had whipped his car around on the gravel and sent it flying. Mason swore as he opened the truck door for Valerie. They eased out onto the road in the truck and headed back into town.

****

Eddie hopped into his car and turned the key. The engine wouldn't turn over. He tried again only to hear it click. After waiting a few minutes, he pumped the gas several times before he turned the key again. Nothing. The door slammed shut when Eddie got back out. He opened the hood not sure what to look for. In frustration, he slammed it shut and leaned against the front bumper. He never liked working on cars, didn't have patience for it. He swore, which helped, a little.

Fifteen minutes later, a yellow Plymouth skidded to a halt beside him. A man in a blue suit got out and asked if he could help. Eddie popped the hood open and leaned inside to look at where the man pointed.

"Could be that wire back there got loose." the man told him. "Give it a wiggle."

Eddie reached in. He heard the man open his own trunk and thought that he went to get his tools. The whack on the back of his head told him something else. Eddie staggered backward, hand on his head, felt the blood oozing through his fingers. Another hit; Eddie fell to his knees. His world spun. He heard the man get back into his car and drive away.

Eddie was still on his knees when he heard the car come back. He pulled himself up onto his feet with one hand and braced himself. Dean walked into view.

"Bummer, man. Who hit you?" his son asked while he scouted the area.

Eddie leaned against the side of his car. "Some bald dude in a blue suit. Never saw him before."

Dean looked up and down the road. He turned back to his father. "You got trouble?" He nodded to the open hood.

"Yeah. Won't start."

Dean bent over the grill, fiddled with wires then asked Eddie to try the ignition again. Eddie did only to hear the click. "It's the carburetor, you need a new one," Dean told him.

Eddie slammed the door and walked to the front of the car. "Well, I can't get one today. I guess you'll have to give me a lift into town. I'll get one tomorrow."

"And leave all those chemicals in there?" Dean pointed to the trunk.

"Then what?" Eddie took out a hanky and pressed it to the back of his head. "I'm getting a headache."

"Wait here, I know where there's one." Dean got back into his car and yelled. "Hide, in case that dude comes back. I'll only be a half an hour." He sped away, leaving Eddie still stranded on the side of the road.

He went for a walk in the woods, in a big circle if only to keep himself awake. Ferns and wildflowers, he had never bothered to learn the names of covered the forest floor. After ten minutes he sat on a rock and waited, listening for any sound of a car. If he strained his neck, he could see the road through the bushes. If that man returned, he'd have a head start to run or a better chance to defend himself.

It was Dean who pulled up. Eddie stepped out to meet him. Dean took out his tools from his trunk and exchanged the carburetor within twenty minutes. "Now try it," he told Eddie while he wiped his greasy hands on a rag. The car started. Eddie let out a whoop.

"Where did you get a carburetor on a Sunday?"

"At the bone yard."

"You mean the auto wreckers?"

"You're solid, man."

****

That evening Troy met Jason by the arcade and was late.

His best friend gave him an annoyed look when he walked up to him. "You still have it?" Jason asked him.

"I still have it." Troy felt it in the pocket of his shirt. "It's right here."

"Good. Because, he's right over there." Jason pointed to a guy in the red bandanna. He was leaning against the side of the building that housed several games. Troy especially liked the ring toss game. They walked up to him albeit a little warily.

The dude known as Jay gave them an amused smile as they approached him. "You two want to score?"

"We have something you might be interested in," Jason said with a squeaky voice. Jay raised his eyebrows, said nothing.

Troy took the sugar cube out of his pocket and showed the dude. "'This is laced. We were wondering if you'd like to buy it from us."

Jay stood up straight. "How much do you think its worth?"

Troy and Jason exchanged looks. "We were hoping to get at least fifty bucks," Jason finally said.

Jay laughed. "How do I know it's laced? How pure is it?"

"It's one hundred percent pure." Troy closed his hand on the cube. "It came from Black Tom."

Jay's eyes widened. "How did you get it? Buy it from him?"

"No. He dropped it," Jason answered quickly. Good comeback, Troy thought.

Jay shuffled his feet. "Do you know who Tom's supplier is?"

"No, only that he's a user. He mixes them himself." Troy lowered his arm to his side, the cube still in his hand. By the look on Jay's face, he knew who Black Tom was.

"Tell me how to get in touch with Tom." Jay looked interested.

"He's in the hospital," Troy said. "He overdosed, isn't doing very well."

Jay watched them for a bit. "I've seen you two around. If you're scamming me, I'll come after you."

"We're not bluffing," Jason said.

Jay backed up; his eyes watching something behind them. "The cops. I'm out of here." Troy and Jason turned around to see Jack walking their way.

****

Troy knew that Jack took longer walks every time he went out. His side seemed to be getting better. He knew it would be a while yet before he could return to work. Jack didn't seem surprised to see Troy and Jason on the beach. He was probably surprised to see them with a well-known local drug dealer, though.

Jay left before Jack got too close. The two boys waited until he stopped next to them. "You should stay away from that guy," Jack warned. "He's trouble."

"We were just talking to him," Troy said. "Don't worry, we don't do drugs."

Jack's eyebrow raised, a sign that he didn't believe them. "What are you up to?"

"Just hanging out," Jason watched a pretty girl walk by. "My dad's awake," he said after she went around the corner of the building.

"I was up there to see him. He looks good," Jack said.

Troy and Jason walked away, Jason still limping. After they stopped further down the boardwalk, Troy looked back through the crowd to see Jack buy himself a drink then take it to a bench where he sat down.

He also noticed a woman walk by Jack that reminded him of Valerie, except this woman had dark hair. The woman smiled at Jack as she passed, he grinned at her. He watched her disappear into one of the booths. Troy wondered how Jack was coping, losing Valerie to Mason. She must have really broken his heart, by the way Jack had been moping. Troy hoped that Jack would heal soon. He deserved happiness.

Troy turned his attention back to Jason and the two girls who'd stopped to talk to them. Eventual, he saw Jack shuffling back home. He noticed Jay about a block away. Jay was leaning against an old building and nodded at Jack as he went by.

After the girls left, Troy and Jason bought french fries. That's when Troy detected an old man sitting on a bench, in the shadows. He had the same description as the man who had attacked his dad the other day.

Troy finished his fries and tossed the container into the trash. He decided to walk up to that man and confront him. Or, at least walk by and get a good look at him. He took no more than ten steps when the man jumped up and bolted. Troy chased him into the parking lot where the man jumped into his car and sped away.

****

Her man was there. He stood on the edge of the creek by Bessie's den. Her new keeper was with him, the one with the long mane. They smiled at her. She felt safe when they were near. The rings hummed in harmony now, peaceful.

Bessie lowered her head and let them pet her. Their touch soothed her, especially after a day like she had today. Two boats tried to run her over. She got them. All three people had drowned after she tipped the boats over. It was good to be home.

****

Dean met Rain at the Stork Club and walked down to the water and then along the shore, westward. He stopped and looked out at Lake Erie, watching the waves roll in. Rain wrapped both of her arms around his arm and leaned into him. He told her the story of how they found his Uncle Mason half dead on the sand. He also told her about his adventure out on the gas rig. Dean didn't know why he felt sad today.

"Come with me." Rain led him to the bottom of the cliff far from cottages and the public beach. She took her sandals off and waded into the water, her long white dress got wet on the bottom. That was one thing Dean liked about her, she didn't care, and she wasn't needy. She was just Rain, and she loved the water, the air and the sand. He couldn't picture her within the confines of four walls. He had always been with her outside. To him she was mystical, and he loved to watch her.

She turned back to look at him, he held out his hand to her. She smiled and ran to him which made him feel special. She didn't stop, grabbed his arm and led him to the base of the cliff. His eyes popped when she lifted her dress off and stood naked in front of him. Her long brown hair blew in the slight breeze. He watched the shadows of the setting sun play on her body. Man, she was beautiful.

Dean took off his sandals and shorts and led her to a place where the cliff jutted out. Here they had all the privacy in the world. He went to her; she ran back further and climbed on top of a large rock. Laughing. She was always laughing. He was always chasing her.

She let him catch her and he pulled her down beside him on the sand. Her fingers curled into his long hair and she pulled him to her. They made love and held each other afterward.

"I don't want to leave," he told her. "I could stay here with you forever."

She didn't look at him, didn't move. "I'm leaving tomorrow. I won't be seeing you anymore."

****

Mason was sitting in his recliner, sipping on a beer and watching the baseball game when his phone rang. It surprised him to hear Sherry on the line. She sounded frantic. "Frank came home this morning," she told him. "Ever since, he's been putting me down. He even slapped me."

"Oh no," Mason thought. "He's never done anything like that before, has he?"

"No. It's like he hates me now. And he's been drinking beer all afternoon. Him and Jason."

"Jason? He's too young."

"I know. I tried to stop him, but Frank told me to get out. He wants to party with his son." Mason waited until she finished crying. She sniffled and continued. "They're both drunk, Mason. Eddie's coming over; I called him. I don't think Jack can handle Frank now."

Mason closed his eyes. "I'll be right over."

He walked into her house ten minutes later, took the half empty bottle away from Jason. The boy slumped against his father's chair, eyes half-shut. Mason picked three dead bottles off the floor, put them back into the case with other empty ones and shoved it away.

Frank swore at him. "Hey, you bastard, that's mine." He lifted himself off the chair and staggered toward it. Mason pushed him back down. Frank hit the chair with a loud thud, arms and legs flailing.

"What are you doing, Frank?" Mason yelled at him. "It's one thing for you to get drunk, but by God, you don't do that to your son."

Frank stood up unsteadily and glared at Mason. "He's my son."

"Yeah, and he's just a kid. Do this shit when he's twenty." Mason helped Jason to the couch. He turned around only to have Frank take a swing at him. In his drunken state, Frank missed and toppled sideways. If it weren't for the TV, the old fisherman would have gone through the front window.

To Mason's relief, Eddie came in at that moment. Eddie stood, hands on hips and watched as Frank went after Mason again. Mason ducked a fist and pushed Frank back into his chair.

"Stay down," he yelled. "Or I'll tie you up."

Eddie stood beside Frank's chair and glared down at him. Frank stayed where he was and glared up at the big man.

"Thanks, Ed," Mason sat on the arm of the couch. "At least he wouldn't dare take a swing at you."

Eddie smiled. "Think we need to tie him up?"

"No, he's settled down." Mason saw Sherry watching them from the kitchen and went over to her.

"I don't know what's gotten into him," she cried. "He isn't the same man, Mason. He's never been abusive before."

Mason put his arm around her. "It's a good thing you called us." He looked back toward the living room. "He's going through a rough patch, sweetheart. He just needs time to get things straight in his head."

Eddie came in. "Jason's sleeping it off." He looked at the two of them and addressed Mason. "I wouldn't be doing that if I were you."

"Do what?" Mason was pushed sideways.

"Get your grubby hands off my wife." Frank glared from Mason to Sherry. "What's been going on?"

"Nothing, Frank," Mason stood his ground.

"Yeah, I know what you're like Mason." Frank's slurred words were hard to decipher.

"There's nothing here, Frank." Eddie pulled at his arm. "He broke up Val and Jack. He's not after your wife."

Frank looked from Mason to Eddie, a sinister smile slowly spreading across his gruff features. "He did what?"

"He went after Val." Eddie watched Mason fidget. "He took her away from Jack."

CHAPTER 18

Dean bolted upright in his bed and looked at the clock. It was only five minutes after four in the morning. What was wrong? His hazy mind registered; his finger was on fire. He looked down at the aquamarine and squinted. It had turned yellow; his finger had swollen up. Panic ran through his soul while he jumped out of bed and dressed as best he could. He didn't know where he was supposed to go or why. He only knew he had to get out of his apartment.

Dean hurried down the hallway. He reached the front door just as he heard tires squealing outside. Mason's truck stopped in the middle of the street. He motioned for Dean to hurry. The young man ran down the steps and slid into the truck. Mason headed toward Picnic Hill.

"What is it?" Dean barely got it out when he braced for the corner.

"Bessie's in trouble." Mason gave him a worried look. "Have you started reading those books yet?"

"A bit. There's a lot there, you know."

"Good. Because I think we're going to have to find out how to deal with things."

"What do you think is wrong with Bessie?"

"We won't know until we get there." Mason skidded to a stop at the bottom of the hill and took two flashlights out of the glove box. "This is our time, kid," he looked over at Dean. "We'll just have to wing it, I guess."

Dean swallowed hard. "Should we take a gun or something?"

"I don't have a gun." Mason stepped out of the truck and walked around the front. Dean met him there. "Maybe we should get Jack."

Dean snorted. "Yeah, like he'd help you right now."

Mason gave him a dirty look before he headed toward the path. "Let's see what it is."

Dean followed silently, listening to the trees sway overhead and rustling at his feet. He jumped when a twig snapped. Mason looked back, "Afraid of ghosts? It was only me."

"No." Dean tried not to sound scared and stayed close to Mason.

They topped the hill and heard a long low moan. Mason stopped to listen. They shut their flashlights off. The moan came again. "It's down by the creek," Mason said.

Dean found the path that led down to the cave. They walked out into the clearing beside the creek and stopped. Bessie was in the water, watching something on shore to their left, low growls came from deep down in her throat. Dean walked along the creek bed, his flashlight off. The moon gave them enough light to see by.

"That's Jay," Mason said behind him, "he's hurt." He bent down beside the young man who bled from the chest. "Jay. Jay, can you hear me?"

Jay moaned and lifted his head. "Shot, I'm shot."

"Who shot you?" Mason looked around.

"A bald guy," Jay gasped. "He's been around lately, watching."

"Watching who?" Dean asked as he knelt beside Jay.

"All of you. Jason, Troy, you," Jay told Dean.

"Where is he now?" Mason asked as he scouted around.

"Split." Jay clutched at his chest. "Hurts."

Mason shoved Jay's hand away, pressed his handkerchief on the wound. He instructed Dean to keep the pressure on it then stood up. "I'm going for help."

Dean nodded and watched Mason run down the creek bed toward the path. When the man was out of sight, he turned back to Jay. "What were you doing out here in the first place?"

     Bessie — The Monster in Lake Erie by Deborah Tadema

Jay gave a sick sounding snicker. "What I do best."

"Dealing," Dean said with disdain. "Way out here?"

"Where the guy wanted to meet," Jay took several painful breaths. "Now I know why."

Bessie swam closer and lowered her head. Jay's eyes widened. "She won't hurt you, Jay." Dean was so relaxed that Jay stopped. "Unless you hurt her first." Dean reached up with his free hand and petted Bessie's nose, "See, she's just like a big ole' puppy."

"That's why the dude ran away. She scared him."

"So, why is this guy watching us?" Dean asked.

"I don't know." Jay closed his eyes.

Keep him talking, thought Dean. "Aw, what were you selling?"

"Just some marijuana."

"Just?" Dean watched spittle come out of Jay's mouth. *Hurry, Mason.* "Do you know who that guy is, his name?"

"I only know him as Parsons."

****

Bessie hated guns. That was what the bald man waved around. He yelled at the younger man as they stood along the shore. They didn't see her beneath the current of the creek she called her own. The young man held out his hand with a small bag in it and demanded money. The bald man snatched it from him, turned to leave.

Maybe he wouldn't have gotten shot if he let the bald man go. The young man went after him, said terrible things to the ugly one who just turned around and fired his gun. That's when Bessie jumped and had no choice. She had to show herself. So, she roared and lifted herself up out of the water.

The bald man screamed and ran down the shore to the path by her den. Bessie chased him, tried to bite him. She missed. He hid behind the trees; she was unable to kill him.

By this time, the man who'd been shot had fallen backward and started to crawl toward the base of the cliff. Blood seeped from his chest. Bessie lowered her head and sniffed at him. He gritted his teeth and looked at her through lidded eyes. In his scent, she detected a faint lingering of her keeper, the one with the long mane. Bessie had been deciding what to do when he came onto the shore of her creek. Bessie's man was with him and they seemed worried about the man who was shot. When Dean talked to her and petted her, she decided she would not kill the man on the ground.

****

It wasn't until he saw Mason run toward him that Dean realized that his finger wasn't hurting anymore. He looked at his hand to see that the ring had turned to its original color. Bessie snorted behind him. He turned to see her submerge into the creek. Too many people, he thought.

Jack was in his uniform. And Valerie was behind Mason. A paramedic dragged a stretcher. Dean gave Mason a questioning look when they stopped beside him. Mason lifted his shoulders and watched the paramedic examine Jay.

Jack walked up and down by the creek, albeit still stiffly, and wrote in his pad. He bent down and picked something up on the end of his pen. He grinned when he walked back toward them. If you weren't looking you wouldn't see the sadness in his eyes. Dean watched as the two men vied for Valerie's attention; saw the way they both looked at her.

"Found the shell casing." Jack gave Dean a plastic bag that he took out of his pocket with his free hand. Dean opened it for him to drop the casing into it.

The paramedic had Jay's chest bandaged and stood up. "Okay. We need to be very careful with him." Mason helped him lift Jay onto the stretcher. Dean walked behind Valerie as the two men carried Jay up and over the hill. Jack brought up the rear.

An ambulance was waiting at the bottom of the hill by Jack's cruiser. After it left, Jack walked up and shook Dean's hand. "Thanks, Dean. He'll be okay."

"I didn't think you were back at work already." Dean nodded toward the police car.

Jack snickered. "Came back this morning. This is my first call."

Jack watched as Mason opened his truck door for Valerie and ran around to the other side. They drove away, leaving Dean there. He grinned at Jack and lifted his shoulders. "He forgot me."

"Not surprised," Jack scoffed. "He only thinks about himself." He put a hand on Dean's shoulder. "Come on, scout. I'll give you a lift."

"It was that Parsons guy who shot Jay," Dean told Jack after they got into the car. "He's been spying on all of us kids. Jay's seen him."

Jack turned the key in the ignition. "I think I need to ask some questions, see who else has seen him around."

"I'll go with you if you want." Dean wanted to know what this guy was up to.

"This is police business, Dean. Why don't you make sure your mother's all right?" Jack stopped in front of Eddie's house.

Dean knew this was a diversion. He nodded at Jack then went into the house. His mother was in the kitchen making coffee. Rachel startled when she saw him.

Dean pecked her on the cheek. "Bessie was in trouble. Mason and I went out to help her."

She looked down at the ring on his hand. "What happened?"

"She was scared. Somebody shot Jay." He saw the surprise in her eyes. "He's all right, they just took him to the hospital."

Rachel put her arm around him. "That could have been you."

"No, Mom. Jay was dealing. I don't do that. Therefore, I wouldn't have been there in the first place." He wiggled free.

"And Bessie? How do I know she won't decide to have you for breakfast?"

He showed her the ring. "Remember what I told you. She won't hurt me." He was getting annoyed now. "She won't hurt Mason either."

He saw the worried look in her eyes before she turned back to her coffee.

****

The next day. "How did you know where I was?" Jay asked Dean from his hospital bed, a look of distrust in his eyes.

Dean glanced at the door before he showed Jay his ring, "Because Bessie was upset. She…"

"That monster? Did you hear her roaring?"

Dean shook his head. "This ring." He held it under Jay's nose. "Whenever Bessie gets upset or is in danger, this ring tells me."

Jay's eyebrows pinched together. "That's the most cockamamie story I've ever heard."

"It's true. Mason has one too. Each ring has its own purpose in keeping her alive." Dean glanced at the door again, pulled his hand back. "I don't know how it works. It just does."

The police officer outside Jay's door glanced into the room. "Shift change, Jay. See ya tomorrow."

Jay waved at the cop and turned back to Dean. "What is it with these rings?"

Dean sat on the edge of the bed. "It seems that Bessie will protect anyone who wears them. She's saved Mason's life a few times already, mine too. In return, we're supposed to help her out when she's in danger."

"So, how did it tell you I was in danger?"

"It didn't. It told me that something was wrong with Bessie. It turned yellow and made me think my finger was on fire, it hurt that much."

"And Mason, his did the same thing?"

Dean nodded. "They call us Bessie's Keepers."

Jay remained quiet for a few seconds. As if thinking out loud, he said, "Maybe we can use Bessie to capture Parsons."

Dean scrutinized his friend. "What do you mean, Jay? Why would a well-known drug dealer want to help the cops?"

Jay looked at the door, then back at Dean. "If I tell you, you must promise not to say anything to anyone, right? Not even Jack."

"Right, I promise," Dean said, wondering what Jack had to do with this.

"It's because I 'm a cop. I'm undercover."

"So, doesn't Jack know?" It took a few seconds to wrap this around the inside of his head. Dean realized that was the reason Jay hadn't been arrested for dealing drugs a long time ago.

"Yes, he knows. He's my partner." Dean glanced at the door. Jay continued. "If he knew I told you my true identity, he'll shoot me himself."

"I didn't even know Jack had a partner."

"No one outside of the force knows." Jay gave Dean a friendly smile. "All the cops around this area know who I am. Just because Jack is the only official cop in town doesn't mean he's alone."

"That's good to know. It takes a load off my mind." Dean felt a little better. Maybe the rest of them weren't in danger after all.

****

Troy sat at the kitchen table watching his mother dry the lunch dishes. His mind, however, was in a different place. A lot of things had happened lately, he needed to put things into perspective. Now, he was thinking about the gas rig blowing up.

"What's eating you, Troy?" Rachel asked after she hung the tea towel on the handle of the stove. "You look like you have something heavy on your mind."

"Aw," he willed his mind to clear up. "Just thinking, that's all."

"I heard that Black Tom is doing better," she said. "He's going to live."

Black Tom? He'd forgotten all about that. He let out an exaggerated sigh. "Remember when we took Jason to emerge when he sprained his ankle?"

"Yes, and you canoed to town."

"Well, Black Tom told me something that I think Mason should hear; probably you too."

"I'll call him now." Rachel picked up the phone and dialed. Troy watched as her slim finger slipped into the holes and pulled the rotary around to each number in turn. It seemed to take forever for it to rotate back to its resting place. He could hear the click-click it made as it went, and the faint sound as it rang through the wires. One thing his parents were glad about was that they were no longer on a party line. Now everything they said on the phone was private.

Troy got a drink of water while his mother talked. "He's coming right over," she told him after she hung up.

He must have flown. Mason was there in minutes; his eyes looking at him as if he was expecting bad news. His mother handed him a beer before he joined them at the kitchen table.

"What's up, Troy?" his uncle asked. "Your mother tells me you have something important to say."

Troy swallowed hard. "When we were in the canoe; well, Black Tom told me that when Bessie's rings are handed down, they have to stay in the family."

"Is that why Dean has one?" Mason looked at his sister nervously.

"I don't know," Troy said. "He said that it's our family curse"

"A curse?" Rachel's hand went to her heart. "I've never heard anything about a family curse, have you?"

Mason shook his head. "No, I haven't either."

"Tom told me that the rings never lie about that."

"Does that mean you're next?"

"I don't want anything to do with either ring. I don't want any part of this thing at all." Troy's angry voice brought Eddie in from the living room. He set a newspaper down on the table in front of him. "What's going on?"

"Black Tom told Troy that Bessie's rings are always kept in the family. He's next in line for one," Mason told him.

Eddie plunked down on a chair. "Ain't going to happen. He's not going to become involved with this, this thing. It's bad enough having one son caught up in this fairy tale."

"It's a curse," Rachel told him. "We can't get around it."

Eddie looked at his son. "If I must, I'll move him to another country. I can tell by his face, he doesn't want to be involved with this."

     Bessie — The Monster in Lake Erie by Deborah Tadema

"I didn't either," Mason said. "If I had known what this ring represented, I wouldn't have taken it from my old man." He looked down at his hand as if disgusted. With his other hand, he reached over and pulled on the ring. It wouldn't budge. "Funny, I had it off this morning, so I could wash up. Now, it seems glued to my finger."

Troy looked at his uncle in horror. "See, we couldn't get rid of it if we tried."

Eddie squeezed his arm. "When is he supposed to take that thing over?"

"When the time is right," Troy said. "Tom told me that someone always comes along when the time is right."

Mason tried to pull the ring off again. "I guess when my time is done."

"He told me to start training, and that Uncle Mason didn't get the training he needed," Troy said.

Mason shook his head. "No, I certainly didn't. I didn't even know I was a keeper until Tom told me."

Rachel covered her mouth with the back of her hand. "My poor boys."

CHAPTER 19

Mason backed his truck out of his sister's driveway with a fogged-up mind. He drove through town taking the back streets just to look at the old style houses he liked. After he turned the corner on Boston Street, he saw Frank standing in the middle of the road. He pulled up beside his friend and called out the window.

"Frank, what are you doing?" Mason leaned against the back of the seat toward the passenger door. "Want a lift?"

Frank got in without saying a word and stared straight ahead. Mason headed toward his friend's house.

"Don't' take me home," Frank demanded. "Take me to your place instead."

Mason drove around the block and parked in the lot. Frank followed him up to his second story apartment. He opened some windows then took out a couple of beers out of the fridge. "What's up, Frank?" he asked as he made his way to the living room where his friend had gone.

Frank watched the curtains on the balcony window billow in and out. "I don't love Sherry anymore." He took a sip of his beer. "One of us will be moving out soon."

Mason didn't know what to say or do for that matter. Frank and Sherry had been high school sweethearts. They've been together forever. "Sorry to hear that, Frank."

"I know I'm supposed to love her. I still love Jason." He gave Mason a tearful look. "I don't want to hurt her, but I do. We've fought ever since I got out of the hospital." He let out a long sigh. "We've tried to keep it from Jason, I know he sees. He senses something isn't right."

"I don't know what to say, Frank. Both of you have been good friends of mine for a hell of a long time." Mason noticed that his friend's bottle was empty and wondered if he should offer another one, especially after what Frank did to his son. He decided he would, he surely needed another one. He got up and went to the fridge, leaned his head against it for a few seconds before he opened the door. All he knew was that Frank had been acting strange lately. It was bound to put a strain on his marriage.

"How do you think Jason will handle this?" he asked Frank as he handed him the bottle.

Frank dropped his shoulders. "I don't know. We plan on telling him tonight." He looked over at Mason who had plunked down in his favorite chair. "My stomach has been in a knot ever since I woke up from the coma. I treat Sherry rough, even in bed. It's like I blame her for what's happened to me."

"She had nothing to do with it, Frank. None of it is her fault."

"Don't you think I know that?" Frank downed his second bottle. He stood and looked down at Mason. "I'm going to get drunk and pass out on your couch, old friend." He proceeded to the kitchen.

"What about telling Jason tonight?" Mason shouted.

"The hell with it, I'll tell him tomorrow."

"I have a date tonight, Frank." Mason didn't want him there all night, didn't want to have to babysit.

"That's fine. Just remember not to bring her back here." Frank let out a chuckle. "Go ahead. I'll be okay."

Mason wondered if he should leave his friend alone tonight, who seemed to want to self-destruct. "Why don't I call Val and have her bring us over a pizza for supper?"

"It's your place. You do what you want."

Mason went into the kitchen and dialed Sherry's number. In a faint voice, he told her where her husband was and not to expect him home tonight.

"Good," she said. "Thanks for letting me know, Mason. You can keep him for all I care." He waited for her to say more, listened to the silence that followed her remark. After a bit he heard the click of the phone and the dial tone.

He took a deep breath before he called Valerie. While he waited he rubbed his temple with his other hand. She answered on the third ring. Mason told her about the change in plans and she agreed to pick up the pizza on her way over. He hung up the phone and wished he had done what Frank told him to do, just go. If he thought it was a good idea he would go over to Val's. He wanted to make love to her tonight, to spend more time with her, alone. Instead, he was about to stay home and help Frank get drunk.

"I was thinking," Frank said behind him, making Mason jump. Frank smiled at him and continued. "Why don't we get Eddie over here, play poker."

"You forget that Val's on her way." Mason was getting perturbed with this man. "And no, we are not going to play poker."

"You're the boss." Frank took out another beer and grinned at Mason as he headed back to the living room. "Does Val like hockey?"

Mason rolled his eyes. "It's the middle of summer, Frank. There's no hockey on TV now."

"I know, I was just wondering." A sly smile crossed Frank's face. "You're much too serious, dear boy."

****

The swings on the beach swayed back and forth as Troy and Jason talked. "If they split, I'm staying with Dad," Jason said.

"Sure, you would. He lets you drink beer," Troy scoffed and slid his foot in the sand as he swung forward on the swing.

Jason gave him a lopsided grin. "I bet he'd let me stay out until midnight, too."

"And what about your mom?"

"Haven't you noticed that she's been taking this out on me? She whacked me yesterday just because I didn't put my laundry away fast enough for her."

"Yeah, a couple of days ago you told me she slapped you on the face."

Jason nodded. "More than once."

Troy said, "Just because your dad acts a little weird doesn't mean she needs to go off the deep end."

"Well, I'm beginning to not like her anymore. This morning she threw a shoe at me."

Troy stopped the swing and thought about how both of Jason's parents have gone loony.

"I've made up my mind. Like you said, Dad may be weird, but his doctor said he should snap out of it. And mom has gotten even worse; and frankly, she scares me now with her temper."

Troy looked down at the ground, saying nothing. Didn't know what to say.

"And the way she swears at Dad now," Jason continued. "She's using words I've never heard before."

"It didn't take them long to fall out of love, did it?" Troy said.

****

Mason showed up first with Valerie and Dean. Eddie and Rachel brought Troy with them shortly afterward. Frank and Sherry greeted them, their faces somber. Jason sat at the kitchen table, a bottle of pop in front of him. Rachel handed Troy a pop after he sat down. The adults held beers. Frank gave a bottle to Dean and gave his wife a look that told her not to cause any problems. Mason saw the look Frank gave Eddie, who ignored it. They all knew Dean drank beer. Troy and Jason, however, were still too young, the law Sherry firmly set down after that episode with Frank and Jason.

"We have a situation," Jack told them after they all sat around Frank's kitchen. "Seems there's this old guy spying on the kids."

Mason didn't miss the look of longing Jack gave Valerie, nor the hate in his eyes when the constable looked at him. "What old guy?" Mason exchanged looks with Eddie. "When?"

"Last week he was at the skating rink watching Troy. A few nights ago, the same guy was down on the beach, watching Jason."

Mason heard the chorus if inhaled breaths. "What does this guy look like?"

"Old. About sixty," Jason told them.

Troy nodded. "Decked out all the time in a new suit, a chrome dome."

"A what?" Rachel asked.

"Bald," Troy told her.

"Did you get a look at his wheels?" Dean asked before he took a sip of his brew.

"He drives a yellow 1963 Plymouth," Jason told them.

Eddie spilled his beer. "That's the guy who attacked me."

They all looked his way with stunned faces, except one. Dean nodded as if he already knew who it was.

"When did that happen?" Mason asked.

"The day we…" Eddie stopped.

Mason figured it out. "It was the time when we took the drugs out of the bomb shelter." He turned to Frank and Sherry. "That's where Black Tom was living, and mixing drugs for Bessie. He was getting her high."

"Yeah, that's when I had problems with my car and Dean got me a new carburetor," Eddie said. "You just got out of the hospital," he explained at Frank's confused look.

Mason told them, "It must be Parsons."

"I only saw his back that day in the hospital," Eddie said, "He was too far away by the time I got to your room. I didn't know it was him."

"It was Parsons," Jack confirmed. "He was the one who shot Jay." Jack looked like he wanted to say something else but decided not to.

"That's what Jay told me," Dean said. "And about Parsons spying on us."

"He told you?" Frank asked. "How did he know all this?" He made his wife move so he could stand against the counter beside Eddie.

Again, Jack looked like he wanted to say something. Didn't. He shrugged his shoulders instead.

"We should call Harback," Mason said.

****

Port Stanley beach was a favorite spot for vacationers to visit. It also was a magnet for all kinds of characters. Dean stood in the shadows and watched Jack at work. He wasn't surprised to see how Jack split up a fist fight. His art of negotiation settled the men down. The three men involved had fought over a girl. The girl herself cowered along the wall of a booth.

Dean looked around to see if he could spot any more cops in the area. If what Jay said was true, there must be at least one more there to back Jack up if he got into trouble. How would he know who it was if the cop was undercover? Why were there so many of them in hiding? Why was Jack the only one in uniform?

He saw one of the men nod his head at another one. They stepped closer to Jack, a deadly gleam in their eyes. That's when Dean walked out of his hiding place. Jack barely had time to acknowledge that Dean was there when he someone jumped him. In a split second, Dean set his fists flying and attacked one of the men. The girl screamed.

A big fist slammed into Dean's stomach. He bent over double and stumbled backward. Out of the corner of his eye, he saw Jack whip out his police baton and swing it. It smashed into the side of a man's head. That man went down. Dean's man came at him again. This time, Dean shot up and connected a fist under his chin. The man's head snapped back.

Dean had his man down. His arms went around his middle as he tried to get his breath back. Jack came up to him and patted his back. "Thanks for the help, Dean. We couldn't have got these guys without it."

Dean looked up and saw that all three of the men were handcuffed. Two men were leading them away; probably undercover cops. "What's going on, Jack? Why the secrecy?"

Jack pulled him aside, wiped the blood from his cheek. "Harback can't make it down here. So, we're looking for Parsons. Plus, there's a major drug deal about to happen. We're just trying to get our plan into motion."

"And Jay, what is he?" Dean wanted to see if Jack would tell him. He didn't have to keep this secret from his friend.

Jack scrutinized the young man he'd known all his life. Finally, he said, "All right. I'll tell you. Don't say anything because this is dangerous stuff."

Dean nodded.

"We spent the better part of a year to set Jay up as a drug dealer. He's been gaining the trust of some go-to guy in the effort to catch the big boss." Jack gave a quick search of the area with his eyes. "We believe that that boss in none other than Parsons himself."

****

Eddie wondered how Jack could put up with Mason after he stole his girl away from him. But, the constable had been in no shape to challenge him. Even now, the cop seemed slow, to favor his side. The knife wound that Black Tom inflicted must still not be fully healed yet. Dean had told him about the fight last night down on the beach and that Jack was able to hold up his end pretty good with all that's considered.

He came up with an idea and called Jack over to his place. Jack's cruiser parked out front of his house; Dean opened the door for him.

"I won't offer you a beer," Eddie told the constable when he walked into the living room. "Not when you're on duty."

Jack took off his hat and stuffed it under his arm. "I can't stay too long. Have to go to court. They're trying to postpone Black Tom's hearing again."

"I'll get to the point." Eddie watched Dean take a seat. "Your knife wound doesn't seem to be healing very well."

Jack's hand went to his side. "I'm still stiff there."

"Well, I'm offering all the other cops from this district a discount at the sporting goods store I'm opening up. And for you, beings you're a personal friend, are going to recruit business my way."

"What store?" Jack's eyes went from Eddie to Dean.

"On Fairlane Street. Mason's helping me with the finances to get started. I'll be running it. I already have some of the equipment downstairs."

"I think this is a good idea, Jack." Dean smiled brightly from one man to the other.

Jack grinned at Dean. "I suspect you had something to do with this, didn't you?"

"We just got talking. I told Dad how well you fought last night with your sore side. You impressed me, Jack. Dad will give you a good deal on some equipment."

"You sure know how to butter up a guy, don't you?" Jack let out a laugh. "Okay, I like your idea, Ed. I can see how this will help all of us." He gave Dean a serious look. "What's in it for you?"

"Nothing, except a job. Dad's hired me to help get things set up. I'm hoping he'll let me stay on afterward." He gave his father a pleading look. Eddie laughed and ruffled Dean's hair.

A slow smile spread across Jack's face. "Maybe a hundred years from now I'll be able to lick Mason." He looked from one to the other. "For more reasons than one."

****

"This is boring," Troy complained. "We aren't allowed to do anything."

"No one said we can't go up the hill. Why don't we go for a hike?" Jason said. "If we stick together, it should be okay."

"Yeah, let's go. I want to get away from here for a while."

The boys left the back steps of Jason's house and headed toward Picnic Hill. "What if that guy is up there? He might shoot us."

"Well for one thing," Troy reasoned, "we aren't going to deal drugs. Why would Parsons be up there?"

"Yeah," Jason agreed. "He's probably looking for us down on the beach. He can't spy on us up on the hill if he doesn't know where we are." After they turned the corner he said, "Something I don't understand is why the cops haven't got him yet."

"You know what I think? I think they're waiting for something big to happen." Troy saw Jason's eyebrows lift. "Well, he's been around this area for weeks now and they just seem to let him walk around. If they wanted him that bad, I think they'd have caught him by now."

"Maybe we should spy on him, see what he's up to."

Troy considered this as they climbed up the hill. It wasn't until they reached the top did they stop and rest. "Look, Bessie's down there." Troy pointed toward Muddy Creek and then waved to her. They turned back toward the other trail. It wasn't long before they emerged from the one beside her den. Troy squinted from the sun as they walked down to the creek.

Jason lifted his arm and Bessie lowered her massive head. Both boys petted her while she checked them out.

They spent time with Bessie before sauntering toward the hill. After that, they got bored. "Want to go into the cave?" Jason asked Troy as if daring him.

Troy didn't want his friend to think he was afraid and said, "Yes, except we don't have a flashlight."

Jason checked the position of the sun. "It'll be light in there for about an hour yet, enough for us to see where we're going."

Troy gave a reluctant nod and said, "Remember, stay to the right."

CHAPTER 20

Eddie stopped in to check on his friends. It was when he found out that Sherry had packed her bags and left while Jason was out. She and Frank had come to a point where they wanted to kill each other and thought it best this way. Maybe it wouldn't hit Jason as hard than if he saw his mother leave. Frank would tell him when he got back home.

She took the family car. "Let her have that old rundown bucket," Frank said to Eddie as they sat at the kitchen table. "Justin's staying with me." He looked down at this coffee and sighed. "She's seen a lawyer, divorce is imminent. I worry about Jason. I don't care about the house, I can move, take my son with me. She can have all the furniture. I just wanted her gone."

Eddie took a sip of coffee then set the cup back down. "Don't you feel remorse for your actions, Frank? She's been your wife for nineteen years?"

"No, not really. All I feel is empty and I don't know why. Bessie sucked the life out of me when she killed my crew. She might as well have killed me too."

"No, Frank. Your son needs you. At least think about that, okay?"

Frank went on as if Eddie never spoke. "The Day of Hell is what I call it. Two of my men are dead, the third has never been found. I missed all the funerals."

Eddie nodded, recalling that two men on the gas rig had been killed the same day, one murdered, the other killed in the storm that suddenly whipped up. And both of his sons were out there?

He almost forgot there was another death out there that day. Ryan had stolen Jack's speedboat and almost sunk them all. It was lucky that the boys made it to the rig, lucky that he and Mason found them.

Frank's hands shook when he looked down at them. As if reading Eddie's mind, he said, "I almost lost my son. And now my wife is leaving me."

Eddie stood to leave. Obviously, Frank was going to blame this all on Sherry.

****

The boys had gone in there to find more sugar cubes. Troy heard an eerie laugh. They ran to the end of the tunnel; the boulder blocked the entrance. He and Jason pushed on it. It wouldn't move this time.

They even tried to move the boulder at the other end, the one that would lead them to the old road, with no luck. All they heard was scraping from the other end of the tunnel behind the rocks. They didn't scream for help anymore. No one, other than their jailer would hear them anyway.

"Who do you think that was?" Jason asked.

"I don't know. I bet it was Parsons," Troy answered. He gave his friend the same look that he knew was on his face, scared to death. Troy didn't need to say anything; the two of them could practically read each other's thoughts. They sat on the cold stone floor, huddled in the bomb shelter.

Troy looked over at the single candle that sat on the table. Its flame had burnt halfway down. He figured they only had an hour left of the dim light. His worst fear would become a reality; total and complete darkness.

The room had been stripped of everything else. No lanterns or books or paper to burn to give them light or warmth. He felt the dampness from the clay and rock wall behind him, smelled the mustiness of the room.

Bessie — The Monster in Lake Erie by Deborah Tadema

Jason screamed as he swatted at a mouse that had touched his arm. The mouse scurried along the edge and out a tiny hole on the other side of the room. Troy got up and blocked the hole with a rag. He didn't think that would do any good. He didn't say anything. It made him feel better.

The boys sat close together, touching each other for reassurance. Troy could hear Jason's breathing that somehow kept him calm. The candle fluttered and went out.

****

Mason left the bed, stepped into his pants, and followed as Valerie padded to her door in her housecoat to answer the insistent banging. He walked around the corner of the hallway and leaned on the wall. Valerie gave her friend a dirty look when Sherry pushed past her with a suitcase. "I just left Frank," she said as tears rushed from her eyes.

Valerie's arms went around Sherry as she led her to the couch. "I'm so sorry," she said as she gazed back at Mason.

Sherry saw the look and waved Valerie away. "I'm sorry. I came at a bad time, didn't I?"

"It's okay Sherry."

"If you don't mind, I'll just stay right here on the couch." Sherry patted the cushion beside her. "Just pretend I'm not here."

"What happened?" Mason decided he better show himself to Sherry.

Valerie gave Mason a worried look. "Sherry's moved out on Frank."

He let out a whistle and walked into the living room. Behind Sherry's back, he gave her a perturbed look. Valerie knew how he felt, and he knew she felt the same way. Sherry had just ruined their night.

Mason faced Sherry with a concerned look now on his face. He bent down to give her a hug. "I'm sorry it had to come to this. I was hoping it wouldn't."

"Yeah, well," She said after Mason straightened up. "Things just kept getting worse."

"What are you going to do now?" Mason asked. "I mean your long-term plans."

Sherry shrugged and said, "I guess I have to find a place to live." She looked up at Valerie. "Tomorrow, I'll get a room, and start looking for an apartment. I don't want to intrude on you two anymore than necessary."

I hope so, Mason thought. She looked over at Valerie. He was about to say something when the phone rang.

****

By the time Eddie walked into Frank's house, Jack was already there. They shook his hands, worried looks in their eyes. "When did you see them last?" Eddie asked as he looked from one to the other.

Frank spoke up. "They were just sitting on the back step. Later I saw them walking down the driveway. I don't know which way they went after that." He ran a hand through his dark hair. "I should have paid more attention. I didn't think they'd get reckless after what we told them."

Eddie said, "When was that?"

Frank looked up after he stared at the floor for a bit. "About three, or maybe it was four. Yeah, closer to four."

Jack went to the phone and called the station. After he talked to dispatch, he turned back to his friends. "I just called for more bodies. We'll wait until they get here."

"You told me that a half hour ago, we should be out there looking," Frank said angrily. "How do you expect to find them if we're in here?"

"Settle down Frank," Eddie said. "It won't do any good going off half out of our minds. I know we'll find them. We need to get organized first."

Jack nodded his thanks. "We'll set up a grid, Frank. I'll get the guys to spread out. Some will take the beach; others will go up the hill." Frank seemed to have accepted this, at least for now.

"I should call…" Frank stopped. "I can't call Sherry. I don't know where she is."

"Aw, I'll call Mason," Jack said. "Maybe his ring will tell us if Bessie knows something."

"I'll call him," Eddie volunteered when he saw four cops walk up to the back door through the window. Frank ran over to let them in.

Jack greeted his fellow officers which gave Eddie time to settle his nerves. Jack laid out his plan to them.

"We can take the beach," Officer Cooper said. "You can have the hill." He looked over at Jack. "If that's what you want."

Eddie listened to the conversation as he made his call, and talked softly after Mason answered.

"Sounds good to me," Jack said, "Why don't you go ahead? We're waiting for one more to show up."

The cops left and headed down to the beach. Jack leaned against the kitchen counter and watched Frank walk back and forth in front of him. "I prefer the hill," Jack said. "I'd rather Cooper and his friends deal with Bessie if she's there."

Eddie piped up. "Got a hold of Mason. He was over at Val's. He's picking up Dean on his way over."

"Oh, ya, I forgot about Dean," Frank said. "Good idea."

****

Tiny lights blinked through the trees like giant fireflies as the men climbed the hill. Their calls were muffled by the vegetation and Picnic Hill itself. At the top they spread out, Dean and Mason naturally headed toward Bessie's cave.

Dean wondered as he followed Mason down the path, why Jack seemed a little nervous around Frank tonight. It wasn't like the constable to keep his distance from his friend like he was, or watch Frank as if he was guilty of something. Maybe he just felt sorry for Frank because his wife ran off on him. Mason said that Sherry was over at Valerie's.

Mason pushed the bush aside and the two of them entered the cave. They stayed to the right and made their way along the ledge. Bessie slowly rose from the water and blinked at them.

"We must have woken her up," Mason said as he stopped to watch her.

"She's not panicking or anything," Dean observed. "I don't think there's anything wrong in here."

Mason stood where he was for a few more minutes then swung the beam of his flashlight around the cave. "You're right," he said and moved to leave. He stopped short and called Dean back. "Look, drag marks."

Dean looked to where Mason's light illuminated. With both flashlights, they followed the marks toward the tunnel entrance. "That's not right." Dean's light showed two huge rocks in front of the entrance way. "Somebody doesn't want us in there."

"Or," Mason said, "nobody to get out."

Dean's mouth formed a big O. Nothing came out. Slowly he backed up. "I'll go get help. There's no way we can move those."

"We can…"

Dean was already on his way out of the cave. He ran a few hundred yards along the creek bed and let out a loud whistle. After several minutes, he saw lights bob up and down at the top of the cliff.

"You got something?" Jack's silhouette asked.

"Yeah," Dean called back. "We think we do."

****

Bessie didn't know the cubs were behind the wall. They were so quiet that she didn't hear them. She had wondered where the extra rock came from. It wasn't there before; it was at the far end of the ledge. She didn't notice it until her keepers saw it there. Someone must have moved it while she was out in the lake. From now on she'd check her den more closely when she came home.

If she had known this, she could have sent for her keepers a lot sooner.

****

Eddie called Rachel from Frank's to let her know that her son was safe and that they'd be home shortly.

Jack thanked all the cops and his friends for all the help they gave him tonight. He sat at the table and faced the two boys. They still had fear in their eyes as they looked from one man to the other.

Eddie gave Troy an angry look. Several times he started to speak only to get choked up.

Frank yelled at them. "What in God's name did you go up there for? You knew you were supposed to stay in town, here at home."

The kids shrank in their chairs. Jack put up a hand to stop his friend. "That isn't going to help, Frank. And if you want to find out what happened up there, let me do my job."

Frank glared at Jack for a few seconds, finally gave a curt nod of his head.

Troy cleared his throat. "We just wanted to," he cleared his throat again. Mason got the teens a glass of water. Troy took a gulp then started all over again. "We just wanted to see the bomb shelter."

"Of all the harebrained…"

"Frank," Jack yelled. "Shut up."

Mason took hold of Frank's arm. "Take it easy old friend. Don't take it out on the kids."

Frank glared at Mason, pulled out of the man's grasp and gave Eddie a sorrowful look. "Just be glad it doesn't happen to you."

Eddie nodded.

"What?" Jason looked around. "Where's Mom?"

Frank's features finally softened. "She's gone, son; just left us."

Jason burst out in tears. Troy laid a hand on his friend's shoulder.

Frank glared at him. "You talked him into it, didn't you? This all because you…" He clenched his fists.

Eddie stepped in front of him. "Oh, no you don't."

It was enough to make Frank think twice. He glared at Eddie for a long time before turning away.

Jack let out an exaggerated sigh. He looked back at the boys. "That's all you did? Someone blocked both entrances?"

Troy's head bobbed. "That's all. I didn't do anything wrong." His eyes never left Frank.

"Haven't you learned anything yet?" Dean asked as if he was innocent of any wrongdoing.

Jason gave a crooked grin. "Yeah, I have." He looked over at his buddy. "Troy screams like a girl."

****

The boys were grounded. Frank had Eddie take him uptown, so he could buy another car. Frank had landed a job at a local factory. His worry now was that he would have to work shift-work. Jason would be alone when he was on afternoons and not get home until 12:30 in the morning.

Eddie said as he drove into the car dealership. "Jason can stay at our place until you get home."

"Thanks, Ed. I'll need someone to keep an eye on him when school starts. It'll be too late to drag him home." He sighed heavily. "I hope that by then Parsons has been caught. I wouldn't feel so bad if I have to leave him by himself for a few hours."

"We can check in on him. Or maybe Rachel can go over there."

"Thanks, man. I don't want to put anyone out. You have your own kids to worry about."

Eddie parked his car and the two of them walked around the lot and looked at the cars.

"This one looks promising." Frank stopped beside a Ford. "Something I can afford."

"How can you afford anything? You haven't worked in over two months."

Frank grinned at his friend. "I got an insurance check from the sinking of my fishing boat; got caught up on all the bills. And since Sherry took our car, I need something to go to work with."

"Good." Eddie felt relieved. "I was hoping you weren't going into major debt."

Frank suddenly looked melancholy. "Sherry's been seeing a lawyer. She's filed for a divorce."

Eddie put an arm on Frank's shoulder. "I am sorry, buddy."

"I just hope she doesn't take off with everything, that's all." Frank straightened when the salesman walked up to him.

    Bessie — The Monster in Lake Erie by Deborah Tadema

Eddie went with Frank on the test drive of the car and waited outside while his friend negotiated a price and eventually bought it. He thought about all the stuff Frank had gone through these past few months. Frank's behavior didn't seem all that strange to him, not what Sherry had led him to believe. What goes on behind closed doors could be a lot different.

Frank came back out, a big smile on his face. "Well, I got it." He waved the keys at Eddie. "Thanks for your help, buddy."

Eddie got into his car. Frank leaned in the window. "That night that Sherry left, said she went right over to Val's." Eddie nodded. Frank continued. "She didn't. Mason said she didn't get there until after ten o'clock. She left our house at about five-thirty."

"She could have just driven around." Eddie wasn't quite sure where this was heading. "Or maybe she tried other places before Val took her in."

"Yeah." Frank glanced over at his new car. "Someone else told me that our car was parked at Jack's apartment."

"There are a lot of people in that apartment building," Eddie reminded Frank.

"Yeah," Frank tapped the hood of Eddie's car. "Only one person that we know."

CHAPTER 21

The lawyer Mason hired got back to him with definite proof that Charles Thomas Brennan was his brother. Mason thought okay, many people went by their middle names. He showed Rachel the papers that said that Tom's mother went by the name, Alicia Charisma Brennan, never married. It gave the dates of his birth and named Tom the youngest of the three of them by a year and a half. Mason had turned forty that spring. Rachel would be thirty-eight in November. That made Tom thirty-six. It also said that Tom was a twin and that the twin had died a couple of months after their birth.

"A twin," Rachel said. "He was a twin."

Mason read over her shoulder. "Well, I'm glad there aren't two of them."

"Dad named the sailboat after Tom's mother." Rachel read the name again. "I wonder if mom knew that." The sailboat that Mason had inherited, the one that blew up.

"I think she did. Remember the fights they used to have?" Mason sat beside her at his kitchen table. He studied the legal document in Rachel's hands.

"You mean the ones that didn't involve her money?"

"Yeah. Something tells me she knew he had another family someplace."

"Isn't there a name for that?"

Yes. Bigamy." Mason swallowed hard.

"They weren't married."

"I know, but they might as well have been."

"Well, I for one don't like our new brother." Rachel turned the page over.

"Me either." Mason drummed his thumbs on the table. "What do you want to do about it?"

"What can we do about it? Nothing. If he's our brother, I guess we just have to accept it."

Mason slapped the side of his leg. "I was hoping that Dean and I were wrong about this. That we missed something."

Brother and sister looked at each other in mutual understanding; keep Tom at a distance. Rachel broke the contact when she put the paper back into its envelope. "So, how are things with you and Val?"

"Fine. Better if she could get rid of that leech." Mason said. "I was hoping she'd let me move in with her. I can't if Sherry's still there."

"Why don't you have her move in here?"

"Because her place is bigger." He looked around his apartment. "There isn't enough room for the two of us in here."

Rachel's head bobbed. "I guess someone has to kick Sherry out. She shouldn't be mooching off Valerie anyway. I wouldn't do that to her."

"Oh?" Mason teased. "You thinking of leaving Ed?"

Rachel gave him a fake shocked look. "Not in this lifetime."

****

It surprised Dean to get a call from Jack so late in the evening. And amazed him at what the constable had asked him to do. He was flabbergasted after it had worked. Jack had distracted the officer that the Chief assigned to guard Jay in his hospital room. He and Eddie smuggled Jay out, took him down to the dock and loaded him onto the pontoon boat. Dean and Eddie took Jay out into the middle of the lake to hide him.

It was a good thing that Jay's wound had healed fast; another that he was able to fight his would-be killer. Both Jay and Jack suspected the officer that was supposed to protect Jay.

"We don't know who we can trust," Jack had explained before he watched them sail away. "For now, I need to rely on you two."

"I never thought I'd be hiding way out here," Jay told them after Eddie released the anchor.

"And I never thought I'd be hiding someone way out here," Dean said. He saw that Jack and his dad had the boat well supplied. Behind his seat, coolers and containers held food to last them a week. A camp stove and lanterns were on the bench along the side with sleeping bags and rain gear. Three fold-up cots stood ready for use that Dean knew, would take up the back half of the boat. Thankfully that half had a canopy over it and clear plastic sides that Eddie rolled up to give them air. Some of the equipment seemed familiar and Dean knew that it came from his dad. He thought about how many times he had sneaked up on his dad, Troy and Jason when they were camping up on Picnic Hill. He snickered when he remembered the time he jumped out at the three of them and made them all scream.

Dean was under no illusions as to why he was there. Jack had laid it all on the line. If there was any trouble, see if you can get Bessie to help you. He looked down at the aquamarine on his hand, hoped that Bessie wouldn't call on him now. There would be no way, unless they used the pontoon boat, to rush to her aid if she ran into trouble.

"Well," said Eddie, as he reached into a cooler and pulled out three beers. "We're about a half a mile west of where the rig used to be."

****

With Eddie gone for a few nights, Troy figured his curfew was lifted. He walked past his mother while she vacuumed and went over to see his best friend. All he knew was that his dad was helping Jack in some secret mission and it had something to do with Black Tom and Jay. This scared him. Why would his father want to have anything to do with a junkie and a dealer?

Troy heard that Black Tom had checked himself out of the Port Stanley hospital by simply walking out. His recovery had been remarkable if you consider he was near death three weeks ago. He was as thin and pale as he had always been and walked on stilt-like legs. Tom

Brennan had checked into the local YMCA and was about to draw on government assistance.

Troy found Jason playing solitary at the kitchen table when he walked in. Troy kicked off is sandals at the door and joined him. Jason shuffled the cards and dealt them each a hand, changing the game to Euchre. Shortly afterward Shannon showed up and asked for Dean. Neither of them could tell her where he was.

"I heard he was with another girl," she said, a hint of anger in her eyes. "Is that true?"

Troy and Jason looked at each other with the silent question. *"Should they tell her?"* Finally, Jason shrugged and said, "I think you should take that up with him."

"I will," Shannon told them and then left.

"Whew, I didn't want to tell her," Troy said. "I think she would have hit us if we told her we saw Dean with Rain."

"Like I think my dad wants to hit Jack," Jason said. "He thinks that Mom went over to her lover's place after she moved out of here."

"She doesn't have a lover," Troy said sternly. "When did she have time to run around on your dad? She spent all of it at the hospital when he was there. I thought she was at Valerie's?"

"There's no proof that she went to his place, only that her car was in his parking lot. Besides, what if she did go to Jack? I like him."

"We all like him," Troy said. "How would you like him as a step-dad?"

"Fine by me. Dad was the one who made her leave, despite what he wants everyone to believe."

After a stretch of silence, Troy spoke up, "My dad's gone away for a few days. My mom doesn't even know where he is."

"You don't think...?" Jason didn't finish.

Troy shook his head. "No, he's not running around on my mom. He's helping Jack out. I think they're going to make a big drug bust or something."

****

Bessie didn't feel that well and hadn't left her den for a few days. Her man came to see her, he looked worried. She didn't think he knew what to do so he just petted her. He coaxed Bessie outside. He must have wanted her to get some sunshine. This did make her feel better, at least a bit.

His friend joined him on the creek bed, the one with no mane. Bessie believed his name was Jack. She liked to say that name in her mind, Jack. It hit like a hammer. Jack. Jack. Jack. She knew her man's name, too. His name was Mason. It reminded her of the rise and fall of the waves. Mason. Mason. Mason. The name she liked the best was of her keeper with the long mane. Dean. Dean. Dean. To her, this sounded like a bird's call.

Bessie focused her mind on the men again and listen to them talk. She liked the sound of her males talking.

****

"I've called Harback. He'll be here in a couple of days," Jack told Mason.

"Good, things will get cleaned up within the police department. Maybe we have to get that done before we go after Parsons."

Jack walked along the gravel and picked up a stick, he twirled it around in his hand while he looked up at Bessie. "I hope we get that bastard before there are more killings."

Mason walked up beside the constable. "I'm sorry, Jack; about Val."

"Yeah, well," Jack looked at his friend. "I knew the moment I saw you on the beach that she'd go running back to you."

"Still, I didn't do it to hurt you."

"I know," Jack sighed. "I still feel lucky, to have had her for a little while."

"There's been talk," Mason hesitated, "that you've been seeing Sherry."

Jack waited for few seconds as if in thought. He turned to Mason. "That day she left Frank, she came over to my place." He whipped the stick into the creek. "She threw herself at me, Mason. Told me how lonely she'd been for years and how she and Frank had drifted apart. She told me how awful it was for her after he got out of the hospital."

"Did you go to bed with her?"

Jack gave a quick nod of his head. "And I've regretted it ever since." He looked back up at Bessie. "It was only one time Mason, and every day since she's been calling me. She wants to move in with me. I don't want her to. We won't last long, we're too different. She doesn't see it that way."

"Have you talked to Frank about this?"

"Hell no! I've been avoiding him as much as I can. It was hell that night the kids went missing, to pretend that I wasn't with his wife when he called me." Jack walked along the shore back toward the cave. "I hate the thought of facing him now, especially when he's been so unstable."

****

Bessie stayed with her men as they walked at a leisurely pace. She saw a flash of something in the trees above them, on top of the cliff. She growled and lifted her head to see what it was. Mason took hold of Jack's arm and ran for cover. It was a good thing he did. Just seconds later the blast of a rifle sounded and the sand at Mason's feet exploded.

****

"Did you bring your gun?" Mason squeezed up against the bottom of the cliff.

"No, I'm off duty," Jack snarled beside him. "I think I'll carry it everywhere with me from now on."

"In the meantime, what do we do about that guy up there?"

"I'll sneak around and go up the path. You keep him occupied, at least until I can get into the trees."

"Yeah, right. All I have to do is get my head blown off." Mason looked over at Bessie. "Maybe we can get her to distract that guy and both sneak up on him."

"Okay, you tell your pet what you want her to do. Frankly, I don't think she'll understand you."

"Dean thinks she's smart." Mason glanced up at Bessie. "You got a better idea?"

"No. Go for it." Jack gave Mason a doubtful look. They waited for a few minutes before either one made a move. There had been no more gunshots, no signs that the man was still there. Bessie swam along the creek, her eyes on the top of the cliff. Her low growl stopped just before she turned and swam back. She settled down and checked in the direction she'd just come from.

Mason took a step out into the open. No shot came. Bessie seemed relaxed. He dared taking another step.

Jack walked out beside him and scoured the cliff top. "I think he's gone."

Mason nodded and the two of them headed toward the path. With eyes peeled, they made it over the hill and into town. "Are we going to get help to catch that guy?"

Jack looked thoughtful. "Who? I don't know who to ask. I certainly don't trust anyone on the force, and Jay is hiding. Eddie and Dean are out of commission. That leaves you and Frank. And Frank will probably want to shoot me himself."

"Maybe we should just leave it until Harback gets here." Mason put a hand on Jack's shoulder. "You need me, I'll be here."

"Thanks, buddy." Jack smiled slightly. "I think that's what we'll do, wait for Harback."

****

As they walked down the sidewalk a red car screeched to a halt in front of the men. Frank Webster jumped out and stormed up to Jack, fists balled up at his sides. "You!"

Jack backed up, hands up ready to defend himself. "Wait. Let me explain..."

"So, you did sleep with her. The rumors are true." Frank took a swing. Jack jumped out-of-the-way.

"Hold on Frank." Mason pushed Frank back. "Sherry ran to him."

"Keep out of this, Brooks. This is between me and him." Frank went after Jack again.

Both Jack and Mason tackled Frank and held him with one arm each. "Listen," Jack tried to explain again. "She came to me that night. It was the only time, Frank."

"What about all that time I was in the hospital? Were you seeing her, too?" Frank's eyes glared with anger.

"No, I told you. It was only that one time, and she's been chasing me ever since."

"That's right," Mason said. "She calls him every night, begging him to let her move in with him."

Frank turned to Mason. "So, he says eh?"

"It's true; I've been at Val's when she calls him." Mason gave him a sympathetic look. "She's getting desperate, man."

So," Frank turned back to Jack and relaxed his stance. "She's good enough for a tumble, but not good enough to live with, is that it?"

"Look." Jack relaxed his grip on Frank. "I thought she only wanted someone to comfort her, to talk to. That's all."

"Yeah, you sure comforted her, didn't you?" Frank tried to take another swing. The other two predicted this and tightened their grip.

"Frank, listen," Jack pleaded. "I didn't mean for it to happen. I honestly don't know how it happened. One minute I was just holding her to let her cry it out. The next we were in bed." He looked into his friend's eyes. "I'd give anything to not have done it, Frank. There is nothing going on between us, just that one night, is all. I am sorry."

"You did kick her out Frank." Mason reasoned. "She had to go somewhere."

Frank looked down at the ground. "Okay, I give. I rejected her, and now you're rejecting her. I wonder who she'll run to next."

****

Bessie should kill him for what he did to her. And she would growl at him all day long if she had to. All she wanted was for him to step away from that tree, so she could bite him. Tom. Humph. He was the one who had poisoned her, gave her drugs and meat. He knew she ate plants. Did he care that her insides tore at her like a knife? No. Nor did he care that her head felt like mush and she saw weird things.

Bessie didn't kill so easily before. Now she would if she wanted to.

****

"Boat!" Dean watched it approach from the north-east that Sunday afternoon. "Looks like Jack's."

Eddie took the binoculars from his son and held them up. "Yes, it is." He let out a sigh. "At least we know it's friendly."

Jay put the gun back that he took out from under his seat. "Maybe now I'll get rid of you two," he joked.

Dean turned to face him. "Just because you can't win at Euchre, sore loser."

"Well, I never thought I'd see that," Dean chuckled after he turned back to watch the speedboat, "Not this soon, anyway."

"See what?" Eddie set the binoculars aside.

"Frank and Jack together, laughing. Not after what Jack just did."

"They must have already had it out." Eddie waved at the men. "I don't see any black eyes."

The speedboat pulled up alongside the pontoon. Jack and Frank stepped aboard and shook everyone's hands. "How's it been out here?" Jack asked after Jay handed him a beer.

"Boring as hell," Jay told him. "When can I go home?"

"Not yet. I called Harback, he'll be here soon." Jack looked at each man in turn. "Someone shot at me and Mason three days ago." He held up a hand. "Neither of us got hit, though. I think he wanted to scare us off."

"Scare you away from where?" Dean asked.

"We were down by Muddy Creek, talking to Bessie. Someone shot at us with a rifle nearly hit Mason in the ankle."

"Bessie's in danger." Dean wanted to take the speedboat to go check on her. He stayed put instead.

　　Bessie — The Monster in Lake Erie by Deborah Tadema

"No, I don't think so," Jack put a hand on the young man's shoulder. "Nobody shot at her."

"I wonder," said Eddie," If there is another place up there, besides the cave where they can hide drugs."

"There must be," said Jack. "There seems to be a lot of activity on the hill."

"So, when will Harback be here?" Jay asked.

"Sometime today. Mason's waiting for him." Jack turned to Jay. "We have to clean up the department first. I don't know who we can trust yet. We have to get Parsons." He faced Eddie. "The kids are getting antsy, being cooped up."

"I know how it feels," Jay said as he walked around. "So, what's the plan?"

"The plan is to let Eddie go home for the weekend," Jack told him. "Frank will replace him." He looked over at Dean. "Sorry, kid. Mason is needed on shore."

Dean looked at Frank. "Are you good at Euchre?"

Frank chuckled. "Not very. Why?"

"Good. Jay will have competition."

Jay hit Dean on the arm. "Smart ass."

"Anything out of the ordinary happen at all out here?" Jack asked the men. They shook their heads. "I guess we should go," he said to Eddie. They headed toward the speedboat when Jack looked back at Dean. "Oh, by the way; Shannon is back, been looking for you. She thinks you're shacked up someplace with another girl."

"Shannon's back?" Dean tried to push past Eddie. The big man held him back. Finally, he gave up. "Tell her I'm not shacked up." He looked at Jay and Frank. "Well, with a girl anyway."

CHAPTER 22

Harback drove into town later that afternoon. Mason Brooks met him at the Port Stanley police station. They greeted each other with slaps on the back. Mason directed him to his apartment. "Did Jack tell you what's been going on at the station?" Mason asked as he unlocked his door. "He doesn't trust anyone in the department."

"He told me," Harback set his suitcase down. "I was surprised he had me meet you at the station."

"Usually, he's the only one there. The officers from St. Thomas only come down when he needs them. He figured it was safe enough."

"So, someone shot at the two of you?" Harback sat in a seat in the living room. Mason got him a beer.

"Yeah, and we have all the kids under lock and key." Mason took a sip of his beer and sat across from the federal agent. "You know about Jay and where we have him?"

"Yes. I think that was a brilliant idea. Who's out there with him now?"

"Dean Jackson and Frank Webster."

"And Jack trusts these guys?"

"With his life."

"Good. I will too." Harback took a drink.

Jack showed up a few minutes later. He didn't waste any time, told them that he just got a call. Sherry Webster was missing.

"And there are only us three who can go looking for her." Mason paced the floor. "Should we get hold of Frank?"

"Not yet," Jack said. "Let's see if we can find her first. I don't want him to panic if he doesn't need to." He headed toward the phone. "I hate to do it. I'm going to call Ed."

"Where should we start? I hope that Parsons hasn't taken to kidnapping."

Harback stood up. "Let's start with her usual haunts and work from there." He looked over at Jack. "Sorry constable, it's just habit."

Jack hung up the phone and grinned at him. "That's fine by me. Eddie said he'll be here in ten minutes. I think we should split up, meet either back here or at the station later." He looked at his watch. "Say ten o'clock."

"Let's meet back here," Mason volunteered. "I'm sure we'll all need a beer by then."

As they headed to the door Jack stopped. "It was Valerie who called. Sherry hasn't been at her place for two nights. She hasn't called or even left a note to say where she was going. All her stuff is still there."

Mason glanced at his watch as they left the apartment. "Val must have just gotten home from work."

****

Mason didn't realize that Tom no longer lived at the YMCA. The man at the desk told him that Tom Brennan left after three nights. He walked out of the building with a headache. It had been days since he even thought about his brother. Should he have kept better tabs on him?

Jack walked around the street corner and up to his friend. "I might have a lead. My informant told me that someone has been living at the old Miller place for the last couple of days."

"The Miller place? That's ready to fall down. There hasn't been anyone in there for..." he stopped and looked at Jack. "Well, since before I left."

"For six years anyway," Jack got into the cruiser. "It's worth a look-see. Coming?"

Mason slid in beside Jack. "I wouldn't put it past Tom to move into a place like that."

The cruiser was parked at the bottom of Picnic Hill. Mason and Jack walked along until they came to an old trail that led part of the way up the south side. They found an old shack hidden in the woods. They stayed behind the trees; it could be Parson's hideout. Mason saw movement through the window. A candle flickered in the window.

Jack looked up through the canopy of leaves. "It's starting to get dark."

Mason nodded, eyes staying on the shack. "It's Tom. Look." He pointed to the door. Tom walked out with a big grin on his ugly face, with only his shorts on. He tossed water out of a pail into the bushes and went back inside. Mason and Jack walked up to the shack and knocked on the door.

Tom opened it and let the two men enter. Sherry was there wrapped in a blanket, her clothes strewn about the tiny one-room place. She gave them a look of defiance. If Jack was surprised, he didn't show it. Mason, however, couldn't hide it.

"You and her?" he looked at his brother and pointed to Sherry. Bile rose up in his throat. How could Sherry end up with the likes of Black Tom?

Tom grinned at them. "What can I say?"

Jack walked over to Sherry. "Did you come here of your own free will?"

Sherry let out a grating laugh. "Yes, I did. And I'm staying."

Mason looked from Tom to Sherry. What did they expect? Every other man in her life had rejected her. First her husband, then the man who stood in front of her now with a disgusted look written all over his face.

Jack shook his head and faced Tom. "Don't you know that there is someone up here with a rifle? He shot at us a few days ago."

Tom said, "It's been pretty peaceful so far."

"I think both of you should go back to town, at least until we catch Parsons." Jack eyed Sherry's clothes on the floor. "It isn't safe here."

"And go where?" Tom looked to Mason. "Will you let me live with you, brother?"

"Can't, I have company. Harback is staying with me until this ordeal is over with."

"See," Tom looked from one man to the other. "I can't afford a fancy place."

"Why did you leave the Y?" Mason barked at him.

Tom gave Sherry a loving look and nodded in her direction. "That should explain everything."

"You should at least go back to Val's," Jack told Sherry.

Sherry gathered the blanket around her, walked over to Tom and put an arm around his skinny frame. "I'm staying with him."

Mason and Jack looked at each other; neither knew what to say next. Finally, Jack said, "I don't have the manpower to give you protection."

****

"I can't make them leave," Jack told Harback. The men had met at Mason's as planned.

Eddie shook his head. "I can't believe it. Sherry and Black Tom. Who would have thought of that one?" He looked from Jack to Harback. "You think that maybe Tom's a good customer of Parsons's? And that's why he feels safe up there?"

"I never thought about that." Harback looked over at Jack. "Did you see any signs of drugs?"

"No, I didn't. But it doesn't mean there aren't any."

"I think we need to keep an eye on that place, just in case Parsons shows up," Eddie said. "Even if Tom isn't connected to that guy, he could still present a threat to him. Parsons could just be biding his time."

"Sherry wouldn't leave him." Mason still couldn't believe this. "Why would she want to hang on to him for?" He shrugged. "It looked to me that he's treating her good. I think he's in love with her."

Jack agreed. "He seemed pretty sure that she wouldn't leave him."

"Maybe he put a spell on her, or something," Mason said.

"What do you propose to do?" Harback gazed from one man to the other.

"I have no idea," Jack said. "This one flabbergasts me."

****

Tom leaned against a tree on top of Picnic Hill and watched Bessie laugh at him. He didn't care. To him, the fly on her nose posed the problem. That fly hummed too loud, the beat of its wings deafened him. Its one big eye stared at him and he became frightened. He couldn't move, the tree held him in place, its branches squeezing him.

He fought for air; his lungs had closed on him. The fly came at him, flew right at his face. Tom screamed and waved his arms frantically at it. Then it was gone. He looked for it under his shirt, in his pants. He panicked when he couldn't find it. He had to find it before it was too late. He had to kill it before that fly killed him.

He considered the trees beside him and wanted to call out for her. Except now, he couldn't remember who that was. All he knew was that a hazy woman walked up to him, talking to him. He wished she would talk faster; her words muffled and slow. He wanted to tell her to run that the fly was going to get her. When he tried to talk, his mouth fell off.

Tom got down on his hands and knees to look for it. Without his mouth, he couldn't hold in the drool that left his face. The woman pulled at his arm. If she wasn't careful he was afraid that she'd pull it off. He looked at her hand. That's when he saw the needle on the ground.

****

That Sunday Mason went with Jack and Eddie out to the pontoon boat. There hadn't been any more threats on Jay's life. He wondered if they should just bring them all home.

Jack had other ideas. "Mason and Eddie are now going to stay out here. Frank has to go to work tomorrow. We don't want him to lose a new job, now do we? And Dean has to make it up to Shannon."

"How's Harback making out?" Jay asked. "Has he made any progress at all?"

Jack nodded. "He's got one of the officers talking. I know now who Parsons's informant is. And we think there are more involved." He looked at his partner. "It's Cooper."

Jay let out a whistle. "I never thought that Cooper would be involved with something like this."

"It seems that Parsons is blackmailing him. Cooper didn't know who to trust either. That's why he's talking to Harback."

"Boat!" Dean's yell stopped them all. They turned to the direction he pointed to. Two speedboats were racing toward them.

"Hostiles!" Jack yelled. "Get armed."

Jay opened the bottom of his seat, took out several guns and handed them out.

"Holey shit, you guys have an arsenal out here," Mason said as he handed a gun to Eddie.

"Take cover!" Jack ducked down behind a stack of boxes filled with food and bedding. The rest all ducked down around him. "They have to shoot first, remember."

The speedboats circled the pontoon, guns blasting as they did. They yelled threats back and forth. It lasted a half-an-hour when suddenly the speedboats took off. Mason stood up after they were out of gun range and watched as the boats headed out further out.

"Boat!" Frank called. Mason turned, ready for another battle. It was the Ontario Provincial Police instead. Harback stepped onto the pontoon boat; the cruiser took off after the speedboats.

"That was a close call," Harback said as he landed on the deck. "Anybody hurt?"

"I am."

Mason's heart stopped. He ran over to Dean who sat against a crate.

Eddie pushed Mason to the side and knelt in front of his son. "How bad, son?"

"My arm," Dean clung to his elbow; a trickle of blood ran down from his shoulder.

"He needs help. We have to get him to the hospital." Eddie was near panic.

"Easy there, guys." Jack squatted down beside Dean and inspected the wound. "He's just been nicked. I'm sure he'll live." He winked at Dean. Mason handed Jack the first aid kit.

Eddie walked to the other end of the boat with tears in his eyes. His fists opening and closing at his sides.

Mason went up to him and put a hand on Eddies shoulder. "He's going to be okay, Ed."

Eddie turned to face him, his face red with rage. "I didn't sign up for this. Not to get my son killed."

****

Gunshots came from the southwest. Mason watched the battle that took place out in the lake. "Look," he called and pointed westward. Bessie was racing toward them, sending high waves in both directions. "She's going to attack the police."

"She's going after the wrong guys." Eddie tried to wave her away.

A high pierced whistle sounded from behind the men who stood along the rail of the pontoon boat. Mason turned and gave the young man a dirty look. Dean took his two index fingers out of his mouth and grinned at the men he nearly deafened. His arm was wrapped in a white bandage, blood seeping through it. "She stopped," he announced as he staggered up to the rail between Eddie and Mason. All the men pointed toward the speedboats.

"Go there!" Mason shouted. Bessie looked from one boat to the other and then swam up to the pontoon. She sniffed at each man and lingered on her keepers as if confused. Both Mason and Dean kept pointing toward the speedboats that now raced toward the police. "Get them," he yelled and pointed again. "Attack!"

Bessie shot out of there so fast that her wake bounced the pontoon boat. High waves sent cargo and people across the deck. Luckily, none of the men went overboard. Jack scrambled to his feet. "She's got it! She's going after the bad guys."

"The police are shooting at her," cried Frank. "Why would they do that?"

"Radio them," Jack told Jay. "Tell them not to harm her, she's helping them."

Jay scrambled over to the radio and called. He came back among the men and said, "They should stop now."

Bessie upset one speedboat; the four men flew into the water. The police boat went after the second one. Later, they rescued the drowning men and drove toward shore.

Mason showed everyone his ring. The blood stone had turned a dull pink that was turning slowly back to its original color. Dean looked down at his aquamarine; it was a pale green and was turning back to its true color

"That's how Bessie knew," Mason told the men. "See? These rings called her."

"I've never seen them work before," Eddie said.

"Well, I think all the excitement is done for today," Frank announced. "We should all be able to go home now."

"Yeah," Jack said. "They know our hiding place. And I think Jay's fit enough to go back to work now, anyway."

"There is one more thing we need to do," Mason said to Jack.

Jack looked from one man to the other, "Oh, yeah. I almost forgot." He faced Frank. "I got a call last night. Sherry is missing."

"Missing?" What do you mean missing?" Frank gave Jack his full attention.

"We found her, Frank. Just remember that she did go willingly." Jack looked at Mason for help. Mason backed up. Jack, Eddie and Harback all took a step back.

"What's going on? Why are you all afraid of me?" Frank stepped forward.

"We found her with another man, Frank," Mason said.

Frank looked at Jack. "Not you?"

Jack shook his head, "Someone else."

"Who?"

"Remember, she went on her own free will." Jack took another step back. "She's with Black Tom."

"Bla…" was all that came out of Frank's mouth before he sank to his knees. His whole body shook while he placed his hands over his face and began to sob.

"Sorry, Frank." Mason walked up to him and put a hand on his friend's shoulder. "Jack and I found them in the old Miller place."

Jack walked up beside Mason. "We tried to get her to leave. She wouldn't." He put a hand on Frank's other shoulder. "Sorry, man."

Suddenly Frank exploded. He pushed Jack back and sent him flying into the steering wheel. Mason stumbled backward into Eddie. The two of them ended up sprawled on the deck. Jay and Harback went after Frank at once. They held Frank's arms while Dean wrapped a rope around him to hold his arms in.

Frank still kicked at his friends and swore at them. He swung his whole body this way and that to get loose. It did him no good. Finally, he ran out of steam and plunked down on a bench. Tears rushed down his face.

Mason and Eddie stood up. Eddie wiped the blood from his lip where Mason had hit him in his fall.

Jack walked up to Mason and said, "I think he took that rather well, don't you?"

Eddie sat next to Frank. "Sorry, man."

Frank looked up and sniffled. "Does Jason know?"

"No, not yet. We didn't tell anyone," Jack told him.

Frank nodded. "Anyone but him." He screwed up his face. "What in hell does she see in him?"

Mason braved a step forward. "I don't know, Frank. It seems to me that those two are into each other hot and heavy."

Bessie — The Monster in Lake Erie by Deborah Tadema

"You mean she's in love with him?"

"Appears so," Jack said.

Frank glared at the constable. "You threw her away. You sent her to that bastard."

Frank jumped to his feet and rushed at Jack. "It's your fault she's with him."

Eddie grabbed the back of Frank's shirt and pulled. Frank landed on the bench with a loud grunt.

"Go to hell," he yelled at all of them.

CHAPTER 23

The men were silent as Mason steered the pontoon boat back to shore. Eddie sat on a crate beside his son then drove him to the hospital. They checked Dean's arm, gave him a tetanus shot before they sent him home. "Like Jack said," Dean grinned at his father. "It's just a scratch. I'm fine, Dad."

Eddie shook his head as they walked up to Dean's door. "You could have been killed."

Dean opened his door and led the way into his kitchen. He turned and wrapped his arm around his father. "I love you too, Dad."

Tears threatened as Eddie held his son.

****

Bessie thought she did something bad. She wanted to kill the men in the wrong boat. By the time she felt the pulse of the rings hit her like a hammer, it was nearly too late. She didn't know who threatened her keepers.

It was a good thing Dean could whistle like that. She never heard such a loud one before. Her men on the flat boat were glad to see her. She checked them all out to make sure they were okay. And she was so glad that she didn't want to leave them.

Bessie felt happy that she knew hand signals. They made it perfectly clear who she should chase. So that's when she raced over to the little boats and flipped one of them into the air. Her friends cheered her on.

She didn't know what to do when the men on the other boat shot at her, the one with the flashing suns on it. After they caught the men in the other little boat, Bessie decided to follow them toward shore. When she got back beside the flat boat her friends all petted her. She thought she did well.

One of her keepers was injured. The pulse of the sky ring was erratic for a while. It was better now. The injury must not be too bad. Besides, Dean walked around, brave even though there was blood on his front leg, ah arm.

Bessie became a little scared when one of the men went a little crazy.

****

As soon as Mason was ashore, he went over to Valerie's. "That sure was some day you had," she said after he told her what had happened earlier. He sat in a plush chair in her living room; she was behind him giving him a shoulder rub. "You still didn't catch Parsons?"

He closed his eyes. "No. At least I didn't see him in either of the speedboats."

"Well, I'm glad all of you guys are all right."

"I just hope that Frank doesn't go off the deep end."

"What do you mean?"

"Sherry's living with Black Tom."

Val's hands stopped. "No."

"Yes. And it looks like they're in love with each other." He reached up and pulled Valerie around to the front. She sat down on his lap. "She made it very clear she wasn't going to leave without him."

"My God."

"No, he's Jason's devil, remember?" he attempted light humor. Mason looked deep into her eyes and kissed her. "I love you," he told her afterward.

"I love you too, Mason."

"You know, Dean and I have gotten a lot closer since I've been back. Sometimes I wish he was my son instead of my nephew."

"And you asked me just the other day if I would have your kids."

"I still do, aw, want kids with you, Val."

She squinted up her face. "Don't you know what menopause is?"

"Sure, I do. It's what old women go through." He was more confused by the minute. "Are you saying that you are going through that now?"

"I'm too old to start having kids, Mason. You should have asked me fifteen or twenty years ago."

"Oh." He sat back in the chair.

"So, if you want kids, I guess you need to look for a twenty-year-old." She stood as if to leave.

Mason jumped up and pulled her into him. "That's not what I want, Val. It's you that I'm in love with. Kids or no kids."

"Menopause can start at thirty-five, Mason."

"I didn't know. I thought it started at say, around sixty or something." He kissed her lips. She didn't respond so he did it again and held it longer. Soon she responded and kissed him back. When the last kiss ended he watched her eyes soften as she looked at him. "Marry me, Val. Please say you'll marry me."

****

Eddie finally got the deed to the store he bought. He showed it to Mason, Dean and Troy. "And this wall is coming down, so I can open it up even more," he told them excitedly. "My office will be in here." He opened the door to a smaller room with a window that overlooked the back alley. "I think I'll carpet this floor."

"This is ideal," Mason told him. "It sure is nice and bright in here, and lots of room for all your equipment."

Eddie watched Dean walk around as he inspected it. "What do you think, son?" he asked.

Dean turned to look at his dad. "It's nice."

     Bessie — The Monster in Lake Erie by Deborah Tadema

Troy had stopped by the front door, in an alcove. He was smiling at his dad. "This is neat."

Eddie walked up and put an arm around his youngest boy. "I'm hoping…" he saw someone walk by the window and motioned to Mason. "Look, it's Sherry."

Eddie ran out the front door and called her back. Sherry turned around and followed him inside his new store. "This is where my sporting goods store is going to be," he informed her.

Sherry gave a quick look around. "This is nice, Ed. I hope you and Mason can make a go of this in here."

"So, what brings you into town?" Mason asked her.

"Just picking up a few things," she looked from Eddie to Mason. "Go ahead, ask me."

Mason shrugged. "Ask you what?"

"What I'm doing with your brother." She gave them a sly smile. "He isn't the monster everyone thinks he is, you know. Tom is a very, very, loving man." The meaning of this hung in the air. "He's just lost, that's all."

"We're all lost, Sherry," Eddie said. "I don't see how he can provide for you. He can hardly look after himself."

"We do all right."

"You seem like you're, ah…" Mason couldn't finish.

"In love? I am in love with Tom Brennan. Is that what you want to hear?"

Eddie and Mason looked at one another as if unconvinced. "I thought you were in love with Jack," Troy said.

"Jack? What can I say about Jack?" She pretended to give this some thought. "Oh ya, he treated me like garbage, just like Frank did." Sherry gave them a stern look. "And they both can go to hell." With that said, Sherry walked out the door.

"Wow, she really is in love with Tom," Mason found a wall to lean on. "I never thought I'd see the day when a woman would admit to that."

"She looks rough," Eddie said in a sad tone. "I wonder how long it will take her to wake up and realize she's living below the poverty line."

****

"Should I tell Dad?" Jason asked his best friend then shook his head. "She said that, in front of you and your dad?"

"Yes, and Dean and Mason. She was proud of it." Troy looked down at the ground.

"Tell me what?" Frank walked up behind the teens who stood around in his backyard. "I take it has to do with your mother," he said with a slight clip to his voice.

Jason hesitated before he said, "Mom told Eddie and Mason that she's head over heals in love with Black Tom."

Frank looked at him as if he could rip his head off. Troy stepped between them. Frank blinked and smiled at the young man. "So, you want to take me on, there, fella?"

"No," Troy's bravado sank, "you better not hit him."

"Is that so?" Frank crossed his arms and huffed. "You think you are man enough?"

"Dad." Jason stepped up beside his friend. "You looked like you were going to hit me, that's all. We know you won't, right?"

Frank took a boxing stance. "Come on, I'll take both of you on." He circled around, bent at the waist with his fists up. "Come on," he coaxed and jabbed at Jason. Jason jumped back unharmed.

"And you." Frank faced Troy. "Let's see what you got." He took a step forward. Frank circled around Troy, jabbed his back.

Troy stumbled a few steps before he turned around and faced him. He saw the light glint in Frank's eyes.

"C'mon, Dad," Jason said. "I bet you wouldn't take Dean on like this."

Frank let out a big belly laugh. Both boys stood there and didn't know if they should move or not. When he stopped laughing, Frank grabbed Jason around his legs and flipped him to the ground. He went after Troy with a growl in his throat and a smile on his lips.

This time, Troy challenged him. Jason jumped on his father's back. The three of them wrestled in the backyard, all in fun.

****

"Who is she?" Shannon asked as she pushed Dean's arm away and reached for the handle on his car door.

"Okay, I'll show you." He turned the ignition on and hit the gas. Grass and dirt sprayed up behind them as they bumped their way across the field at Lover's Leap.

She looked at him wide-eyed. "You're going to let me meet this other woman you've been seeing?"

"Yes." He grinned at her. "And I wouldn't let that temper of yours loose on her if I were you."

"So, you just want me to hand you over to her without a fight?" She glared at him. "If that's what you want, I have three words for you."

The car hit the pavement and shot forward. Dean turned the wheel and they skidded onto the road. He had to slow down as they drove through town. He told her little, grinning all the way. The car stopped at the bottom of Picnic Hill and he took her by the hand and led her up the path.

"She's a lot bigger than you are, so I'd be careful." Dean felt her heated gaze on his back as he led her down the other side, toward the creek bed. "This here is Muddy Creek. This is where she lives."

Shannon crossed her arms in front of her and huffed. "Yea, right, I know…Holy cow! What's that?" She took a few steps back and hid behind Dean.

"That is Bessie," Dean said with an amused smile. "See? I told you she was bigger than you are."

"That's the other woman?"

"Yep and she likes me." Dean walked up closer to Bessie and reached up to her. Bessie lowered his head and sniffed at him. "She won't hurt you, Shannon. If you don't threaten her, or me."

He petted Bessie's nose. "That's a good girl," he crooned to her." "That's my big old pet." He waved Shannon over. She backed up further.

"Not on your life," she said, her eyes wide in fear.

"She won't hurt you, Shannon. I need for her to get to know you." He waved her over again. "If she knows you as a friend, she'll protect you."

"Protect me from what?"

"Me," a gruff answered from behind her. Someone grabbed Shannon by the hair on the back of her head and pulled her into the trees. Bessie raised her head and growled. Shannon screamed. Dean ran toward his girlfriend. A shot rang out. He skidded to a stop.

"Stay back," the man yelled.

Dean couldn't tell who he was. "Let her go," he called. "She's done nothing to you, let her go."

"Don't move, or she'll get the next bullet." A man all dressed in black dragged Shannon into the bushes. Bessie swam back and forth in distress. Dean's ring began to pulsate.

"I'm here, Bessie. Don't knock my finger off," he snapped at her.

Dean turned back around. Shannon was gone. He stood where he was for a few seconds and wondered if he dared to move yet. Finally, he let out in his breath and ran toward the path.

****

Bessie didn't know what he would do. She didn't know how far he would go. He was a bad man and she should have killed him a long time ago. Who made up the rule that said she couldn't kill a keeper?

****

Mason took Valerie over to his sister's.

Eddie looked over at Valerie who stood quietly in Mason's arms. "And what are you beaming about?"

Valerie pulled out her hand that she had hidden behind Mason and showed them her diamond ring. "We're getting married."

 Bessie — The Monster in Lake Erie by Deborah Tadema

"Congratulations." Rachel hugged and kissed the two of them.

Eddie shook Mason's hand and gave Valerie a big hug and kiss. He held her at arm's-length, "You aren't pregnant, are you?"

Valerie slapped at his arm. "No. I don't think I can handle diapers now." She looked over at Mason.

"So, when is the wedding?" Rachel asked.

Mason held up his hands, "I'm leaving all that up to her." He gave Valerie a loving look. "I'm just around for the ride."

"When we got married," Eddie teased, "Rachel wanted me to wear a pink tux."

Mason looked at him in mock horror, "I hope Val has better taste than..." He looked down at his own ring. It was vibrating, and his finger was starting to swell. "Oh shit. It's Bessie."

****

"I didn't mean to give your dad a bloody nose," Troy said as he Jason ran down the street. "We were only playing."

"I know," Jason gasped, "you whacked him a good one with your elbow." They stopped at the corner and looked back. "He's not coming."

"I saw him go into the house. Maybe he won't come after us." Troy bent at the waist, hands on his knees to catch his breath. "He started it."

"I know. I think we should stay away from there for a while."

"What do you want to do?" Troy straightened up.

"Let's check out the Miller place," Jason said as if daring his friend. "I want to see where my mother is."

"I don't think we should go up on the hill." Troy looked down the street toward Picnic Hill. "We could get into worse trouble with your dad."

"Well, I'm not going back there until he has time to cool off." Jason started toward the hill. "I'll go by myself if you don't want to come."

Troy caught up to him. "All right, I'll go with you. He's the devil, remember?"

"I figure if my mom sees some good in him, maybe he isn't that bad."

At the bottom of the hill, the boys looked up at the path that led to the old shack. Jason glanced at Sherry's old car beside him and scowled.

"You sure you want to face Black Tom?" Troy asked. "What if he's there?"

"I only want to see my mother. I'm sure he'll let me." Jason put on a brave front even though he was shaking. Jason started up the hill. Troy followed.

"He needs to clear this path better," Troy said as he held back a branch. "It would..."

"Shh," Jason pulled on his friend's sleeve. "I heard someone scream."

"Don't scare me, Jason. It woe..."

"Listen, I heard it again." The nervousness of Jason's voice made Troy turn around and look at his friend. He remained quiet until they heard a scream come from the top of the hill. Jason looked toward his left; the shack was down that way. "What should we do?"

"We better see who that is." Troy went off the path and headed upward. "Someone could be in trouble." He was about to step into a clearing when Jason pulled him back and hid in the bushes.

"Look, over there," he whispered. "That's Shannon."

"Why is she tied up like that?" Troy ducked down.

Jason watched as the man shoved a cloth into Shannon's mouth. She strained against the rope that held her to a tree. Tears streaked down her face. The man clenched his fist and hit her on the side of the head. Her body slumped against her restraints her head flopped forward. Jason and Troy looked at each. It took a few seconds for them to digest what had just happened.

Jason whispered, "Where's Dean? Surely she wouldn't come up here by herself?"

Troy pointed to their right. His brother lay the ground, looking like he was out cold. "He's tied up now."

The man had his back to them all this time. Troy held his breath as the man ran his fingers through Shannon's hair. He went over to Dean and gave him a kick in his side. Dean didn't even grunt. Troy's stomach lurched.

        Bessie — The Monster in Lake Erie by Deborah Tadema

Shock and horror held him rooted to the ground where he hid. The man turned around and looked right in his direction. Troy's heart pounded loudly in his ears. All he could do was hold on to Jason as Black Tom came toward them.

CHAPTER 24

"Come on out boys," Tom said angrily. Troy wanted to run. He couldn't, his legs became spongy and wouldn't move. Tom stormed up to them and pushed the bushes aside. "I said get out of there."

Troy stood up and led Jason into the clearing. Tom glared at them and told them to stop halfway between Shannon and Dean. Troy looked around for a weapon, saw nothing within easy reach. He wished now that he had thought about that earlier. He could have snuck up on Tom and hit him over the head with a log.

Tom glanced into the woods then back at the boys. "What are you doing up here? You're going to ruin everything."

"We, ah," Jason looked over at Shannon. "We heard her scream."

Tom turned and glared at the girl tied to the tree. "Should have knocked her out sooner, I see." He faced the boys again. "I'm going to tell you to do something and you're going to follow it to a tee."

Both boys nodded their heads.

"Good, because if you don't," Tom gave Jason a wicked smile, "your mother will die."

Jason's Adam's apple bobbed several times before he gave a slight nod of his head.

"You're going to run all the way to the shack, where your mother is and stay there." Tom stepped closer. Troy could smell his rank breath. Tom stared at Jason. "You'll stay there and protect her. Don't let anyone in unless it's me." He faced Troy. "And you won't say one word about what you saw up here today, got it?"

Tom waited a half a second. "Say you'll do what I told you."

"I will," Troy said in a girly voice. Jason said the same. Tom gave them a satisfied smile and told them to go.

The boys ran as if their lives depended on it.

****

Dean lay on the ground motionless and pretended he was dead. He kept his breath shallow and fought hard not to scratch the itchy spot on his leg. His arm where the bullet had grazed him throbbed. He realized that his wrists and ankles were bound. When Tom kicked him, he bit down on his tongue, so he wouldn't make a sound. Already his body was sore, and his head hurt where Tom beat him. Dean was too weak to move. And there was the matter of the gun that Tom hid under his shirt. He watched with his one eye through the hair that covered his face, and he listened. He almost groaned when he saw Troy and Jason. It was just like Tom to scare them out of their wits.

Behind them, he could see Shannon. His tearful eyes watching Tom's every move. Dean swore he would kill Tom, especially after he touched her like he did. It surprised him when Tom let the boys go. It was only a few minutes later that Dean found out why and fought hard to stay conscious.

Parsons walked into the clearing with a cloth bag in one hand. He looked from Shannon to Dean. "Well, well. I see you've found them." He gave Tom a satisfied grin and walked up to Shannon and lifted her head. "She's a beauty, isn't she?"

Tom stood where he was and watched Parsons with a scowl on his face. "You bring the drugs?"

"Right here," Parsons walked over to Tom and gave him the sack.

Tom opened it and smiled. "Your money is over there." He nodded at a green sack on the ground by Shannon. "Now, this deal is done, right?"

"Sure, Tom. First, you have to do one more thing for me." Parsons narrowed his eyes. "If not, your woman will find someone else in her bed tonight."

"You wouldn't dare." Tom looked deadly. "You keep your filthy hands off her."

"I won't if you do one more thing." Parsons walked up to Dean and stared down at him. "You will wake this guy up and hold him." He faced Tom. "While I have a little fun with his girl over there."

****

Mason stood with Eddie, Frank and Jack beside the cave and watched Bessie swim back and forth in the creek. "She is upset about something," he said as if to justify her actions.

Jack searched the area. Mason walked up to the edge of the creek and held up his hand. Bessie stopped and sniffed at him. "Whatever it is, girl, we'll make it right."

"Over here," Jack called. Mason and Eddie looked down at the drag marks in the gravel. "Something sure happened here."

"Shit," Frank said as he ran a hand through his hair. "I hope the boys didn't come down here."

"Well, I'd be hiding if I was the one who gave you a bloody nose," Jack laughed and pointed toward the trees, "looks like someone was dragged into there."

Frank touched his nose. "It wasn't all that bad. Probably looked worse than it was. It sure scared them."

The men started to follow Jack's lead when they heard a gunshot. They froze and looked at one another. "That didn't sound good," Eddie said. Jack pulled out his police revolver and ducked into the trees, the rest of them following close at his heels.

"I don't know where that came from," Frank said when they stopped at the top of a hill. He looked up at the next one as if he dreaded to climb up there too.

"Here," Eddie pointed to footprints in the dirt. "They went up there," he looked up at the very top of the hill. "Maybe we should spread out."

Mason and Eddie went straight up while Jack and Frank went around along a ridge that would eventually end up at the top of the hill. "Did you tell Jack about you and Val?" Eddie asked as he pulled on a branch and hefted himself up.

"Not yet," Mason grabbed the same branch.

"You better tell him soon. Don't let him find out from someone else." Eddie waited for Mason at the top of a knoll.

"I know." Mason caught up with his friend. "I'll tell him to..." A gunshot came from the direction the other two men had gone. "I hope Jack didn't shoot Frank."

Eddie gave Mason a worried look. "That first shot came from up that way," he pointed over his shoulder. "That was a different gun."

****

Jason and Troy didn't stop until they burst through the door of the little shack. Troy slammed it shut and slid the deadbolt into place. Jason looked around and cried, "She's not here."

"Now what do we do? Tom is going to kill us for letting her get away." Troy backed up from the door. "We're supposed to keep her here and protect her."

"You think I don't know that?" Jason snapped. "He could be killing Shannon and Dean. Didn't you hear the gunshots?"

"I heard." Troy walked toward the bed then turned around. "Listen."

Jason got down on his knees, lifted the blanket and peered under the bed. "Mom? What are you doing under there?"

"Gunshots," she said. "Frank's after me."

"Dad isn't even here," Jason helped his mother climb out. "Are you all right, Mom?" He studied her face as she stood up and adjusted her clothes. "Have you been taking drugs?"

"I wouldn't be surprised if Tom got her to take some," Troy said as he looked around the room. "See, there's some over here."

Jason led Sherry to a chair. She looked up at him and smiled. "You're a good son, you know? You've always been a good boy." She reached up and smoothed his hair.

"How can you live in a place like this, Mom?" Jason gave her a disgusted expression. "You don't even have running water." She was dirty and thin but didn't seem to notice. Troy knew he longed for the mother she once was, one that took pride in her appearance, had her hair done at the salon once a month. Sherry always dressed nice and kept her nails painted. Now they were cracked and jagged with dirt embedded in them.

"I'm happy here, son. My Tom knows how to make me happy." She grinned at Troy, "Frank isn't as good a lover as Tom is." She shook her head. "Not even close."

"Mom. Troy doesn't need to know that, and neither do I." Jason gave his friend a look of desperation. "She must be high on something."

"Try one of those," Sherry pointed by Troy's elbow to a small pile of hand-rolled cigarettes on the shelf. "It's only Marijuana. That will make you feel better."

"No, Mom. Troy doesn't want one of those." Jason held his mother back as she reached for one.

"I think I should hide these," Troy picked up the cigarettes and looked around. "I guess there isn't any place to hide them in here." He set them back down. "She'll only find them anyway."

Jason startled when someone pounded on the door. Troy jumped back against the shelves, feeling his heart hit the floor.

The pounding on the door persisted. "Let me in. It's Tom."

****

Mason ran into the clearing and knelt beside Dean. "Dean. Dean, can you hear me?" He reached down, rolled the young man over and untied him. Dean's eyes blinked. "Dean, it's your uncle. Tell me you're all right."

"Mason?" Dean looked around as if he didn't know where he was. "Where's Shannon?" He tried to sit up, fell back down.

"Take it easy, son." Mason helped him sit up against a tree.

"She's over here," Eddie said. Mason looked behind him for the first time. Eddie had untied Shannon and caught her as she fell to the ground. He eased her down and tried to pull her top closed where someone had ripped it open. "She's out cold." Finally, he took off his own shirt, wrapped it around her then sat on the ground. With her head on his lap, he lightly tapped her cheeks.

Mason heard Dean groan and turned back to him. "What happened here?"

"Black Tom snatched her. I chased him, but he ambushed me."

"Tom did this?" Mason had never felt more betrayed as he did at that moment. It was several heartbeats before he could focus again. "Did he shoot at you?"

"No. He killed Parsons." Dean lifted his arm slowly and pointed. "He is in those bushes over there."

Mason stood, walked over and parted the bushes. Parsons lay sprawled out in the mud with a single hole in his chest. He felt for a pulse that he knew wasn't there. "He's dead," he told Eddie who now stood beside him. "One shot, through the heart."

Jack and Frank walked up to them. "Well, whoever killed that bastard is a hero in my books," Frank said.

Eddie and Mason both gave him a dirty look. "You going to kiss Black Tom's feet?" Eddie said with disdain. "He beat the shit out of Dean and tied Shannon to a tree. Is he still your hero?"

Frank and Jack looked behind them. "Sorry," Frank said. "I didn't know."

Jack went over and checked Shannon. "She's out cold," he said as if he couldn't believe it. He glanced at Eddie's shirt on the girl and then sad eyes looked over at Dean.

"Tom shot Parsons when he tried to ah; he was going to rape her." A tear slipped down Dean's cheek. "And I couldn't even move."

"What all did he do to you?" Jack faced Dean. Mason wanted to hear this, so he stood beside Dean.

"He came at me from behind and just kept hitting and hitting. When the stick broke, he used his fists. I think I blacked out for a while."

"We'll get you some help Dean, both of you." Jack stood up, looked over by the bushes and shook his head.

Mason glanced over to where Jack was watching. Frank had just pissed on Parsons's body.

****

Jason slid the bolt sideways and sprinted to the back of the room beside Troy. Black Tom stepped in and shut the door with a bang. He barely got it locked when Sherry ran up to him and jumped into his arms.

"Tom, Tom I missed you." She plastered kisses all over his face.

He chuckled before kissing her hard on the mouth. His arms embraced her, and she leaned into him. When the kiss broke he looked at her with a shine in his eyes. "I missed you too, babe." He gently led her to the chair she had just sprung from. He turned his attention to the boys.

Troy thought he was about to get sick. Never had he seen Sherry throw herself at a man like that before. What did Tom have that Frank didn't? Even Jack was a better man than this.

"Thank you, boys," Tom said as he held out his hand.

It took all of Troy's being to take that hand. Somehow, he managed to touch it, snapped it back. Jason shook the hand just as quickly. Tom didn't seem to notice because he went back over to Sherry and went down on one knee.

She leaned over and kissed him. Then she looked up at the boys. "This is my man now and I love him with all my heart." Sherry gave Jason a strange look that made Troy tremble. "If anything happens to him, you might as well kill me too."

****

Troy didn't know that his uncle had a soft side to him. Tom always seemed harsh and came across like a man with no soul. As he watched him with Jason's mom he saw that Tom could be vulnerable too. This was Black Tom in love. Who would have thought?

Tom got Sherry a glass of water from a picture in the tiny fridge powered by a generator outside. Troy had seen it as they ran into this dump.

  Bessie — The Monster in Lake Erie by Deborah Tadema

The water came from a well out back. He compared this shack to the bomb shelter that Tom used to live in. Although the bomb shelter would make a neat fort, he preferred it here. At least this place had windows.

His ears picked up when he heard someone at the door. It sounded like Jack who called out to Tom. Tom stayed where he was and stroked Sherry's hair as if no one else existed. Someone tried the door handle then knocked. At the same time, Troy and Jason ran to it and slid the bolt back. Mason hugged both boys while Jack pushed past them.

"Where is he?" Jack held out his gun.

"Right..." Jason turned around. "He was just right there." He pointed to the empty space by his mother.

"How long ago was that?" Mason asked as he stepped into the room.

"About two seconds ago," Troy said. "He was right here when we opened the door."

Jack stopped in front of Sherry. She cowered from him, so he kept his distance. "Sherry, it's just me, Jack. Where did he go? Where's Tom?"

Sherry looked past Jack to her son. "Jason, tell your father that I despise him."

Jack shook his head and stood up. "She's high. I won't get anything from her now."

"Well, he must have some way of getting in and out of here without using the door." Mason opened a cabinet. He shut it before he turned to the boys. "Your fathers are taking Shannon and Dean back to town. Tom roughed them up pretty good."

"How did you two end up in here?" Jack checked under the bed.

"We heard Shannon screaming," Troy said. "Then Tom found us and told us to come here."

"He said that my mom was in danger and we were to keep an eye on her until he came home." Jason screwed up his face as he watched his mother pull strands of her hair out of her head.

Mason and Jack exchanged looks. "Doesn't sound like a guy who just beat and tried to rape someone, does it?" Jack gave Sherry a sorrowful look. "Something sure doesn't add up."

"He did kill Parsons," Mason reminded him. He walked over to Sherry and squatted beside her. "Sherry, it's Mason. How are you doing?"

"Mason, you're back are you?" She patted his arm. "Did you know," she whispered, "that Jack stole your girl? He ..."

"Sherry, do you know where Tom is, I need to talk to him?"

Sherry looked under the table where she sat. "He's in the basement."

Mason crawled under the table, lifted a hatch and jumped down under the shack. Moments later he stuck his head up through the opening. "He just crawled under here and went through a hole at the back," he informed them.

****

Jack went out and checked around the back of the shack then came back in. "He left a trail easy enough a toddler could follow," he told Mason. "I have a feeling he wants us to go after him."

"What do we do with these guys?" Mason nodded toward the boys. "Think we should have them take Sherry back to town?"

"I'm not going anywhere," Sherry piped up. "And you can't make me."

Jack let out an exasperated sigh. "No, we can't. Not as long as she isn't in any danger and can provide for herself."

"Is she in any danger, do you think?" Mason asked.

"No," Jason said, "not from Tom, anyway." He gave his mother a disgusted look. "They're in love," he said with disdain.

Jack gave Sherry a look of regret before he cleared his throat. "I think you boys should go home. Mason and I are going to see if we can catch up with Tom." He looked at Jason. "Your mother will be fine up here."

"Are you going to shoot him?" Troy asked Jack.

"Not if I can help it," Jack said. "You boys better get going."

Mason thought about the time Tom stabbed Jack. How easy would it be for him to pull the trigger?

Jason walked past Sherry and didn't even tell her goodbye. She looked up and watched him walk out the door. Troy gave his uncle Mason a quick hug before he followed his buddy. Jack checked his pistol, then he and Mason went out behind the shack.

"I hope he doesn't double back and go after them," Mason said as the two men watch the boys go down the path.

"I don't think so. Looks like he's heading toward the lake." Jack followed Tom's trail. Tom had kicked up pine needles as he went or left deep shoe impressions in the mud. They followed this trail up along a ridge and down the south side of the hill. Jack and Mason walked out onto the beach about two miles from town, the mouth of Muddy Creek not too far away.

"Think he met a ship?" Mason asked as he looked out over the lake. Tom's footprints had him walk right into the water. "Damn it, he disappeared again."

Jack walked along the shore and pointed in front of him. "No, he didn't. He came back out here."

CHAPTER 25

"And they say that my dad is nuts." Jason walked beside Troy on the sidewalk. "My mom sure has gone loco."

Troy didn't answer that. Instead, he said, "I'm supposed to tell Valerie where Mason is."

They turned the corner toward Jason's house. "I'm starved. You want a grilled cheese sandwich?"

"Sure," Troy walked up the back steps and opened the door for Jason. "How about five?"

"You should call your mom, too." Jason headed toward the stairs.

Troy called Valerie and his mom at work. He told her that Dean and Shannon were in the hospital that Frank and his dad were with them. He didn't tell her any more than he had to over the phone. She'd find out later what happened today.

Jason came back down and opened the fridge, reached in and took out the sliced cheese and the margarine. Troy took the bread out of the breadbox and set it on the counter by the stove. He lifted out a frying pan while Jason buttered the bread. Troy got the flipper out of the drawer.

Frank walked in while the boys were eating their lunch. Troy was glad he sat on the far side of the table. Frank, however, didn't mention how Troy had given him a bloody nose. He eyed them and sipped at a beer.

"Dean has a concussion," Frank set his bottle down. "Shannon's scared out of her wits. They'll both be out of the hospital in a day or two."

"That's good to hear," Troy said and pushed his empty plate away. "Jack and Mason are still chasing after Tom."

Frank was quiet for a bit before he looked over at Jason. "Dean said you went to the shack. You see your mother?"

"Yes, she was there." Jason fidgeted in his seat. "She smokes Marijuana. I saw her."

Frank's face twisted in pain. "Maybe we should get her out of there."

"We tried that," Troy said. "She won't go anywhere without Tom."

"How could she live in a place like that?"

"I don't know," Jason said. "She's very dependent on him."

****

Mason and Jack followed Tom's footprints in the sand to a set of wooden stairs that took them up the side of the cliff. When they reached the top, Mason looked back at the lake and thought that this would be a good place for pirates to stash their loot. He had heard of places like this along the shores of Lake Erie, secluded with an inlet where small boats could come close to shore. Rum and whiskey had been smuggled into Canada during the prohibition. He didn't think any of these places existed anymore.

An old cottage stood in an open area surrounded by trees and hills. "This is the perfect hideout," Jack said as they headed toward the cottage. Before they entered it, Jay walked out into the sun and squinted at them. "Jay?" Jack asked. "What are you doing here?"

"Come inside," Jay led them into the kitchen where Tom sat at a crude table, his back to the far wall. Mason gave him a dirty look before he sat down beside his brother. It took all his might not to rip into the guy.

Jack fingered his gun. Jay asked him not to. "We'll tell you what's been going on before you decide to take Tom in." Jay sat down between Tom and Jack on one of the mismatched wooden chairs. "I've been getting all my drugs from Tom, here. Tom is or was my middle man. He was getting them from Parsons. It was Tom who found out how Parsons was smuggling them into this town." Jay pointed out toward the lake. "Right out there, and then he'd hide them in here."

Mason looked over at Tom, "Why did you attack those kids?"

"Let me tell you," Tom inched away from his brother. "I didn't kidnap them. That was Parsons. By the time I found them, he had both kids tied up."

"Dean only saw you there." Mason fought to keep his temper in check. "You tried to rape Shannon."

"No, no. That was Parsons. I kicked Dean to save his life. Parsons wanted to kill him. He was the one who tried to rape Shannon. That's why he's dead."

Jack held out his hand. "Give it to me."

Tom looked perplexed. "The gun? I don't have it."

"What did you do with it?" Jack's face turned red with rage. "You shot Parsons. Where's the gun?" He stood up and reached over the table.

"I don't have it," Tom cowered in his seat. "It's gone."

Jack looked from him to Jay. Jay shrugged. "He didn't have it when he came in here."

Jack sat back down. "What did you do with it, throw it in the lake?"

Tom shook his head. "I don't remember."

Jack glared at the man and everyone knew he didn't believe Tom. "What were you doing manhandling Shannon?"

"I was trying to undo the rope. I didn't touch her like that." Tom's scared eyes looked from one man to the other. "I stumbled into that scene after Parsons left them there. Except he came back. When I heard him coming I kicked Dean to keep him quiet, he started to make sounds."

Mason tried to sort things out in his head. "One thing I don't understand is why you would hurt your successor as Bessie's keeper, seems to me you'd want to help him."

　　　　Bessie — The Monster in Lake Erie by Deborah Tadema

"I do," Tom said eagerly. "That's why I gave him the ring, so he could take over and I'd have time to, to..." he looked at Jay.

"To help me out," Jay told them.

****

"I still have to arrest you for murder, Tom," Jack said. "Or the very least, drug possession. Plus, your trial is in three days for what you did to me." He fingered his gun again. "And this time, there will be no more delays."

Tom nodded. "I'm sorry about that. It was just instinct."

"You can't keep getting away with this kind of stuff, Tom," Mason said. "You assaulted me too, remember?"

"I know. I'm learning." Tom looked up at the ceiling. "Sherry is helping me with my temper. She's telling me what's right and wrong."

Holy cow, thought Mason. It's like the blind leading the blind. "You really depend on each other, don't you?"

Tom looked back down at his brother. "I've never had a good woman like her before."

Mason didn't know what to say to that, so he let it be. He swore at himself in his mind because he had started to feel something for Tom, other than loathing.

"So, Tom could plead self-defense in shooting Parsons," Jay said. "I'm sure we can convince everyone in town that Parsons went after him. We all wanted Parsons out of our lives anyway."

Jack yelled at Jay, "That man killed in cold blood." He pointed to Tom, jabbing his finger in the air with each word. Tom shrank back a few more inches. Jay didn't even blink. "What's going on Jay? I thought you were my partner."

"I am."

"Why are you going behind my back all the time? How come I don't know what you're up to?"

"Look, Jack." Jay kept his gaze level. "I don't know all the things you do either. Remember, I'm still undercover. Now we must confiscate the boat that smuggles in the drugs. I need Tom's help in this."

Jack gave Tom a look of scorn. "Why?"

"Because Cooper trusts him, and I think that your man Cooper is in this deeper than he wants us to believe."

"I've seen him," Tom piped up. "He helped unload the boat for Parsons. Plus, he's been taking some of those drugs away in a truck."

"To where?" Jack asked.

"I don't know."

****

Dean sat up in his hospital bed and lifted his spoon of Jell-O to his mouth with some effort. His whole body protested at this simple movement and made him jerk in spasms. He captured the spoon between his teeth and then slowly pulled it out. The Jell-O slid down his throat in one big gulp. Harback came into the room as he lowered the spoon into the bowl. "That sure looks painful," he said as he walked up to the bed.

"I don't even want this stuff." Dean dropped the spoon into the bowl. "I just wanted to see if I could feed myself." He lifted the bowl and Harback set it on the table for him. "Have you seen Shannon?"

"Yes, just came from there. She's doing well, physically. Mentally, I don't know yet." Harback pulled up a chair. "I need for you to tell me exactly what happened, Dean. And don't leave a single thing out, okay?"

Dean closed his eyes and brought up the image of him and Shannon on the creek bed with Bessie. "Some guy all dressed in black pulled Shannon backward into the bushes. I couldn't see who it was because he stayed in the shadows, plus he was behind her." He opened his eyes and looked past Harback as he spoke. "As I started to run toward them, there was a gunshot."

"Did that man fire a gun?"

Dean focused on Harback. "I just assumed it was him. He yelled at me to stop so I did."

Harback nodded for him to continue. Dean said, "He dragged her back. I looked up at Bessie for just a second. She was growling and my ring," he rubbed the ring with his fingers. "It started to act up. When I turned back around they were gone. I ran after them. Followed her screams. I heard a scuffle up ahead. I found Shannon on the ground and bent down to see if she was all right. That's when I was hit over the head." He rubbed the bandage around his head. "I hope they didn't cut off all my hair." Dean let his arm fall back down onto his lap. "I remember a cloth over my mouth and nothing for a while."

"That cloth probably had Chloroform in it to make you black out." Harback sat forward in his seat.

"Next thing I remember, I kinda came to and saw Shannon tied to the tree. I tried to get up, but someone had tied me up too. That's when I saw Black Tom. He..."

"You didn't see Parsons there?"

"No. Not until later." Dean paused before he continued. Harback waited patiently. "I kept going in and out of consciousness. I know Black Tom kicked me. He kept saying he was sorry and didn't want to hurt me. He did. At one time I saw him over by Shannon, he was doing something to her. I couldn't see what." Dean started crying.

Harback handed Dean a handful of tissues from the box by his bed. "I'm sorry you had to go through something like that, Dean. He waited until the young man got hold of himself. "Then what happened?"

Dean blew his nose, let his head fall back against his pillow. "Tom saw Troy and Jason in the bushes and called them out. Tom talked to them for a couple of minutes before they ran away. He kept checking the bushes as if he was expecting someone." Dean looked at Harback in confusion. "Parsons showed up a couple of minutes later. He threatened to hurt Tom's new woman. He turned away from Tom and went up to Shannon. She had been unconscious throughout all of this, by the way." He took a few breaths before he could continue. "Next thing I remember was him and Parsons arguing." Tears erupted from his eyes again. "Parsons wanted Tom to wake me up, so I could watch him rape Shannon. That's when Tom shot him, I think."

Dean blinked his eyes several times. "I know I blacked out again. When I came to Dad and Mason were there."

Harback nodded. "Where were the rest of the men who went up there with him?"

"My dad cut Shannon loose and lowered her to the ground. I told Mason where Parsons's body was and those two went over to see. Jack and Frank came up a few minutes later. Jack checked Shannon over and then came over to me. I told him and Mason what had happened. Frank pissed all over Parsons. At least that's what they said. It sure looked like it to me.

"Jack pulled rank and had Eddie and Frank take me and Shannon down the hill. Dad practically carried her all the way; she came to about halfway down. Frank helped me. I think Jack wanted to get rid of Frank."

"Why do you think that?"

"Before they arrived, I heard another gunshot. From the direction they came from."

Harback nodded again. "Where did Mason and Jack go?"

"They were going after Black Tom. They went in the same direction the boys went."

"Thanks, Dean. You were very helpful today." Harback stood up. "Both Tom and Parsons were wearing black, weren't they?"

****

Dean felt someone by his bed before he opened his eyes. His mother bent over and gave him a kiss on the cheek. "Hello, sleepyhead. How are you doing?" Rachel said as she looked down at his bruised arm. He could practically read her mind. *He was lucky that he didn't have any broken bones.* She pushed back a lock of hair from his face, the bandage on his head now gone.

"Hey Mom," Dean pushed the button to raise the bed. "I'm not doing too bad. The doctor says I'll be out of here by Friday."

"You should stay in your old room for a few weeks to recover."

He shook his head. "No, mom. I'll be fine." He saw tears in his mother's eyes as she turned to glance out the window. After a few moments, she pulled a tissue out of her purse and dabbed her eyes. She faced him again.

"Yes. I guess you're right. You are your own man now." She squeezed his arm. "You and Troy are growing up too fast."

"Hi, Dean," a female voice came from his doorway. He sat up further and blushed.

"Rain, what are you doing here?"

Rain walked up, stopped on the other side of the bed and gave Rachel a shy look.

Rachel looked from one to the other before she excused herself. "I have to get going anyway." She gave her son a kiss on the cheek and then left the room.

Rain took hold of Dean's hand and kissed his knuckles. "I heard what happened to you, I'm sorry."

"I thought you left," he considered her sad green eyes. "I missed you."

"I missed you too. That's why I came back."

"For me?" Dean sat up a little straighter. "I thought I'd never see you again."

"Well, I'm back now. I'll be waiting for you," she looked around his room and then back at him. "I need you, Dean."

****

The sky ring was not seeing the sun. It made Bessie feel listless. She was vulnerable because she didn't care what happened to her now. Her keeper was injured. She was not sure if Tom did this or that other man. Dean was the keeper she loved the most, she really missed him.

The blood stone's erratic pulse made Bessie think that her man was upset about something. She didn't blame him, someone tried to kill Dean. Was it wrong for her to have deep feelings for her youngest keeper?

****

Jack was still fuming as he and Mason made their way back over the hill toward town. "That bastard sure took us the long way around, didn't he?"

"Yes, and all we had to do was cross over this hill and end up back to where we began." Mason stopped and waited until Jack looked up at him. "What are you going to do now?"

Jack stopped, studied a tree as if collecting his jumble of thoughts. Mason knew he was trying hard not to take this out on him. "Well," Jack continued, "Jay sure is protecting that brother of yours and I don't know why." He shifted to his other foot. "I don't like this one bit. The first thing I'm going to do is have a talk with Harback."

Mason nodded. "He's still staying at my place." They jumped over a small stream. "We heard another gun shot up there. Do you know what that was?"

Jack gave him a look of surprise. "I didn't hear another gun shot. Are you sure there were two?"

"Yes. Ask Ed. It came from the direction we thought you were in."

"And so, you thought it was me?" Jack shook his head. "This could change things. If there was a second shooter up there, we must find out who it was, and why they were there."

Jack walked on. Mason stop behind him after just a few steps. Jack turned to see his friend's troubled face.

Mason put his hand on his arm. "I need to tell you something, Jack. Val and I are engaged."

Jack's face flushed before he pulled away from Mason. He walked off in another direction and then stood and looked at nothing. That's when all his pent-up emotions spilled over. He cried.

Mason walked up behind him. "I'm sorry, man. I didn't think it would hit you this hard."

Jack leaned against a tree, finally pulled himself together. "It just seems that everything is going wrong right now. I'm beginning to wonder if I did the right thing when I protected Jay. And I don't understand how Black Tom gets away with breaking one law after another with no apparent consequence." He waited until Mason stood in front of him. "He sure has a horseshoe up his ass."

"Jay did promise that he'd be in court on Wednesday."

"And do you think he'll keep that promise? I don't. I have a feeling that Jay's going to smuggle Tom out of the country, so I can't get to him."

"We better find Harback."

The men continued down the hill. They reached the bottom of Picnic Hill and walked up to the police cruiser. Jack clasped his door handle. "You keep her happy, Mason. Or else you'll have me to contend with."

Mason opened the passenger door. "I hear you, buddy."

CHAPTER 26

Troy walked down the hall in the hospital with his best friend and saw a girl come out of his brother's room and turn the other way. "Isn't that Rain?" Troy asked.

"If it is, Dean's in trouble," Jason snickered. "Think he can keep Shannon from finding out?"

"Probably not." Troy watched Rain turn the corner. "I don't know which one to vote for either. I like them both."

They walked into Dean's room and greeted him. "So," Jason gave him a crooked grin, "your other girlfriend is back."

Dean pinched his eyes closed. "What do you want?"

"We came to see how you are and you act like your mad at us," Troy teased as he walked up to the bed. "I think Bessie's lonely, too."

Dean swatted him. "You let me deal with this. Don't say anything to Shannon."

"Sure," Troy saw the wink Jason gave him. "Tell us how you do it, Dean."

"Get out of here," Dean chuckled. "With friends like you, who needs enemies."

"That's what we want to talk to you about," Jason said. "How well do you know Black Tom?"

"He's worried about his mother," Troy explained. "Do you think he'll hurt her?"

Dean looked from on to the other. "I don't really know. He does seem to really care for her. He's done some weird things too."

"She's taking drugs now." Jason's eyes misted over. "After all the lectures she's given me, she goes and smokes up right in front of me and Troy."

"All I can say is that I hope you stay away from drugs. Look at what happened to Tom. Next time he might not be so lucky."

"I wish I knew how to get her down off that hill," Jason told them. "I don't like her being up there. Tom had all kinds of drugs there."

"And Jack didn't arrest him for possession?" Dean asked. "That's odd."

Troy and Jason gave each other guilty glances. Finally, Troy spoke up and told Dean about the sugar cube they found in the bomb shelter.

"And Jay bought it from you?" Dean asked.

"Yeah. He paid forty bucks for it." Jason said. "He didn't even tell us if it was laced or not."

Dean checked the door before he said, "Didn't you guys know that you sold it to a cop?"

****

"I didn't know that Jay was a cop," Troy said as he and Jason walked down the sidewalk later.

"Dean said he was undercover. If he is, how come everybody knows about it?"

"You think he'll arrest us for selling drugs?" Troy looked behind him as if he thought that the cops would be there.

"I don't know. I'm scared. You should have just left the sugar cube right where it was."

"It was your idea to sell it." Troy gave Jason a dirty look.

"Yeah, and you got your half of the money for it too." They crossed the street and went into an apartment building. A woman with a poodle in her arms brushed by them as they climbed the stairs. "You think he's home?" Jason pushed open a fire door at the top of the stairs.

"Well, Jack isn't home, and I saw Mason's truck out there." Troy knocked on a door. Mason answered it and waved them inside.

The boys walked into the living room where Jack, Harback, and Eddie greeted them. Troy went over and sat on the arm of Eddie's chair. "Hey, son," Eddie said as he rubbed Troy's back. "Some heavy stuff going down, isn't there?"

Jason sat beside Jack on the couch. "I just want to get my mom away from Black Tom."

The men all glanced at one another. "We all do, son," Mason said. "None of us think she's safe up there."

"You saw the drugs he had," Jason addressed Jack. "Why didn't you arrest him?"

Jack looked at Harback who nodded before he answered. "Because there is a lot more going on. We're hoping to get a much bigger score."

"Is that why Tom is still running around loose?" Troy asked.

"I don't like it any more than you do," Jack told the boys. "Some people think that Tom can help us bring down a bigger fish."

Harback leaned forward in his chair. "Have you told anyone what you've seen up there?"

"Just my dad," Jason said. "I told him that Mom smokes Marijuana and that she's in love with Tom."

"That's all?" Jack asked.

Harback told both boys. "The less that gets out the better."

"What about my mom?" Jason asked Jack again.

"First of all," Jack said, "she's an adult and has gone up there on her own free will. Unless Tom abuses or threatens her there isn't much I can do. As far as the drugs are concerned, we just told you about that. There is also a lot of cash involved in this."

"Jack," Harback said as if he didn't want him to tell the boys too much. "Whatever we discuss here can never be repeated, right boys?"

Jason looked over at Troy, both boys nodded their heads. "Well, all I can say is that Dean is in trouble," Troy said.

"Why is that?" Mason asked.

 Bessie — The Monster in Lake Erie by Deborah Tadema

"His other girlfriend is back," Jason said.

"What other girlfriend?" Eddie's eyebrow lifted.

"Rain, his hippie girlfriend," Troy said.

****

Later that day Jack asked Eddie to go with him to see Frank. Eddie went, reluctantly; knowing he was there if Frank went off the deep end again. He leaned against the wall mostly listening to them argue.

"Why would I go up there?" Frank asked Jack. "I don't care what she does anymore."

"She's still your wife, Frank. And Tom has already got her into drugs." Jack leaned against the kitchen counter. "I just don't need you going up there half mad about something and causing us more problems."

"Look," Frank said, "I can't keep Jason from seeing his mother." He raised a fist. "That bastard better not get him involved in drugs or I'll kill him myself." The fist slowly lowered, Frank looked at the floor. "That's all I worry about."

"Those are pretty strong words, Frank," Eddie said

Frank looked up at him. "That is a promise."

Jack sighed and seemed to be giving his friend the benefit of the doubt. "For now, keep the kids from going up on the hill." He looked from Frank to Eddie. "I have a feeling that it's not going to be very stable up there."

"What do you mean?" Eddie asked.

Jack looked out of the screen door. "With all the drugs and people running around up there, I don't think it's safe."

Frank leaned against the fridge. "You think that Sherry's in danger, don't you?"

Jack gazed back at Frank. "I don't know. Tom will protect her if he can." They were silent for a few seconds before he asked, "Did you hear a second gunshot when we were up there?"

Frank looked confused. "I thought I heard something. I couldn't tell if it was a gunshot or not. It seemed so far away. Why?"

"Mason and I both heard one," Eddie said. "Dean did too."

"I thought Dean was unconscious all that time?"

"He went in and out. He remembers bits and pieces of what went on up there." Jack stood up straight and stretched. "Now all I have to do is fill in the blanks."

****

Mason kissed Valerie goodbye and left her apartment. He drove his truck over to the hospital and whistled as he walked up to the front door. Shannon greeted him on her way out. "Mr. Brooks." She held out a hand. "I want to thank you for saving me from, from..."

"You're quite welcome, Shannon. I didn't do it alone, you know?"

"I know. I'll thank Mr. Jackson too. He was the one who carried me all that way." A tear slid down her face. "He gave me his shirt." She swallowed hard.

"Shannon, ready to go?" Bill McCurdy walked up to them and shook Mason's hand.

"I was talking to Ed earlier. I told him that from now on Dean needs to stay away from my daughter." Bill looked apologetic. "I don't want her in that situation again."

"It wasn't anything he did, he..."

"I know, Mason. It's just the company he keeps sometimes." Bill patted Mason's arm. "Not you, of course."

"Did you tell Dean?" Mason asked Shannon.

She looked down at the floor. "Yes, I just came from his room." Tear-filled eyes looked back up at him. "I'm sorry," she glanced at her father then left.

"I am too, Mason. I liked Dean a lot." Bill followed his daughter.

Mason watched them go before he went up to his nephew's room. Dean was pacing back and forth when he entered. "Glad to see you up and about, son. Just ran into Shannon and Bill. Sorry about the bad news."

Dean stopped and faced Mason. "Yeah well, I was going to break off with her, anyway." He waved a dismissive hand.

"Who is this Rain?"

"She's just Rain." Dean smiled, "She's the girl I'm in love with."

"How much do you know about this girl?" Mason sat on the bed.

"I know that she lives with her brother and that her parents live in Hamilton."

"Who is her brother?"

"I don't know. She doesn't like to talk about her family."

Mason walked over to Dean and gave him a manly hug. "Just be careful what you get yourself into."

"I will." Dean walked over to the window after Mason let him go. "That's the appeal, I guess. She's mysterious."

****

Wednesday morning Mason stood beside Jack in the county court-room and waited for the key witness. Finally, this hearing was about to start, and he hoped there would be no more delays. It surprised him that Tom Brennan showed up for his trial by judge. Jay had brought him in last night, as he promised, to spend the night in jail. Tom had fidgeted in his seat for the last half hour; his lawyer gave him last-minute instructions. Jay wasn't here today, which, Mason knew, made Jack nervous.

Tom looked behind him several times to give Sherry a sorrowful look. She'd smile sweetly at him and gave him words of encouragement. Even from where Mason stood, he could see how Tom felt about her. In a way, it would be sad to see him in jail for the attack now that he had just found love. He put that in the back of his mind. They were here to put that bastard away and if not this time, he knew that Jack would get him eventually.

The big doors at the back of the room swung open and Dean walked in. Valerie, Eddie, Rachel, and Frank came in after him. Jack's lawyer walked up to them and directed Dean to his seat. It wasn't lost on any-one that behind the defense was only one person. Sherry never looked over to the prosecutor side and kept her head held high as if in defiance. Even Tom's brother and sister sat with the opposing team. Frank sat between Valerie and Eddie and never even acknowledged his wife.

The judge came in and the room went quiet. Dean was the first one on the stand. He gave his statement on how he found Black Tom in the Stork Club, passed out. He was clear and precise, and Mason saw the pleased expression on Jack's face. Jack must have felt the pain when Dean told them how he found him with a knife in his side. Jack's eyes closed, and he held his side where the knife had entered his body.

Jack gave his statement and showed the judge his scar from the knife wound that Tom had inflicted on him. Tom gave his word that he didn't attack Jack on purpose and that he was drunk and didn't know what he did until later. He looked pathetic up there on the stand with ill-fitting clothes, the innocence he portrayed. Mason had seen that look before, the one that could give you the impression that Tom was just a kid.

Throughout the hearing, Mason watched the Judge and tried to read him. Sometimes you could tell how things were going just by the way the man acted. This Judge gave nothing away, which irritated him even more than he already was. In the end, Tom won over some stupid technicality. While everyone sat in stunned disbelief, Tom jumped up and gave Sherry hugs and kisses. He took her by the hand and walked toward the doors with a big smile on his face.

Jack quickly followed them and stopped Tom as he reached for the door handle. "Tom Brennan, I'm putting you under arrest for the murder of Delroy Parsons."

****

"I didn't kill him," Tom protested as Jack held his arm and nodded toward the officer that stood just inside the door. The officer took out his handcuffs and put them on Tom.

Sherry shrieked and tried to push Jack away. Frank pulled her back and whispered something in her ear. She slumped into his arms. Tom gave him a dirty look as the officer led him away.

"Wait," Mason yelled as he walked up to them and faced Tom. "What did you just say? You admitted you shot Parsons when we were on the hill."

Tom grinned at him. "You didn't find a gun, did you?"

Dean stood where he was and felt confused. He knew he saw Tom shoot Parsons. Didn't he? Doubt crept in his mind as he tried to think back to that day. He knew that everything Tom did came into question. All he saw was the man's back and couldn't swear that he was one-hundred percent sure that he saw Tom shoot Parsons. If only he didn't go in and out of consciousness he could better recall the events as they really happened.

He heard the gun go off. There was the mysterious gunshot that followed. No one had been able to figure that one out yet. Dean looked at Tom and saw not a killer but a man who didn't seem to understand what was happening. Mason looked back at him and all he could do was shrug his shoulders.

Dean sank back into his seat and watched the officer take Tom away. Jack and Mason sat, one on each side of him. Jack looked sick. "I don't believe it," Jack said. "He did tell us he shot Parsons."

Mason nodded. "It wouldn't be the first time he's lied."

"You saw him, didn't you?" Jack asked Dean.

"He had his back to me. Just like his back was to me when he said he didn't rip Shannon's blouse." He sucked in his breath as his body started to spasm.

Mason glanced over at Jack. "At least we can charge him for assault."

"I'm going to," Jack said with conviction. "And I don't care what Jay wants. That bastard is going to get whatever I can throw at him."

Eddie walked up to them. "I think someone got to the Judge." He nodded toward the door that led to the chambers. "How else could he have gotten off with such a stupid thing."

"I certainly agree," Frank said as he watched Sherry leave the room.

"Who else could have done it?" Valerie asked, squinting at Dean. "Are you all right?"

Dean gave her a weak grin. "I just want to go home."

"You still need a lot of rest Dean. I think you're overdoing it." Valerie looked at Eddie. "I think someone should take him home."

****

There was a very fast boat that had docked by the cottage that Bessie saw her man and Jack go into after they followed Tom. Four men unloaded sacks and took them up those long stairs. One of them used to work on the rig. She thought he was a friend of Ed's. It took them only a matter of minutes and then the boat sped away. Bessie followed it straight across the lake to the south shore.

****

Mason kissed Valerie before she headed back to work. Valerie smiled at him, saying, "See you tonight."

Dean headed toward the doors after Valerie left. Mason turned to Jack. "What's going to happen next?"

Jack watched Dean walk down the aisle. "I don't know. I have to think things through." He looked back at Mason. "Have Harback give me a call when you see him."

Mason nodded and then headed out of the courthouse. Eddie fell in step beside him. "You think Dean will be safe at his place?"

"Something bothering you, Ed?" Mason stopped. Dean turned around.

"I was just wondering about that other gunshot we heard up there, that's all. What if Tom wasn't the only one there? What if that other person was the one who killed Parsons?"

Jack took notice of the exchange and walked up to them. "I think I'm going to go back up there and see if I can't find this gun Tom had."

"I'll go with you," Eddie volunteered. "I think we should scour the hill."

"Count me in," Frank said. "Just let me check in on Jason first and I'll meet you there."

"Yeah," Mason said. "Why don't we meet at the bottom of the hill in about ten minutes?"

"If you want, I can take Dean home," Rachel said. "And I can check in on Jason," she addressed Frank. "That way you'll have more time before it gets too dark to see."

"She has a point," Mason said. "Are you sure you don't mind?"

"Not at all," she smiled at the men.

Eddie gave her a kiss. "Thanks, sweetheart."

CHAPTER 27

All four men walked around the clearing where they found Dean and Shannon earlier. "If Tom shot off a gun, where is the shell casing?" Frank asked as he scrutinized the area. "Tom would have been about here, according to Dean. I don't see anything."

"He could have picked it up," Eddie said. He was looking around the area where Shannon was tied up.

Mason checked along the route where Frank and Jack came up from. This is where he thought he heard the second shot from. "I have a gun," he shouted and stood back. Jack ran down the hill to him and took out a plastic bag out of his pocket.

"Good job," he said to Mason as he picked it up with a rag and dropped it into the bag. "It looks like it's the right caliber." The two of them searched the area for more evidence, finding nothing.

"Bullets," Eddie called from atop the hill.

"Bullets?" Jack said to Mason as they ran back up the hill. They found Eddie in the bushes to the left of the clearing. He showed them a bunch of bullets scattered on the ground.

"Looks like someone dropped them," Mason said as he held back a tree branch for Jack. After Jack had them all picked up and secured in a bag, the three of them walked back toward the clearing.

Frank stood in the place where Dean was. "I didn't see that there when I helped Dean down the hill." He pointed to a shell casing. "He would have laid on this."

"That doesn't make sense," Mason said.

Jack let out a huge sigh. "We're being set up, guys."

"You saying someone planted this stuff for us to find?" Eddie ran a big hand through his hair. "Why?"

Mason waited for Jack to answer. Both Eddie and Frank turned, looked behind them and froze. Mason did the same and knew by their reactions that something terrible had just happened. Jack was in the middle of the clearing with his hands up in the air. Sherry stood on the far side with a gun aimed at him.

"You took Tom away from me. It's your fault he's in jail." The gun wavered as she spoke.

"Sherry, he's got to answer for the things he's done." Jack kept his voice even. Mason knew he feared for his life. He inched his way to the right and saw Eddie go to the left.

"Stop," the gun pointed from one to the other. "I'll shoot all of you." Her deadly eyes rested on her husband. "Are you hiding behind Jack, Frank? Coward. You have always been a coward."

"I'm not hiding," Frank stepped forward. When he did this both Mason and Eddie widened the gap even further. "Look, honey, you don't have to do this, we..."

"Don't call me honey! I'm not your honey." Sherry aimed the gun at his head. "Both of you," she grinned. "I can get both of you."

Mason took another step. Sherry whipped the gun in his direction. Eddie ran toward her. The gun went off. Sherry dropped the gun and ran into the bushes.

****

As the boys walked down the beach Troy reached over and tugged down on Jason's swim trunks.

"Hey!" Jason swatted his friend on the arm.

Troy pulled back and laughed. "I didn't think you saw me."

Jason tried to look stern, couldn't quite pull it off.

Troy hit Jason back.

"Yeah? You're the biggest pervert I ever saw." Jason backhanded Troy and then ran down the beach. Troy chased him.

They stopped when they ran out of breath and leaned on each other for support. Troy looked out at the lake. "This is where we found Uncle Mason."

"It seems so long ago now, doesn't it?" Jason plopped down on the sand.

Troy watched a speedboat skip across the water in the distance. "I wonder if they're smuggling drugs. It sure is fast." He sat down beside Jason and picked up a stick that he dug in the sand with. "A lot has happened this summer, hasn't it?"

Jason was still for a bit before he spoke. "I wonder what's happening in court today."

"I know. Things seem so messed up as far as Black Tom is concerned, isn't it?"

"One minute I hope they fry him and the next I hope they don't, so he can look after my mom."

"Me too," Troy watched some girls down by the water.

Jason poked his arm. He turned his attention to the base of the cliffs. "Isn't that Rain? What's she doing with Jay?"

Rain and Jay were talking as they headed toward the hill. Troy eventually stood and said. "Let's head on back."

They opened the door to Jason's house to find everyone there. Sudden fear ripped through Troy as he looked from one person's sad eyes to the next. He realized that Frank wasn't there.

Rachel was standing next to Eddie beside the fridge; she sniffled and blew her nose when they walked in. Jack stood up from a kitchen chair and motioned for the boys to sit. Eddie went over to Troy and put his hand on his son's shoulder. Mason walked over and stood beside Jason.

"We have bad news for you, Jason," Jack said. "Your father was shot today." Tears ran down his face. "He was killed."

Jason sat in his chair completely stunned. "Who? Who would want to shoot my dad?"

Mason sat down next to him and pulled his chair close. He hugged Jason's head to his chest and said in a low voice, "Your mother."

"No!" Jason shot up. "She wouldn't shoot my dad. She just wouldn't. She loved him."

****

Bessie cowered inside her den. Both rings told her that something sad had happened. She hoped they didn't blame her because she didn't do anything wrong. She did hear another gunshot up on the hill earlier today. There have been many shootings this summer. She cocked her head to the side. Did she hear that? It sounded like a wolf howling.

****

"Is my mom in jail?" Jason asked the grown-ups that had made their way into the living room.

"She has disappeared," Jack told him. "We looked all over up there for her after she ran."

"So, both Mom and Tom will go to prison?"

The phone rang. Jack went into the kitchen and picked it up. A few seconds later he hung up and gestured for Mason and Eddie. In a faint voice, he told them. "Tom's been howling all night in his cell." He looked at the clock on the wall. "It's already past midnight."

"How does he know?" Eddie said. "He must know that something has happened to Sherry."

"What? We couldn't find her." Mason looked back toward the living room. He was glad that Valerie was to spend the night with Rachel.

"You think she might have committed suicide?" Eddie asked.

Jack rubbed his eyes and yawned. "I think we should all get some rest and convene in the morning."

"I'll stay here with Jason tonight," Mason volunteered. "I don't think he'll get much sleep; frankly I don't think any of us will."

"Yeah," Eddie said and called Troy. "Let's go home, son."

Troy glanced at friend, shook his head. "I'll stay here with Jason."

Eddie nodded then left with Rachel. Valerie gave Mason a kiss and followed them out.

Mason went back into the living room and hugged Jason. "Why don't you two go upstairs and try to get some sleep. I'll be here if you need anything, okay?"

Jason nodded before he followed Troy up the stairs.

Mason turned to see Jack hang up the phone. "I just called Harback," Jack told him as he walked over to the recliner. "To tell him where we're staying tonight."

Mason sank into the couch and looked around the room. This was his friend's house. Frank had been one of his best friends since public school. How could he be gone? How could his wife of nearly twenty years just up and murder him?

Suddenly all the pent-up sorrow was too much to hold in. He lowered his head to his knees and let it all out. Jack was beside him in seconds and put his arm around Mason. Mason put it around his buddy. Together, they cried.

****

The phone rang. Jack jumped to his feet. Mason squinted at him and rolled over on the couch. It was early, too early. He had just dozed off when Jack tapped his shoulder. "Harback wants us at the station."

"What time is it?"

"Seven."

Mason rolled over and opened his eyes. "It isn't even human time yet." He sat up and ran his hand through his hair. "Why so early?"

"He wants to question us." Jack headed to the phone. "I'll call Val and see if she'll stay with Jason."

Mason nodded, flopped back down. "Tell her to bring my toothbrush."

"She's at Ed's, remember? I have to tell him to show up, too."

Jack tapped his shoulder again and this time, Mason got to his feet. "I'm up," he said as he staggered into the kitchen to make coffee. "Have you checked in on Jason this morning?"

"I'll do that right now." Jack headed up the stairs.

A few minutes later Troy came downstairs, his hair hadn't been combed and he yawned as he sat at the kitchen table.

Eddie walked in ten minutes later with Valerie. Mason could tell by the looks in their eyes that neither had much sleep last night. He probably looked just as bad. Valerie went straight into Mason's arms. He inhaled her scent and held her close and told himself that he needed a shower. As soon as he saw his son, Eddie went over and gave Troy's shoulder a squeeze. Eddie parked himself in a kitchen chair and put his elbows on the table and hands under his chin as if it was too heavy to hold up on its own.

Valerie put bread in the toaster and then turned around. "You guys need to eat something."

Mason looked down the hall. "I think we lost Jack. He went upstairs over a half an hour ago."

"Eddie put his hands down. "He must be counseling. God knows Jason will need it."

Valerie handed Mason his toast that he ate absent-mindedly. It was hard to swallow. He forced himself and felt a little better. Eddie picked up one of his and took a bite. Troy ate as if he was starving. Jack walked down the hall and into the kitchen. Valerie handed him a plate and a cup of coffee.

"Jason is one messed up kid," Jack said as he found a seat.

"What will happen to him now?" Valerie asked as she sat down with her own plate. "God knows Sherry won't be there for him."

"That will depend on if any relatives show up and offer to take him in," Jack said. "If nobody does, he'll end up with Children's Aid and be fostered out."

"Shit," Eddie said. "What else does he have to go through?"

****

Jason walked down the stairs and into the kitchen. His eyes were red. His muffled crying had kept Troy up all night. Mason jumped up and gave him a big hug. Jason hung on to him and held in his tears. After a bit Jason pulled away, only to be engulfed in Eddie's strong arms. Troy figured that Jack had given Jason a hug while they were upstairs.

Valerie gave him a kiss on the forehead and handed him some toast. He sat in the chair that Mason had just left and watched as the men all left the house. While Troy helped Valerie with the dishes, Rachel walked in with a casserole dish. Valerie commented that it seemed that that's all they did lately was eat Rachel's food.

"This is just a salad," Rachel told them as she put it in the fridge. "You don't need to heat it up."

"Thanks, Rachel," Jason muttered. He waited until the women sat down before he asked, "Where is my dad?"

Valerie and Rachel glanced at each other before Val said, "He's in the basement of the hospital."

"So, he's in the morgue," Jason said. She nodded and sniffled.

"That's what we need to talk to you about," Rachel said. "Did your father have any life insurance? Do you know where his bank book is?"

Jason shrugged. "They never talked to me about that kind of stuff. They have one of those safes in their closet, his closet." Jason led the way up to his father's bedroom. Troy sat on the edge of the bed waiting to get kicked out. No one seemed to mind that he was there. Val and Rachel slid the safe out and looked at it.

"It's locked. Do you know where the key might be?" Rachel asked.

Jason went over to the dresser. Troy wondered what it felt like, prying into his father's personal things. Was it up to Jason to go through his dad's stuff and get rid of it all? Finally, Jason found a key on a shoelace and handed it to Valerie. She opened the safe and took out forms and papers and sat on the bed with them. She handed Rachel a brown envelope. "This is a life insurance policy," she smiled at him. "At least you will get something."

Rachel pulled a folded paper out of the pile and opened it up. "This is from Hart's Funeral home. It looks like your parents bought plots a long time ago." She looked up from the paper. "I think you should appoint an adult to look after this stuff for you. It doesn't matter who. Just think about it, okay?"

   Bessie — The Monster in Lake Erie by Deborah Tadema

"Good idea," Valerie said. "Someone you trust to handle your affairs. We need to get hold of this guy." She waved a paper at Rachel. "Your father has some investments." She looked up at Jason. "Someone will have to look into that."

"What about the house?" Jason asked as he looked from one woman to the other.

"I don't know," Valerie said. "I guess it'll depend on what happens with your mother. She held up another legal looking paper. "This is the deed to it right here. It has both of your parent's names on it."

Jason sat on the bed beside Troy. "This is all complicated stuff, isn't it?"

****

Mason and Eddie sat in the police station and waited their turn to go into Jack's office and give their statements. After he talked to them individually, Harback had all three of them at once. He sat behind Jack's desk with his fingers steepled and elbows on the hardwood. Eddie thought of the last time he was there. It was when his only worry was, who wrecked his campsite. Now he was here because he witnessed a murder and Harback had interrogated them for over an hour each.

"Your stories all line up," Harback told them as if relieved. He looked down at his notes. "Sherry held a gun on Jack. You two split up so she wouldn't have you all bunched up." He pointed to Eddie. "When she wavered, you ran toward her and the gun went off. That's when Frank was hit right between the eyes, is that right?" He looked up.

"That's how it happened," Ed said and looked down at the evidence on the desk. "I think that's Tom's gun."

"This will all get tested." Harback leaned back in the chair and looked over at Mason. "It seems that we have ourselves another problem." He sat forward and shook his head. "Your brother's fingerprints don't match up with Tom Brennan's."

"What?" Mason's face went white. Eddie forgot to breathe. Jack looked at Harback as if he had just grown horns. "What do you mean, don't match up?"

"He's not Tom Brennan. At least the one that lived at the address we have."

"So, are you telling me I don't have a brother? What about the proof my lawyer found?"

"I think that there is a brother out there somewhere, the real Tom Brennan. Just not this guy."

Eddie remembered to breathe and saw Mason's body shake. "So, we should see if we can find his real brother."

Harback nodded. "I would if I were you, Mason. In the meantime, I'm going to hold that guy in there until we find out just who in hell he is."

CHAPTER 28

Eddie took Mason home and then called his wife to come over. Mason wanted Valerie and Dean to be with him too. Right now, he felt naked without them nearby. When they arrived, he told them what they had just learned.

"So, are you saying that Black Tom isn't related to me?" Dean asked. "That's a relief."

"I pleaded for Jack to let me in the cell with that ass hole, so I could punch the shit out of him," Mason told his sister and motioned for Valerie to get them all a beer from his fridge.

"Yeah, you should have seen him," Eddie said. "It took three of us to hold him back." He took the beer that Valerie handed him. "I wouldn't be surprised if Jack went in there instead. He was really pissed off, too."

"So, who is he anyway?" Valerie asked. She sat at the kitchen table and held Mason's hand. He lifted it and kissed her knuckle.

"Nobody knows. All we know is that he's not Tom," Mason said. He looked over at Rachel. "Now we need to find our real brother."

"Well, all I can say is that guy has been one big lie after another," Eddie said after he pulled up a chair and sat on it. "We can't believe a word he says."

Dean lifted his hand and scrutinized the aquamarine on his finger. "You think these are a lie too?"

Mason looked at his own ring. "I don't know. I honestly can't tell you."

"They do work," Rachel said, although a little skeptical. "They have warned you of danger, and Bessie has helped you when you needed it."

"That just might be the only thing Black Tom hasn't lied about," Dean said. "I've read some of those books. They all seem to say the same things, and they all mention these rings. It seems they have been around for centuries." He added. "There is no mention of them having to be kept in one family."

"That was a clever ploy if Tom knew that Dean was your nephew," Valerie said.

Mason felt his face drain of blood. "How could he have known?" He looked from Dean to Rachel. "He knows a lot about our family."

Dean watched him for a long time, his face expressionless. Mason held his arm. "I love you, Dean. I always have. This doesn't change anything."

Finally, Dean spoke. "I just hope we don't have to drag Troy into this." He looked down at his ring then at the people in the room.

They remained quiet for a while and sipped on their beers, each in their own thoughts. Rachel spoke up. "I guess we need to find our brother." She looked at Mason. "Maybe he can give us some answers."

****

If it hadn't been for him; he knew Jason wouldn't have made it. He leaned on Dean throughout the funeral. Between him and Troy, they kept Jason from collapsing. Yet the day went by slowly and in a haze.

It was bad enough that Jason's father was dead, even worse because his mother had killed him. Dean saw the looks of pity people gave Jason, heard their whispers and speculations of the murder. Jason told him that he didn't care what they thought. He just wanted it all to end.

One person said that it was a shame that Jason had to endure this alone that his mother should have been there for him. Jason wasn't alone, Dean thought. His best friends were there. All the adults he'd ever loved, except his parents, were there. They made sure that Jason had never been alone since that terrible day, four days ago.

Bessie — The Monster in Lake Erie by Deborah Tadema

Rachel, Valerie, Eddie, Jack and Mason all stayed close and cried just as hard as Jason did. It was Dean who caught him when he almost fainted. He had always been there for Jason, just as he was there for his brother. He wondered about this as they followed the hearse to the gravesite.

Dean stumbled after the crowd to where a hole had already been dug. He watched as Eddie, Mason, Jack, Harback and another cop carried the coffin to the site. Jay must have still been undercover; he thought and wondered how the bad guys didn't know this if everyone else did.

They said prayers that he didn't know or cared about. He bowed his head with everyone else and mumbled amen at the ends of them. He felt Jason sway beside him and held his arm. Troy gave him a small nod of his head as if in thanks and squeezed Jason's other arm.

Tears ran down Jason's face when they lowered the coffin. He stepped up to it and told his father goodbye. Mason finally pulled him away and Rachel talked to him on their way back to Eddie's place.

Sandwiches and drinks were served. He ate little. Dean wanted to grab a handful of beer bottles and go up to Troy's room and get drunk. He wanted to go up the hill and kill Jason's mother because she took Frank away. None of these things he did. Instead, he just sat on the couch beside Jason and brooded.

Several people walked up to Jason and gave their condolences before they went home. He talked to them. Dean figured he didn't really know what he said. It wasn't even dark outside yet when he followed Jason up to Troy's room and sat on the twin bed he always used. That's where Jason took off all his clothes and dropped them to the floor. He got in under the covers, pulled the blanket over his head. Dean sat on his brother's bed and stared into the darkness.

****

To give support to Jason wasn't the only reason why Mason and Jack spent several nights at Frank's house. They were worried that Sherry would show up and cause problems. Jack also wanted to arrest her for her husband's murder. The day of the funeral, Jason spent the night at Eddie's.

Despite all their efforts, Sherry had vanished. "I think someone is hiding her," Jack said as the guys sat around in the police station, "just like they must have hidden Parsons."

"She didn't even show up at the funeral," Eddie said. "Maybe she knew there would be cops watching for her."

"She could be in China by now." Mason put his feet up on Jack's desk and leaned back in his chair. Jack swiped his feet off and Mason nearly tipped over.

Eddie chuckled and then asked, "So why didn't you guys find out about Tom's fingerprints beforehand, he's been arrested often enough?"

"We don't fingerprint for petty crimes," Jack answered. "I don't know why the arresting officer didn't when that bastard tried to carve me up."

"Who took him in that time?" Mason asked.

Jack stood and went over to the file cabinet, unlocked it with a key from his belt and pulled out a thick file. "All this is Tom's," he told his friends. He sat back down in his chair and set the file on his desk. After he scanned through several reports he pulled one out. "Says here, it was our young Officer Cooper."

Jack put the report back in the file and closed it. He sat at his desk for several seconds and didn't say anything. Mason and Eddie exchanged glances. Eddie started to say something when Mason cut him off, "Shh, he's thinking."

Jack looked over at Mason. "Has Harback given you any clues as to where he has Cooper hidden?"

"No, I haven't been home much these days. When I'm not babysitting with you, I'm spending the night with Val."

Jack quickly glanced at the file cabinet but not before Mason saw the sadness in his eyes. He hoped that Jack would find someone soon, so he could get his mind off Val. It surprised him that Jack still remained his friend. To cover up the awkward silence that followed Mason made a little joke. "Now we know why Jack is getting bald, he thinks too much."

"What were you going to say, Ed?" Jack asked.

"I was going to say that maybe it was a mistake. Maybe Cooper just forgot to get the prints."

"Maybe," Jack muttered.

****

Dean waited until his mother went to work before he left the house. If she had her way he'd be stuck there until he was thirty. That was the main reason he had his own apartment, his mother relied on him too much. She needed to lean on his dad, now that he wasn't working on the rig anymore. He'd told her a hundred times that he was fine. He needed fresh air and exercise, so he headed to the beach to find Rain.

She wasn't on the boardwalk, he went down to the water and walked along the shore. The warm breeze off the lake felt good, he took off his shirt. Before he knew it, he was at the secluded place where he'd taken Rain several times, so he could be alone with her. This was their private spot; this was where he came when she left him, to feel close to her.

Dean walked around the base of the cliff and stopped short. A man sat in the middle of the clearing with his back to him. Rain sat cross-legged and was facing him as she talked. Hurt, betrayal, and disbelief surged through him in a rush. This was their secret place; she was his girl. He turned to leave and staggered back the way he'd come with tears in his eyes.

"Dean." Rain ran up to him and grabbed his arm. "Where are you going? Come back."

He stopped, refusing to look at her. "Who are you seeing, Rain?"

"Just you," she looked back at the cliffs. "Please, come with me. I want to introduce you to someone."

"No thanks. I don't need to meet your new boyfriend." He tried to pull away from her grasp.

"He isn't my boyfriend, Dean. Please." Gently she guided him back to where the man sat on the sand. As they approached, the man stood and turned to face them. "This is my brother, Dean."

All he did was stare at him. The man held out his hand. Dean hesitated before he shook it. "Your brother?"

"Yes Dean, Rain is my little sister," Jay said and motioned for him to sit down with them.

Rain pulled him down with her and smiled nicely at him. "Jay is my brother, and he is a cop."

"Why are you meeting way out here?" Dean looked from one to the other. "Don't you live with him?" he asked Rain.

"Do you know where we live?" Jay asked him. Dean shook his head. Jay answered his own question. "We rent a cottage up on Feather Heights. It's a bit far to walk to all the time. So, we meet here occasionally."

Rain leaned into him. "This is why I never took you home; it might have compromised my brother's identity."

"And you knew about us?" Dean asked Jay.

"I knew."

"And you didn't say anything? Why didn't you say anything?"

"I had to make sure you were clean first, Dean." Jay looked up at the cliffs that nearly surrounded them. "And I knew about Shannon."

Dean felt his face go hot. "I aw, didn't mean to..."

"It's all right Dean." Rain pecked him on the cheek. "I knew about her too."

He looked into her eyes. "Yet you stayed with me, why?"

"Remember I left you? I went back home to our parent's place to get over you. Jay told me that Shannon went on vacation and it didn't seem to bother you too much."

"You seemed more upset after Rain left you," Jay put in. "When you came to see me in the hospital, I saw the look on your face when I mentioned her name. That's when I knew which one you were really in love with."

"And while I was back home, all I could think about was you." Rain turned Dean's head to look into his eyes. "You are the reason I came back, Dean. You scared me. I've never felt like this for anyone before."

"I couldn't get you out of my mind either," Dean told her. "I love you, Rain."

Jay got up and walked away.

****

Bessie watched the cubs come down the hill by her den and waited for them. The two were in deep conversation and didn't watch where they were going. She watched for them, made sure they were safe. One of them seemed very upset. She greeted them and let them pet her. They smiled sadly up at her and then continued the conversation.

"Everything changed after my dad died," Jason said. "I just don't feel like doing anything."

"That's why I made you come outside, get some fresh air."

"I know, and I thank you."

"You're still grieving, Jason. This is going to take a long time for all of us to get over."

Bessie sensed that someone was watching them as they meandered along the creek bed. There! Over by the base of the cliff by the bushes, she saw someone and growled a warning. The boys stopped, looked up at her and then to where she was looking. A female stepped out, Tom's mate.

"Jason," she said and checked behind her. "It was an accident, Jason. I didn't mean to kill your father. The gun just went off."

"Mom?" Jason stepped closer.

"Don't." She backed up. "Don't come any closer."

The cubs stopped. "You have to turn yourself in, Mom," Jason pleaded.

"Just tell them it was an accident." She looked at her son as if to hold him in her memory. "I love you, Jason. I miss you." She turned to go.

"Mom! Come back." Jason ran to where she was just a second ago. He stopped by the bushes and looked back at Troy. "She's gone."

"She couldn't have gotten too far," Troy searched the area. "She couldn't have just vanished."

"Hey! You boys. What are you up to down there?" This was a voice Bessie had never heard before and stood guard over the cubs. The man was on top of the cliff and shaded his eyes with his hand. "Did you see her? Where is she?"

"Who?" Troy asked and gave Jason a nervous glance. He pointed to where the man was.

"That killer, that's who, she's still running around up here some-where."

"No, we didn't see anybody," Jason yelled up at him. "We're just treasure hunting."

"I suggest you get out of here, it's not safe."

Troy studied the man while Jason asked him why not.

"Because, if you don't leave." He aimed a rifle at them. "I'll get you."

The boys ran back to the cave and ducked into the den. The man on top of the cliff stood where he was and laughed.

****

Eddie went over to the police station to talk to Jack about finding Sherry Webster. They were discussing it with Harback when the door opened.

"Ah, here he is," Harback said as Jay walked in and closed the door behind him.

Jack gave him a dirty look, "Well, there's my invisible partner."

"That's my fault," Harback said. "I've kept him busy." He looked over at Jack from behind the constable's desk. "He's still infiltrated in the drug gang."

Jay walked over and sat in the chair next to Jack. "I missed you too," he gave Jack a hug. Jack pulled away. Eddie laughed then stopped at the dirty look Jack gave him.

　　　　Bessie — The Monster in Lake Erie by Deborah Tadema

"What have you got for me, Jay?" Harback smiled warmly at his cops.

"I've found out the name of the guy who took over after Parson's death. His name is Rick Hall."

"I've heard of that name before," Jack said.

Eddie choked and coughed. Jay got up and slapped his back until he stopped. He sat back down and said, "You know him?"

"He was my motor man. Why?" Eddie wiped the tears that formed in the corners of his eyes.

"He's taken over for Parsons," Harback said. "I thought I recognized that name. And I cleared him." He slouched in his chair.

"Cooper says there will be a big shipment Friday night while the town's busy with the Labor Day dance at the Stork Club." Jay turned to his partner. "It's to take place up at that cottage you were at, Jack."

"That's where Cooper was all this time," Jack gave Harback a dirty look.

"I know, Jack. I should have told you sooner." Harback apologized. "I was just trying to keep things simple and you had your own job to do."

"What's the plan?" Eddie asked.

"I think it's time we did a big bust and nail these guys once and for all," Harback said. "I'll call St. Thomas and have the Chief send us re-reinforcements."

"What about Sherry Webster?" Jack asked. "We haven't caught her yet."

"We'll get her," Harback said. "Right now, I want to concentrate on this drug bust."

Jay nodded and said, "And if we happen to run into her on that hill, we'll get her."

Eddie nodded. It surprised him that Harback included him in police matters.

"And if you don't," Harback smiled, "I have a plan that might bring her in." He leaned forward in his chair. "I think that Black Tom has some drugs and about five thousand dollars hidden someplace. Dean said he saw two sacks up there. Nobody's seen them since."

CHAPTER 29

"So, Jack won't let you in to see Tom. I can see why," Dean told his uncle. He had gone over to Valerie's apartment for lunch. Afterward, they took tall glasses of ice tea into the living room.

"Yeah," Mason said, "he thinks I'll kill the bastard through the bars."

"They still haven't figured out who he is?"

"No, and Harback and the Feds are looking for the real Tom." Mason let out a big sigh. "Man, I wish I never met Black Tom."

"He's been a thorn in everyone's side this summer, hasn't he?" Valerie said. Mason squeezed her hand.

"About what we talked about earlier," Dean said. "I think it's a clever idea."

"Are you sure?" Mason asked. "This will affect you and Troy too, you know?"

"I'm sure."

"Will you come with us this afternoon to tell them?" Valerie asked Dean. "I have a feeling it will help."

Dean shrugged and said, "Sure."

After they finished their ice teas, the three of them went over to Eddie's. Rachel called Troy and Jason into the kitchen where they all sat around the table. Valerie gave Mason a gentle nudge and he cleared his throat.

"We," he looked at Valerie first. Eddie nodded for him to continue. "Val and I have been doing a lot of talking...and we want to, that is..."

"Holy cow, Mason," Dean stepped in. "I've never seen you at a loss for words before."

Mason looked at him annoyed and then smiled at Jason. "We want to know if you want to live with us."

Jason glanced around at the people in the room with a shocked expression.

"You don't have to decide right this minute," Valerie told him. "Talk it over with others if you want, make sure if this is what you want first."

"For how long?" Jason asked.

"For as long as you want. This will permanent," Mason said. "If you do, we'll start looking for a house." He nodded toward the brothers, sitting side by side. "And Troy and Dean can stay with you sometimes as well."

Jason said. "Dean's already like a big brother to me anyway."

"I am?" Dean arched his back. "I didn't think of it that way before."

Jason and Troy watched each other in silent communication. Dean knew that the two of them were so close that they didn't need to talk. They seemed to be able to read each other's minds.

"I want to," Jason finally piped up. When all eyes turned in his direction he repeated it. "Troy and I had already talked about different scenarios of what could happen to me. Besides living here, you two are my next choice."

"Is that settled?" Valerie asked.

"It's settled," Jason confirmed.

"Good, now," Valerie addressed the teen. "Rachel is going to be my Maid of Honor.

Mason said, "And Jason can hold me up at the altar."

****

Harback asked Dean to meet him at Mason's apartment the next night. When he walked in, Jack and Eddie were there. Mason came in shortly after and said, "I just got invited to my own apartment."

"You haven't slept here in two weeks, Mason." Harback reminded him with a chuckle. He looked around and said, "It's becoming just like home."

"You want it, you can have it," Mason told him. "I don't need it anymore."

"Well, you know, after we crack this case, I was thinking of retiring." Harback went into the tiny kitchen and brought out a handful of beers. After he handed them all one he nodded to Jack.

Jack took a sip of his and then addressed the men in the room. "We have the results back from ballistics. The bullet that Jay was shot with came from the same gun that shot Parsons. The bullet that killed Frank definitely came from the gun Sherry had. A different weapon."

No one breathed for a few heartbeats before Mason let out a whistle. "So, you're saying that Tom didn't shoot Parsons?"

"No, he didn't. My guess is that he fired in the air, maybe to scare him, I don't know," Jack told him.

"Who shot Parsons?" Dean asked.

"We don't know," Harback said. "I'm thinking maybe one of his own men."

Eddie sat forward. "The boys were down by Muddy Creek yesterday. Some guy was up on the cliff and threatened them with a rifle."

Jack looked at him stunned. "Why didn't you report it?"

"I just found out about it an hour ago. They said that Bessie was there and growled at him. He told them to leave because it was too dangerous for them there. And he was looking for Sherry."

"Another thing," Harback said. "Rick Hall has taken over for Parsons."

Mason looked over at Eddie. "He was the one who found Hal Johnson. You think he might have pushed Hal over the rail?"

"Someone sawed the rail enough to weaken it," Eddie said. "Ken Hennessy told me, it should have been in his report."

"Maybe Rick did push Hal over," 'Dean said. "That might explain things."

"Shit," Jack said. "How will we prove that?"

****

Labor Day. Mason and Valerie went over to Eddie's. Dean took Rain with him. They made sure that none of the teens left the house after the barbecue they had. Everyone stayed in the living room with nervous tension. The cops were on the hill.

Harback warned them to stay inside tonight. Most of the police from St. Thomas had come down, people thought because of the holiday celebrations. Some did stay in town, mostly to keep drunks off the streets. The police boat had gone out. They were all armed and wore bulletproof vests.

It wasn't until after 2 A.M. when Jack showed up. The kids had all gone to bed. Dean snuggled with Rain on the couch, they were dozing. The adults were in the kitchen with cups of tea in front of them. "We got them," he announced with a grin. "You can all go home now."

Rain stumbled in the room half asleep, Dean right behind her. Jack looked at her and said, "Your brother is fine. He's taking our prisoners in." He looked around the room. "I gotta go."

After he left Dean drove to his apartment. They slept in the following morning. Dean woke up to find Rain awake. "I love you," he said.

"I love you, Dean. Let's move in together."

"I thought you were going back home soon." He played with her hair while he gazed into her deep green eyes.

"I don't want to. And I know I'm in Jay's way."

"I can't think of anything I'd rather do." He grinned at her.

Rain pushed his long hair back from his face. "You really look like your father, you know?"

"We'll have to split the rent. I was thinking of going back to school."

"I get a good allowance from my parents every month."

Dean sat up. "I don't want to live off you, Rain. I'll be working soon."

"You won't. I'm sure you'll still be able to work at your dad's store part-time if you want and go to school."

"And what will you do?"

"I've been thinking of going to college. I want to take writing courses."

"You write? I've never seen your work." He kissed her, felt her melt in his arms.

****

Mason and Dean went up the hill to check up on Bessie. "I think she hid in here," Mason said as they walked along the ledge inside the cave. Bessie had greeted them and seemed calm.

"She's probably used to all the guns going off by now," Dean patted her forehead. "That's a good girl," he crooned to her. He looked down at his uncle and noticed he seemed a bit down. "What's wrong?"

"They're going to let Black Tom go, drop the murder charge."

"What about him assaulting me and Shannon?"

Mason reached up and laid a hand on his nephew's shoulder. "Harback is hoping that Tom will lead them to Sherry. And the sacks you saw."

Dean studied Mason's eyes. "I did see two sacks that day, one of them was green."

"Nobody doubts you." Mason brought his hand down. "We think Tom hid them before he went to the shack."

"Who's going to get close enough to nail Tom?"

"Jay and Officer Cooper are going to keep their undercover until they get this settled."

"Wouldn't Tom have seen them take the rest of those guys in?"

Mason shook his head. "Apparently, they took Tom downstairs and put him in solitary confinement before they went on the raid. He didn't see them."

"Tom's going to get away with what he did to us?"

"No, he won't. Harback is just putting that off until later. He wants to throw the book at Tom."

Dean watched Bessie for a bit and then looked back at Mason. "Rain's going to move in with me."

Mason smiled. "You need any help just let me know. You need money?"

"Can I borrow some, just for next month's rent? I'd ask dad but he's not getting much on unemployment."

"Dean," Mason put his arm around his nephew's shoulder. "I'll give you enough money to get you by for a while. Get one thing perfectly clear. You never, ever, borrow from me, got that?"

Dean grinned at Mason.

****

Troy and Jason pulled their jackets closed as they walked along the beach a few days later. "It sure turned cold in a hurry, didn't it?" Troy said as he looked out at the angry waves that bashed against the cliffs ahead.

"Yeah," Jason glanced up at Picnic Hill. "The leaves are turning color. Soon winter will be here."

Troy stepped over a dead fish. "You're worried about your mother, aren't you?"

"Sometimes I want to go up there and find her, tell her how much I miss her. I want to take a gun with me and kill her like she did my dad."

They walked along with no clear destination in mind. After a while, Troy said, "I'm sorry about this stuff you're going through."

"Yeah, well." Jason kicked at a piece of driftwood.

Troy found a log and sat down on it. Jason joined him, and they watched the lake. "I asked dad why he and mom didn't ask you to stay with us," Troy said. "He said that they were talking about it when Mason approached them. Mom worries that if we spent too much time together, we might end up hating each other. And the fact that my dad's not working made them hesitate. Mason told them that he and Valerie can afford to give you everything you need. And we can still be best friends."

"I thought about your dad not working. And I know I'm welcome at your place any time." Jason stood up and continued his walk.

Troy caught up with him. "I'm glad you're moving in with Mason and Valerie. I think it'll work out. Don't you?"

"Yeah, I do." Jason gave Troy a knowing look. "And I don't want to listen to you snoring for the rest of my life."

Troy ignored the tease. "I don't know who else I'd rather beat on the swimming team at school."

"Look! Up there!" Jason pointed to the top of the cliff. "That's Mom."

"Are you sure?" Troy squinted at the figure that was too far away to identify. He saw another silhouette walk up behind the first one. The first person dove into the lake.

Jason screamed and ran toward the bottom of the outcrop. "He pushed her! Black Tom pushed her!"

****

Troy caught Jason and pulled him back before he dove into the high waves. "Get a grip," he yelled at his buddy. "We have to get help. You go in there now, you'll drown."

Jason struggled to get away from Troy's grasp. "That's my mom. He killed my mom." Tears of frustration and anger slid down his face. "Let go of me."

"No. Stop fighting me." Troy punched Jason in the stomach. Jason doubled over and staggered backward. "Now will you listen? We have to get help."

Troy pulled Jason back along the shore toward town. In their desperate need to get help, it turned into a race. Troy let Jason get ahead of him. They ran right into the Stork Club and used the pay phone in the lobby. Troy was the one who told Jack what had just happened. They sat on a bench to catch their breaths.

A few minutes later they heard sirens and went back outside to meet the police. Both Jack and Harback got out of the car and ran toward the boys. Jack got there first. Jason told him what he had just seen. "I know it was Black Tom," he said. "He pushed my mom into the lake."

"Show me," Jack followed the boys down along the shore. Harback struggled to keep up with them.

          Bessie — The Monster in Lake Erie by Deborah Tadema

They stopped where the boys were earlier, Jason pointed to the top of the cliff. "That's where they were."

Jack down at the bottom of the outcrop. "I've called the firemen. They're bringing their boat around and are going to drag the lake for her, Jason." He put his arm around Jason's shoulder. "Just hold tight."

Harback caught up to them out of breath. "I'm too old for this," he complained. He took Troy aside. "Did you see his mother up there?"

"I saw somebody. I don't know if it was her or not." Troy gave Jason a sad look. "And there were two people up there."

It seemed to take forever for the firemen to move their boat to where Jack pointed to. For over two hours the boat went back and forth along the bottom of the cliff. Strong currents made it difficult to keep the boat on course. After a bit they gave up and headed back into town.

"Looks like they didn't find anything." Jack led Jason back toward his cruiser. "I need both of you to come to the station and give me a statement. Can you do that, Jason?"

With tears in his eyes, Jason nodded. Troy opened the car door for him. Before he got in beside his friend Troy heard someone say, "I wonder what they're being arrested for."

He didn't answer, he didn't care what people thought. He knew the truth. His parents would know the truth.

CHAPTER 30

After the boys gave their statements, Harback took them to Eddie's and stayed with them with a plane-clothed officer. Jason was on a suicide watch. Jack didn't want to wait for backup from St. Thomas. He asked that Eddie, Mason and Dean help him look for Black Tom.

"This time, lock him up and throw the key away," Mason told him. "I'm getting tired of the swinging door you guys give him."

"I'm not the one who keeps letting him loose," Jack said as they climbed the hill. He stopped on level ground and looked at each man when they reached him. "Maybe we should make sure he doesn't get off this hill alive."

Four set of eyes looked back and forth at each other. Mason was the first one to give a nod. "Are you sure?" Jack asked him. "He could still be your brother."

"He's not my brother," Mason said. "My brother is out there somewhere." His arm swept over the hill toward town.

Jack looked at Eddie for his answer. Eddie held up his hands. "Hey, I'm all for it. That bastard has caused enough heartache."

Dean gave his go-ahead and the four of them made an oath that they were all in this together. Whatever happened today would be their secret.

Tom was easy to find. Mason thought later that maybe it had been a little too easy. He was on the top of Picnic Hill where the boys slid down the embankment. The four of them walked up to him. Dean huffed, "He's high."

Tom sat against a tree with a needle still in his arm. Diluted eyes gave no indication he knew they were there. Mason asked Jack, "What do you want to do?"

Jack looked down at the man and said, "Maybe we won't have to do anything." He nodded toward the needle. "Hopefully that stuff will kill him."

"What is it?" Eddie asked.

"Heroin," Jack told him.

"I thought he did LSD." Eddie looked disgusted at Tom.

"He does anything he can get his hands on," Dean said.

Mason considered his options and paced the area. Bessie rose up in the creek and watched them. He turned to his friends. "Let's push him over the edge, maybe Bessie will finish him off."

"I think she'd love to, after what he has put her through," Dean said. "I wouldn't blame her."

"Do we all agree?" Jack asked them.

"Let's do it." Eddie bent down to lift Tom up.

Jack rushed to the other side and helped Eddie stand Tom up. Tom drooled down the front of his shirt and laughed. His eyes looked out into space and he remained limp in their arms. Jack asked the men one last time.

Suddenly Tom yelled and pulled away from them, he ran straight ahead and disappeared over the edge. The men stood on top of the cliff in shock. Down below was his sprawled-out body on the creek bed. For a long time, Tom didn't move.

"Think he's dead?" Dean asked.

"That fall shouldn't have killed him," Mason said. "Maybe the combination of that and the drugs did him in."

Bessie had swum away when Tom flew at her. She stayed by her den and watched the men on top of the cliff. "I think we should go down there and check," Eddie said.

By the time the men made their way to the path and down the hill, Tom had pulled himself up and was on his feet. They could see him stumble as he made his way toward the lake. "Tom, stop!" Jack yelled. Tom kept going as if he didn't hear.

Mason called Bessie. She swam up to the four men and sniffed at them. He pointed to Tom and said, "Go get him, girl."

"Attack!" Dean yelled at her.

Bessie turned her massive head and growled at Tom. "Attack," Dean repeated and pointed again. Bessie swam after her former keeper.

"Call her off!" Jay shouted at them from on top of the cliff. He pointed his gun at Bessie. "Call her off or I'll shoot her."

"Shit," Jack swore. "You better call her off, Dean."

Dean shouted for Bessie to stop. She did and looked back at them as if confused. She lifted her head and roared. She charged after Tom again. "Bessie, stop," Dean shouted again.

Jay followed her with his gun. "Make her stop," he yelled.

Dean ran after Tom and yelled for Bessie to stop again. By the time she did, Tom was near the base of the cliffs that blocked his access to the lake.

Jack ran up to him as Bessie lowered her head and blew at Dean. He reached up and petted her. "Sorry girl. I know how much you wanted to get back at him."

"Yeah," Jack said. "I wish she could have had her way with him."

****

Jay slid down the cliff face in the same place where Troy and Jason did earlier that spring. He charged up the creek bed toward Jack. "Run," Eddie told him. "We'll stop him."

"I won't run," Jack stood his ground. "Stay close."

"What in hell were you doing?" Jay yelled as he approached the group.

When he was within a few yards Jack said. "He killed Sherry this morning."

Jay stopped in mid-step and gawked at his partner. "How do you know?"

"I have an eyewitness who saw him push Sherry off the tall cliffs and into Lake Erie."

Jay looked past Jack. "Are you sure it was him?"

"That's what my witness says."

Mason looked back at Tom. Tom had walked behind some bushes. "Man, he's got to be sore."

"So," said Jack, in an angry voice. "Once again you come to that bastard's rescue."

"I didn't rescue him," Jay said. "I kept you four from committing murder." He looked over at Bessie. "That was cruel."

"Bessie owes him," Dean said. "Tom used to drug her."

"Still," Jay said. "The end result would have been the same. And I don't think that any of you would be able to live with yourselves afterward." He looked down at the ground. "Believe me, when I tell you that it'll eat you up inside. There will come a point when you think the only way you'll get rid of the guilt is by committing suicide."

"You make it sound as if you experienced that," Dean said.

Jay nodded. "I have." He looked at Jack. "Before I moved to Port, I was investigating a homicide in Toronto. There was another man who beat the system, just like Tom has. He broke away from me and jumped in front of a subway train." Jay looked at each man in turn. "I was there to kill him."

Mason checked behind him. Tom wasn't there.

"I came so close, murdering that man," Jay said. "I got pissed off because he jumped before I could push him." He sniffled. "I ended up in therapy for three years after that. And I almost lost my badge."

"Are we just going to let him get away?" Eddie asked.

"No," Jay pulled himself together. "Let's go and arrest him."

****

Bessie watched the men go after Tom. She wanted so much to kill him. She felt the vibrations of both rings. Her body twitched like she had been hit by lightning. Tom, she needed to kill him! She had to answer the call of the rings, had to stop. Why did Dean make her stop?

****

"You think my mom was a bad person," Jason accused Rachel.

"No, I don't. I think that Black Tom got her hooked on drugs and that she didn't know what she was doing anymore."

"I hope he rots in jail," he said with conviction. "I'm glad they caught him."

That was after they found Black Tom half way up the hill. He had stopped in a small clearing and leaned against a large rock talking to a tree.

"Now," Rachel told him. "You have to sell the house. The money will go into the estate for you."

"Does that mean I'm rich?" Jason asked. Then he lowered his head. "That won't bring my parents back."

"No, nothing will," Rachel gave him a hug. "I'm so sorry you have to go through all this."

"Valerie says I have to try to put their murders behind me. I don't think I ever will."

"I don't think any of us will," Rachel told him. "We just have to learn to deal with it the best we can. And get on with our own lives. I hope that you won't let this ruin you, Jason. You have a lot to live for."

"Yeah," Jason said.

Rachel put her arm around his waist. "I think you need to get over your anger first before you can grow as a person."

"I'm not mad at you," he said. "I don't know what I'm mad at."

"That's all right, Jason. It's your way of dealing with your loss. I know you've been crying a lot. So, have I."

"I swore at Ed this morning before he left for work." Jason pulled away from Rachel. "I didn't mean to."

"I'm sure he'll get over it," Rachel said.

"Why are you and Eddie always so nice to me?"

"Because we love you. We've always thought of you as part ours."

"You don't want me to live here," Jason said.

"That's because we can't afford to feed you," Rachel half-joked. "The real reason is because we're nervous that you and Troy would end up hating each other. That I couldn't live with."

"Besides," Rachel continued. "Mason has already partitioned the courts." She put her arm around Jason, "You're going to be the family he's always wanted."

"Why didn't he have kids?" Jason asked.

"Because he never settled down. And now that he's ready, it's too late for Valerie to start having babies." Rachel let Jason go. "I tried to warn him."

****

The gang was at Eddie's for what they figured was the last barbecue of the season. The men stood outside with various brands of beers in their hands. The women were in the house preparing salads and cutting up fresh vegetables.

"Jack doesn't know what he's missing," Mason said as he flipped a burger. "It's too bad he had to work today."

"He'll be here later," Eddie said and zipped up his jacket. "Man, it feels like it could snow."

"Here we go," Mason piled the burgers on a plate and handed it to Dean. He shut the lid on the barbecue to let the coals burn down and they went inside. The women had the table set and they all sat around. "Looks good," he said as he eyed the food.

The phone rang. Dean answered it being he was the closest to it. His face drained of color as he listened. Mason stood back up. Everyone waited in silence.

Dean hung up and looked around at everyone. His eyes rested on Jason. "That was Jack," he said. "They found Sherry's body. She washed up on shore near where she went in."

Jason's tears ran down his face as he looked at the people in the room. To Mason, it looked like he wanted them to tell him it was a lie and that his mother wasn't dead.

Dean finally got his bearings and said. "He wants someone to go down there and, and...."

"I'll go," Valerie said and stood up. Everyone knew she was to give a positive identification.

"I'll go," Eddie said as he got up from the table. As he reached for his jacket in the closet, Mason took out his and helped Valerie into hers. Dean stood up. Rachel started to put the food into containers. No one was hungry now.

Jason got up. "You don't have to do this, Jason," Eddie said. "We can do it for you."

"I know." He put on his jacket. "I need to be there, to make sure it was her I saw."

"Are you all right, son?" Eddie asked Dean. "Maybe you should stay here. Watch over your mother and brother." He nodded to where Troy still sat at the table, looking down at the floor.

Dean shook his head. "I'll be okay." He opened the door and stepped outside.

****

Harback met them halfway across the sand and looked from Jason to Dean, "It might be a good idea if you two stayed here. It's not a pretty sight."

"I'm going," Jason said defiantly and walked by him. Dean just followed the men as they trudged down to the water.

Jack greeted them with a nod. He stood by a bloated corpse that looked more like a whale than a human. Sherry's bruised arms had seaweed wrapped around them and some of her clothes were torn. One shoe was gone, and three toes pushed out from her sock. One side of her face as bashed in, her hair tangled in knots. Valerie bent down and examined the body, and then she stood up and walked a few feet away.

Jason swayed. Mason and Jack each took an arm and led him toward some driftwood. "That's my mom," Jason said. "That's my mom."

"We know, Jason." Jack sat Jason down on the log. "We didn't want you to see this."

Jason sat where he was and stared out at the lake. Mason stood by him while Jack went back to the body. He was barely aware of the men from the coroner's office that came with a black bag and put Sherry into it. The men all helped carry her to the black station wagon that waited in the parking lot. Mason guided him along. Jason sobbed as he watched them take his mother away.

Mason and Eddie led him to Eddie's car and took him back to the house. Valerie hovered over Jason like a mother with her cub. He didn't seem to mind, he probably needed someone to comfort him.

Eddie plopped into a chair with his jacket still on. Mason and Dean took theirs off and hung them on the backs of their chairs before they sat down. Dean took an object out of his pocket and handed it to Mason. "Sherry was lying on this."

Mason took it and turned it over in his hand. He looked up at Jack with a white face. "It's my watch, the one Black Tom stole from me."

****

For the next few days, Eddie walked around like he was half asleep. The store remained closed until after Sherry's funeral. The autopsy performed on her didn't reveal if someone had pushed her from the cliff top or if she jumped. Tom told everyone that she jumped, and he tried to stop her. Eddie had his doubts. However, Tom did seem genuinely upset with her death. Maybe for once he was telling the truth.

He had to get out of the house, to get away from the crying and sadness. Eddie went to see Rick Hall in jail. He stood in front of the bars and glared at the man he once trusted. Rick sat on his bunk and looked everywhere except at him. Eddie glanced at Tom two cells down before he addressed Rick. "I want to know if you used the gas rig for your dirty work. I want to know if you killed Hal Johnson."

Rick looked up at Eddie with fear in his eyes. He must have sensed that it was over for him because he told Eddie the truth. "I had drugs hidden all over the place," he said. "Parsons used the rig as a holding place until I could smuggle it out." He looked around at the other men that Jay had brought in with him. None of them threatened him so he continued. "He figured that nobody would look for it there." Rick stood up and walked around his cell. He stopped in the middle of it and faced Eddie. "None of us knew that Jay was a cop."

"Who shot Parsons?" Eddie asked. Rick didn't answer.

"He did," one of the other inmates said. "He was supposed to shoot Tom."

"Me?" Tom yelled and ran to the front of his cell. He grabbed the bars and rattled them. "You bastard, I'll get you."

Jack rushed in and smacked Tom's fingers. "Get back! Settle down, or you'll go back into solitary." Tom yelped and stepped back. He looked at Jack with an angry face and rubbed his knuckles. Jack took Eddie by the arm and led him out.

"What happened in there?" Jack asked after they settled down in his office.

Eddie took a big breath before he told him. "One of the guys just told me that Rick killed Parsons. He was aiming at Tom."

"At Tom?"

Eddie didn't know how much the constable knew. Police business meant that Jack couldn't tell him everything. "So, what's going to happen to those guys in there?"

"They'll be transported to St. Thomas for trial. The only one that won't be going is Tom."

"Why is that?"

"He wasn't apprehended in the raid. And all I can charge him with is assault and drug possession. He wasn't caught trafficking like those others were."

"What about Sherry? I know that bastard killed her."

Jack shrugged. "We don't have any proof of that. Jason may or may not have seen Tom push Sherry. Troy couldn't tell who was up there with her. Tom might have tried to stop her from jumping, I don't know." He leaned forward in his chair. "Believe me, Ed. If I could get him on a bigger charge I would."

"So, once again, Black Tom gets away with a minor and will be out walking our streets again," Eddie said in a huff. He stood to leave. "Someday, somebody is going to get him."

CHAPTER 31

Mason showed Valerie the letter he got from his lawyer. She read it and then looked up at his stricken face. "We can't get Jason unless we're married and have enough accommodations for him. What's the problem?"

"That means you won't get a big wedding. We'll have to go to the justice of the peace soon because if we don't do it, we could lose him. I don't want him to end up with Children's Aid."

Valerie pulled him close. "We'll do whatever we need to, so we don't lose him. I can cancel the hall and band I've hired. We don't need all those flowers and I can buy a cheaper dress, one that won't take months to get altered. I haven't confirmed with the caterer yet, so that won't be a problem."

"See," Mason said. "You'll miss out on your special day. And I don't..."

She stopped him with a kiss. He pulled her into him. When they parted she smiled his and told him, "You were the one who wanted a big wedding, my dear. I'll be just as happy if we get married in Eddie's backyard by the new pond he put in."

He raised an eyebrow. "You've been talking to Rachel, haven't you?"

"We knew this could be a possibility." She watched his eyes light up. "And we do like that little house by the lake. Why don't we take Jason up there this afternoon and show it to him? If he likes it, we can buy it beforehand."

Mason nodded. "And I can move right in. Harback says he'll take over my apartment."

"What do you think?"

"I think you're the most beautiful woman I've ever known." He gave her a kiss that lasted until she melted into him. When they parted, he looked deep into her eyes. "I love you so much, Val. Let's get married next weekend."

****

With the drug ring squashed, Jay wasn't undercover anymore. He was in Dean's apartment when Troy and Jason went over to bug Dean. As soon as they saw the cop Troy wanted to run.

"If he wanted to arrest us," Jason said. "I think he would have done that by now."

"What makes you so sure?" Troy stood just inside the door and watched Jay talk to Rain in the kitchen.

"He knows where we live," Jason said impatiently. "He could have come and got us any time."

"Come on in," Dean said as he walked out of the bedroom with a big grin on his face. He looked around his apartment. "How do you like it?" Rain had painted the walls and added pictures. And there were more knickknacks on shelves and pillows on the couch.

"Fine," Troy said and kept the wall between him and Jay as he checked out the place. It had two small bedrooms, one used for storage. The bathroom was a decent size and that was pretty much it until Dean led them into the kitchen. Troy walked in behind Jason.

Jay stood up from the table and showed them pictures in an album. He pointed to one and grinned. "This is Rain when she was six."

The boys bent over the album and studied it. "Is that your real name?" Troy asked Rain.

"No. My real name is Rayanne. I've been called Rain since I was little."

Troy noticed that Jay was watching him closely. He excused himself and practically ran into the bathroom. He locked the door and sat on the edge of the bathtub. With his head down between his knees, he began to hyperventilate. Big breaths, he reminded himself. Slowly the dizziness faded, and he could breathe normally again. After a few minutes, he washed his face and stepped out of the bathroom.

Jason gave him a concerned look when he joined them again. Jay was glancing between him and his friend. "You two shouldn't deal in drugs you know?" he said in a stern voice. "At least know who you are dealing with when you do sell drugs."

Troy fell into a chair. "We won't do it again." He saw Jason's face turn red.

"It's a good thing that sugar cube wasn't laced," Jay grinned at them now. Dean held back his laughter. Rain smiled at the two of them. "Don't worry," Jay said, "you don't have to pay me back." He held out his arms as if in surrender. "That's the risk we take buying off the street like that."

Dean burst out laughing. Jason hit him. "It isn't funny. We thought he was going to lock us up."

Jay's features softened. "I thought I'd let you two stew about it for a while and I hope you won't do something so stupid like that again."

Troy and Jason looked at each other. Both shook their heads. "We promise," they said.

****

It was a cool day in early October when Valerie and Mason stood in front of the Justice of Peace. The pond beside them glistened in the afternoon sun. Colorful leaves floated down on top of the guests from the big maple tree near the fence. Mason stood beside Valerie in nervous anticipation. He vaguely remembered saying his vows, knew that Valerie said hers. He kissed his bride and whispered that he loved her in her ear. "I promise to be true to you," he told her.

The crowd erupted in cheers. He and Valerie posed for pictures. They all went inside the house. It had started to rain. That was fine. Mason didn't even feel it.

Dean handed out beers as the adults entered and Eddie toasted them. Mason saw the look in his friend's eyes. *Treat her right, or else you'll have to deal with me.*

"Where are you going on your honeymoon?" Tracy asked.

"To Niagara Falls," Valerie said. "We're only going away for a week. We want to get back home and move into our new house." She gave Jason a big squeeze.

"Thanks, Jason," Mason told him. "You almost forgot her ring this morning, didn't you?"

Jason laughed. "I think I was more nervous than you were. I couldn't even tie my tie right."

Rachel put a record on the player and guided Mason and Valerie into the living room for their first dance. They swayed together. Mason didn't even remember if he moved his feet. Soon others joined in. Everyone had a partner except Jack and Jay who danced together.

"Stop leading" Jack complained. "You always want to take charge."

"And you like to whine about it," Jay pulled Jack closer and gave him a kiss on the cheek. "Now behave." He led Jack around the floor. The others stopped and watched and couldn't keep straight faces. When the song ended the room erupted in laughter and applause. Both men gave deep bows and headed into the kitchen for another drink.

Mason walked up beside Dean. "If there is any trouble, with you, Bessie, these kids, you call me right away."

"I got it. We've been over this before." Dean straightened his uncle's tie.

Mason's arms went around his nephew. "I will always love you." He turned, placed his other arm around Jason and gave him a squeeze. He saw Troy over by the window and gave him a loving smile. "I love all my kids," he said.

****

Two weeks later, Mason and Valerie were in a cute little bungalow at the base of Picnic Hill. It was the second last house on a dead-end street before the hill became too steep to build on. The long backyard gently sloped down to the beach. Mason stared out the big back window from his living room at Lake Erie. If he looked way over to his right, he could see the place where Bessie had rolled him onto the sand. Melancholy set in as he thought of the events of this last summer.

His dark mood centered around one person. Was Black Tom his brother? Did he blow up the *Charisma*? Was he innocent of murder? Drug trafficking? He was glad that at least Tom would have to answer to beating up Dean. Mason wondered just how involved with Parsons Tom really was. He concluded that they would never know. Tom had a way of twisting the truth until you ended up with more questions than answers.

He turned around and forced a smile. Valerie was looking inside a box and chatting easily with Troy. He and Dean had come over earlier to help them get settled. Troy giggled at something, but Mason knew of the sadness in his eyes, as there was in all their eyes. With their help, Mason hoped that he and Jason would be able to overcome the horror they'd gone through this year.

Jason came out of his bedroom and grabbed another box. He gave Mason a gloomy look and took it into his room. Mason went into the kitchen where Dean had the table full of dishes he had unpacked. He took his jacket out of the closet and put it on. "I need some air," he said and walked out the door.

He didn't have a destination in mind. He ended up in Bessie's cave. She snorted as she swam up to him. He petted her and talked softly to her. It seemed he was only there for a few minutes when Dean came in.

"I figured you'd be here," he said as he stopped beside Mason. He reached up and stroked Bessie's nose. "The last book I read says that she'll stay in here and hibernate for the winter."

"I noticed she seemed a little sluggish lately." Mason sat down along the wall.

Dean followed him. "Just after you left the house, you got a call from Harback. He's found your brother."

We meet   We Part
We hope to meet again

Other books by Deborah Tadema

Break in The Wind

No Honor Between Brothers

Abandoned Honor

Restless honor

Check them out at debtadema2.com

www.ingramcontent.com/pod-product-compliance
Lightning Source LLC
Chambersburg PA
CBHW070427120726
47910CB00003B/675